TRISKELLI3N
THE GATHERING

WILL PETERSON

WILL PETERSON is the pseud-onym of Mark Billingham and Peter Cocks. Mark is the bestselling author of a number of adult crime novels while Peter is a popular children's TV writer and performer. Mark and Peter have worked together previously on many much-loved TV programmes such as *Maid Marian and Her Merry Men*, *Knight School*, *Big Kids*, *The Cramp Twins* and *Basil Brush*.

TRISKELLI3N
THE GATHERING

WILL PETERSON

**WALKER
BOOKS**

First published 2010 by Walker Books Ltd
87 Vauxhall Walk, London SE11 5HJ

2 4 6 8 10 9 7 5 3 1

Text © 2010 Mark Billingham Ltd and Peter Cocks
Cover design by Walker Books Ltd

The right of Mark Billingham and Peter Cocks to be identified
as authors of this work has been asserted by them in accordance
with the Copyright, Designs and Patents Act 1988

This book has been typeset in Fairfield

Printed and bound in Great Britain by Clays Ltd, St Ives plc

British Library Cataloguing in Publication Data:
a catalogue record for this book is
available from the British Library

ISBN 978-1-4063-1968-2

www.walker.co.uk
www.triskellionadventure.com

For our children, again

Triskellion:
the story so far...

While staying in the quaint, peaceful and deadly village of Triskellion, American twins Rachel and Adam Newman have discovered that they are anything but ordinary. Caught up in a terrifying and bizarre adventure, they have also been befriended by a mysterious boy called Gabriel, a traveller who seems to know more about them than they do themselves and whose strange powers they seem to share.

Powers that make them feared ... and hated.

The twins quickly find themselves pursued – not only by the sinister Hope Project, but also by their ruthless and psychotic uncle, Hilary Wing. Since the motorbike crash that should have killed him, Wing appears to have become all but indestructible and able to reinvent himself at will.

Having escaped the research lab and survived a harrowing race across Europe, Rachel and Adam are now in possession of two Triskellions: the powerful amulets that appear to be the source of their unique abilities.

They go into hiding in Australia with their mother, Kate, and friend, archaeologist Laura Sullivan. But there are those who will never stop hunting them, and when someone they believed to be dead comes calling, it's clear that dark forces are closing in once more.

Rachel and Adam's new life is about to take the strangest and most dangerous twist of all…

prologue:
western australia

Molly Crocker stared across the yard to where the boy was working, cursing herself as she spilt the lemonade and reaching for a cloth to clean up the mess. When she looked up again, the boy had moved out of her line of sight and there was a large bee butting gently against the window from outside.

Zzzzz ... dnk. Zzzzz ... dnk.

Molly thought it was a bit early for bees, but it wasn't a complete surprise. Everything was going haywire with the climate these days. Global warming was never out of the news.

She was careful not to spill any more as she carried the lemonade outside, down the steps from the porch and out across the front yard to where the boy was painting one of the fence posts.

"Here you go," Molly said. She handed the cold drink across. "Looks like you could do with this."

The boy, whose name was Levi, had been working at their place for the last couple of weeks. He'd mended the roof on one of the barns, fixed the gate on the paddock where Molly's horse was kept and done some basic plumbing inside. He was sixteen, Molly guessed – about the same age as she and Dan were – and according to their mother, the Aboriginal tribe he belonged to had been living in the area for over forty thousand years.

Levi drank half the lemonade in one gulp. "Thirsty," he said.

While Molly waited for the glass, she stared around the compound. It was isolated for sure – their closest neighbour was seven kilometres away and it was half an hour in the truck to the nearest shops – but it was a nice place to live. They were only ten minutes from the sea and got to go surfing after school or ride horses in the hills whenever they fancied it.

Debbie, their mum, and Mel – the woman who shared the house with them – reckoned they were lucky.

They all had a pretty good life.

Molly wiped the sweat from the back of her neck and tried to remember how long they'd been here. Was it two years? Something like that...

Levi handed back the glass. "Thanks, Rachel."

Molly blinked. The glass slipped from between her fingers and shattered on the ground. "Excuse me?"

At that moment, Dan waved from the other side of the yard as he walked back to the house. Levi waved back enthusiastically and called out, "Hi, Adam."

Molly watched as her twin brother stared back, confused, before walking back to the house a little faster.

"What did you call me?" Molly asked.

"I called you by your name," Levi said. "Your name is Rachel, but you've forgotten. You've forgotten everything."

Molly stared. The boy was making no sense, and yet ... something was swimming forward from the recesses of her mind: something struggling to come into focus.

"I think maybe you should go," she said.

Levi didn't move. "It's good that you forgot; that you all started a new life. It was the only way you could stay alive. But now it's time to remember again."

"You're crazy," Molly said. She turned at a noise from the house and saw Mel and her mum marching quickly towards them across the yard. Dan was walking nervously a few metres behind them. Mel was carrying the shotgun.

"What is my name?" Levi whispered.

Molly stared, held by the boy's intense green eyes – funny how she'd never noticed that they were green before – and saw a beach.

An explosion and a boy running. Rocks falling and a ball of flame rising high into the sky. She felt desperately sad for no reason, and the word came out of her mouth without her brain telling it to: "Gabriel."

The boy smiled.

"Hey!" Mel was shouting as she, and Dan and Molly's mother got closer. Mel raised the shotgun. "Get the hell off our land right now. And don't come back."

"You'd best do it," Molly said.

"I need you," the boy said. "You and Adam."

"Need us for … what?"

Mel and the others were only a few steps away. "Didn't you hear me?" Mel screamed.

"There are people in the shadows," Levi said. "They've stayed hidden for a long time, working quietly to destroy you – all of you."

Molly nodded. She could feel the danger and remember the urgency and the pain. She remembered running and running…

"You've been hidden for a long time, Rachel, but it can't go on for ever. It has to stop. It's time you came out of the shadows."

"Why?" Molly said. She hadn't been aware of the clouds gathering, and the first fat raindrops felt cold and heavy. "Why now?"

The boy's eyes darkened. "Because they're coming…"

part one:
the dreaming

1

Molly, or Rachel as she was beginning to think of herself again, padded across the floorboards of her bedroom and looked out of the window.

She already knew what she would see.

Just the action of getting out of bed and looking from the window had resonated with something deep in her memory. A wave of déjà vu swept over her. She had been in this position before; she had done this before; she had *felt* this before. And sure enough, there, across the yard, the boy sat under a tree, sheltering from the rain that had barely stopped for two days now.

He had disappeared when Mel had threatened him with the gun, but Rachel had known he would come back. He would always come back.

He was that kind of boy.

Rachel had been having flashbacks since the boy, Levi … Gabriel, whatever his name was, had called her by her old name. It had unlocked something buried in her mind: a past as dim and distant as her childhood in New York, as shadowy as her memory of her father; a past her mind had deliberately locked away to allow her to move forward and forget the traumas that had forced her to go into hiding on the other side of the world.

Images had begun to come together – an English village, a chalk circle, a beach, some caves – but whenever Rachel had tried to remember more, her brain had felt as if it would burst.

She had tried to link the pictures and recall the people in her mind's eye, but her head would spin until she felt nauseous. She would have to sit down and clear her mind for fear of being physically sick. It had been as though her brain was preventing her from dredging up the past: protecting her from it.

And when Rachel had pulled Adam into the sitting room after Mel had chased the boy off their land, it had been clear that he felt the same way.

"He called you Adam," Rachel had whispered.

Adam had clutched his head between his hands, trying to keep his thoughts straight. "I'm Dan," he'd said. "Dan Crocker. My mum calls me that; my friends call me that. That's who I am. End of story."

"I know; I know," Rachel had agreed. "And I'm Molly. It says so on my passport. But when he called me Rachel and you Adam, something clicked. It was like a window opened in my mind and bright sunlight streaked through."

Rachel had seen from her brother's face that the same window had been opened in his mind, but he had decided to shut it firmly again. He had shaken his head rapidly from side to side and left the room, slamming the door.

Rachel pressed her palms against the glass of the window and watched the rain drumming on the corrugated steel that covered the wood store. The boy under the tree seemed unaware of her presence and oblivious to the rain that filtered through the branches and soaked his dirty shirt. Rachel's head began to throb again and she leaned her forehead against the cool windowpane.

Rachel.

She heard the voice in her head. Then again.

Rachel?

She quickly drew her head away from the glass, and the boy under the tree turned to look at her. His white-toothed grin was clear against his dark wet skin.

Listen to me, Rachel, the voice in her head said. *You can hear me, can't you?*

Rachel nodded.

Good. You're coming back gradually. Still some way to go, but at least you can hear me. You've had time to rest. We need to get going…

Where? Rachel asked with her mind. *Where are we going?*

Walkabout.

Rachel was familiar with the word. Mel had used it. It

was an Aboriginal phrase. Aboriginal youths would "go walk-about" at the age of thirteen or so, disappearing into the wilds and tracing the Songlines, or paths their ancestors had taken thousands of years before. They would try to recreate the heroic deeds of their forefathers.

It was a rite of passage.

Mel had said that the Aboriginals were the oldest continuous culture in the world, and that every lump and bump of the Australian landscape was sacred to them. Every rock and pebble told a story; every river and stream had a meaning.

Rachel looked out past where the rain had drilled tiny craters into the red mud and the gum trees beyond, to the line of hazy blue mountains that slumped across the horizon. Mel had told them about the Darling Scarp: a range of hills that the Aboriginal tribes said were the sleeping body of a giant mythical snake-being which had crawled across the country creating lakes, streams and rivers.

Rachel imagined for a second that she saw the whole line of hills undulate and move as if it were breathing; a trick of the light created by the rain dribbling down the windowpane.

Rachel. The voice in her head snapped her back to reality. But this time it was a different voice. Her brother's voice.

Rachel, Adam said again. *I can hear you. I can hear what you're thinking. I can hear what* he's *saying.*

I can hear you, too, Rachel answered with her mind. *And you called me Rachel.*

Another voice chimed in, tuning into their frequency:

someone who could read *both* their thoughts. The boy...

Welcome back, Adam, Levi's voice said. *Now we're getting somewhere. You're beginning to get your memory back.*

There was a silence. Rachel looked across the yard at the Aboriginal boy, who had got to his feet and was drawing a shape in the wet mud with a stick. He looked up as Adam's voice came through again, faint ... anxious: *I'm not sure I want my memory back.*

There was nothing wrong with Mel Campbell's memory.

She remembered every step of their hellish journey here: getting two teenage kids and their mother, all on the verge of mental collapse, halfway around the world. She remembered the lies and subterfuge she had been forced into in order to escape the clutches of the shadowy organization for whom she had been working.

She remembered coming back to Perth, not only a place where she felt safe, but one where she was familiar with every street and alleyway, with an Aboriginal-like knowledge of the bush land that spread for thousands of kilometres beyond the city. It helped that this place was so remote: as close geographically to the wilds of Borneo as it was to Sydney. If they could start a new life anywhere, then the sparse vast space of Western Australia, which housed just over a million people in as many square kilometres, was the place.

The place where Mel Campbell had grown up as Laura Sullivan.

She, too, was watching the boy from her window.

She saw him look up and smile.

Laura had guessed that threatening the boy with a shotgun would not deter him. She had done it out of fear as much as anything, because if the boy was who she thought he was … if he was from *where* she thought he was … then their quiet life was about to be thrown into turmoil once again.

A couple of years ago she had promised the twins' mother that she would protect them. She had promised to keep them away from the probing of scientific organizations and not to lie to them as she had been forced to do in the past.

Laura took a deep breath and pulled on her long Driza-Bone raincoat. She would have to try and reason with the boy, at least. She stepped out into the rain and splashed across the muddy yard to where the boy sat under the tree.

"Hi," she said.

The boy grinned, as if he had won an argument.

"Listen, I'm sorry about the … you know, about pointing a gun at you."

"No worries," he said.

"We were afraid, you see. I promised them…"

"What did you promise them?" the boy asked.

"I promised to keep them safe; I promised to protect them from anyone who might want to hurt them. They've been through enough."

Levi looked hard at Laura.

"I promised their mother," Laura added.

"That's a promise you can't keep. You know you can't."

Laura looked at the bruised grey sky. A wet bee wove through the raindrops towards her, landing on the trunk of the tree. Another followed it, then another and then twenty or so more. They crawled over the wet bark, wiggling their abdomens: signalling to one another, before forming a line and weaving about until they'd created the outline of a symbol.

It was one that Laura had not seen for some time, and the instant she saw it, she knew that the boy was right.

She could not keep her promise. She could not protect them.

2

"**Y**ou promised me!" Kate Newman screeched across the breakfast table, banging her fist so that the mugs jumped and the coffee splashed.

"I promised you I wouldn't lie. And I haven't." Laura looked at the two empty places where Dan and Molly – Adam and Rachel – would have normally sat.

"You said you'd protect them," Kate said.

"I've done my best." Laura looked her friend in the eye, before getting up from her seat and putting her arm round Kate's shoulders. "I've done what I can for all of you. But I can't protect them from *who* they are, or *what* they are, any more than you can."

Kate was silent for a moment, digesting Laura's words, and then she nodded. The women had become close in the two years they had spent together. They had bonded, delighted that this new life in rural Australia had suited them all so well. They had also been relieved that something in the kids' mental make-up had enabled them to wipe their memories clean. Neither Rachel nor Adam had seemed to have any recollection of the time they had spent in England two summers before, nor of their traumatic adventures evading the Hope Project across Europe. And neither Laura nor Kate had had any intention of reminding them. They'd lulled themselves into a false sense of security and clung to this idea of a new start like a comfort blanket – a blanket that had suddenly been whisked away when they had woken to find Rachel and Adam gone.

"So who do you think the boy is?" Kate said.

"It might sound stupid, but I think he's Gabriel. Or at least, someone very much *like* Gabriel."

Kate's face drained of colour. Nothing would surprise her after what she had come to learn about her children – what she had been through with them – but the mention of Gabriel's name gave her a sinking feeling of dread and panic.

"No," she said. "Not here. I mean he didn't *look* anything like Gabriel."

Laura shook her head. "I know, but I'm beginning to think he comes in different shapes and sizes. Even if he's not exactly the same Gabriel we used to know, he certainly knows who the kids are."

"We've been stupid," Kate said. "We thought we were safe out here in the middle of nowhere, but *because* we're the only people for miles around we're easy to find. If Gabriel can find us, so can *they*." Kate couldn't bring herself to say the name of the Hope Project, the organization that had abducted her children, tortured her son and nearly killed them all.

"I don't agree," Laura said. "I think our cover here has been perfect, but I think Gabriel could find them wherever they were in the world."

"It's time to move."

"Where?" Laura asked.

"Home. New York." Kate's voice cracked with emotion when she said the words. "They can only have been gone a couple of hours. Just get them back here and we'll be off. We can disappear completely in a big city."

Laura saw the strain on Kate's face and suddenly felt the fear herself: the urgency to get Rachel and Adam back. It was like the panic of a parent who one moment sees their child playing on the swings and then the next sees that he has vanished.

"I'll go after them," she said. "There's only really one direction they can go in, and as long as they're on foot they can't have got far."

But as Laura grabbed the keys to the old Jeep, she knew in her heart of hearts that it would not be as simple as that.

Rachel and Adam were still not quite sure why they had agreed to go with the boy Levi to Perth. Without even being aware that they had come to any decision, they had left with him in the middle of the night and had found themselves cold and hungry at the bus station at dawn.

He must have been very persuasive, Rachel thought, as she took a seat next to her brother on the bus. She felt perfectly calm, as if leaving her mother and Laura behind were the most normal thing in the world. She'd barely given them a thought – it was as though something, or someone, had banished any negative thoughts from her mind.

She looked at Adam. He smiled, every bit as relaxed as she was.

The bus pulled out of the station and emerged into the bright morning sun that flashed off the mirrored buildings of Perth's financial district. The light in Australia was brighter than anything Rachel and Adam had ever seen before. Somehow the sky seemed higher and bluer, and the whiteness of the light made everything around them seem crisper, more sharply focused, and hyperreal.

Levi had dumped himself in the seats in front of the twins. He pushed his face between the seat backs and, grinning his white-toothed smile at them, said, "We're on our way."

"Where?" Adam asked.

"Kalgoorlie," Levi answered.

Adam shrugged. The name sounded vaguely familiar, but then many of the Australian names sounded similar to his ears. It may have been somewhere he'd heard his mother and Laura talk about. "What's in Kalgoorlie?"

"Gold." A voice that sounded as if it had been baked dry in the sun croaked from across the aisle. Rachel and Adam turned to see a man leaning across to speak to them. He could have been sixty, maybe older ... or younger. His age was difficult to guess because his face was deeply creased and weathered brown, and his glittering eyes were almost concealed beneath lids that looked as if they had spent a lifetime squinting against the sun.

"Gold?" Adam repeated.

"Expect you'll be going to seek your fortune, eh?" the man said, putting down his newspaper. "Like thousands before you."

Adam said nothing, and Rachel smiled.

"The Golden Mile, they call it. My great-granddad came out from Scotland a hundred years ago and started digging. He was a millionaire by the time he was thirty."

"Wow," Adam said.

"All gone now, mind. His son – my granddad – gambled most of it away, and my dad drank the rest. That's Kalgoorlie for you. From nothing to a million and back again all in a hundred years. Boom and bust."

"And are you in gold?" Adam asked.

"Kind of. I'm a jelly man."

Rachel and Adam looked stumped, both imagining a job to do with making cakes or party food. The man didn't look like a cake-maker, and he saw the confusion on their faces.

"Jelly – gelignite, high explosives. I used to blow holes in rocks."

"What for?" Adam asked.

"To get the gold out, mate." The man mimed an explosion with his stubby fingers and blew his lips out in a "Boom!" He had clearly enjoyed his work. "Of course, the Abos kicked up a great big stink, complaining that we were blowing up their special fairy-story places. Mind you, you can't so much as *fart* on a rock without upsetting the Abos."

Rachel and Adam winced instinctively at his use of the word "Abo". It was derogatory, and they felt embarrassed for Levi, sitting in front of them. Adam coughed nervously, and, breaking eye contact with the "jelly man", the twins stared straight ahead. A second later, though, the man grabbed Adam by the wrist.

"Listen," he whispered, "I've been watching you two since you got on the bus. You look like good kids, so let me give you a word of advice." Adam looked into the man's deep-set eyes as the hand tightened on his wrist. "Stay away from the Abo kid. He'll get you into trouble, believe me. A quarter of our prisons are full of Abos, and Abo kids are twenty times more likely to commit crimes. It's a fact. I read it in the paper."

Levi stood up and gave the man a look that could have split rock itself. Adam wrestled his arm free, and Rachel felt the hair on the back of her neck begin to prickle.

"Excuse me, sir," she said, "but that must mean that seventy-five per cent of the prisons are full of people like you. You said your great-grandfather came here a hundred years ago and started digging and that your other ancestors had gambled and drunk whatever profit he made from exploiting the country. Hardly anything to be proud of, is it? Well, the Aboriginals have been here forty thousand years longer than you and your grandparents and, unlike you and your family, have done nothing but treat the land with respect. And I think that's something *you* should respect."

"Now, listen here…" the man said. "We've done more for this country in two hundred years than they've done in forty thousand." He was about to say something else, but, seeing the look on Levi's face, he decided not to continue. He grabbed his newspaper and fanned it out in front of his face, shielding himself from Levi's gaze. His voice grumbled out from behind the paper. "Don't say I didn't warn you."

And as the Aboriginal boy continued to stare, the jelly man's newspaper began to smoulder…

3

Kate Newman sat on top of the suitcase and bounced. She squashed down the clothes inside, then clicked the catch shut and twisted it: her family's few possessions secure under lock and key.

Hauling the case from the bed, she stood it next to the other bag in the doorway of Rachel's bedroom. She looked out of the window and down the rough path that led from the house. The sun had already dried up the rain of the day before, and in the distance she could see a cloud of dust being churned up by the wheels of an approaching vehicle.

She smiled, relieved. Laura had done well; she'd only been gone a few hours. She had presumably found the kids on the road to Perth, as Kate had thought she would. Kate pressed her face close to the warm windowpane and her heart suddenly jolted in her chest.

Laura's Jeep was red, battered and old. The vehicle, now only a hundred metres or so away from the house, was black, shiny and very new.

Kate quickly pulled the curtains across the bedroom window and threw herself back against the wall. She was breathing heavily and her heart was pounding. She waited, listening as the tyres rumbled across the yard and the vehicle came to a halt outside. She heard the ratchet of the hand-brake and the slam of a door.

She waited.

There was a loud rap on the front door.

Kate swallowed hard; they never had visitors here and neither did they want them, especially *now* … while she was alone. There was a second knock and Kate realized that the door was unlocked. Whoever was outside would be able to let themselves in. There was nowhere to run; she would have to go down and face them.

The door opened slowly just as Kate reached it, and she shaded her eyes from the strong sunlight to see a man standing on the porch. He looked crisp and smart, as if the heat of the day had not touched him. He wore pressed chinos, a black polo shirt and sunglasses.

"Hi," the man said. His accent was American and he sounded friendly enough.

"G'day," Kate replied, trying to sound Australian and disguise her trembling voice.

"Sorry to bother you, ma'am. I'm from the Beekeepers' Consultative Committee for the Government of Western Australia."

The name sounded preposterous. Kate might have

laughed had she not been so terrified.

"We're doing some research into a thing called Colony Collapse Disorder or CCD. Ever heard of it?"

Kate thought that she might have and nodded. "Isn't it a disease that's killing off bees in America?" she asked. "You're American, aren't you?"

"I am, but it's not just in America, ma'am. It's here as well. The hives are down by fifty per cent in WA. And we don't even know whether it's a disease or if it's caused by some other phenomenon: pesticides, phone signals or something else altogether. So we're just doing a survey of all the bee-keepers in the area, to work out the health of our hives."

Kate nodded again.

"So are those hives active?" the man asked, pointing across to the paddock.

Kate was surprised. She was hardly aware of the two old hives buried among the long grass. "I don't think so," she said. "They were here when we moved in."

The man made a note on a clipboard.

"And how many people live here?" His voice sounded different. More businesslike.

"Oh ... I live here ... by myself," Kate stuttered, trying to sound light and cheery, and failing.

"But you said 'when *we* moved in'." He looked at Kate for confirmation.

"Oh yes, there's a lady who lives here too," Kate said as if suddenly remembering. "A friend."

The man raised an eyebrow, and made another note. "So," he continued, "not alone, then?"

"No. Not exactly." She was beginning to wonder what on earth this had to do with bees.

The man studied his clipboard for a moment and whistled between his teeth before looking up at Kate. "It's just that you seem a bit confused about who does live here. It's you, your lady friend … no *kids*?"

"No," Kate lied.

"No … *twins*?" The man glanced across at the BMX bikes leaning against the fence.

"No," Kate said again, her face reddening.

"OK, that's fine, then. Thanks for your time."

"No problem," Kate said, ready to close the door.

"Yeah, thanks," the man said again. He looked down at his clipboard once more. "Just to be sure – the names Dan and Molly Crocker mean nothing to you?"

Kate shook her head, fighting to control the tremble moving through her body.

"It's just that I have them listed as living here." The man stepped forward and showed her the names printed on a sheet.

Kate shook her head again.

"If you're sure," the man said. "Or perhaps the names Rachel and Adam Newman might jog your memory?" He smiled, his voice deadpan.

Kate tried to slam the door, but it wouldn't shut.

Looking down, she saw the American's shiny boot was wedging it open. She pushed her full weight against it, but with her legs trembling like jelly she was no match for the man as he forced his way in…

The isolation had been one of the main reasons why Kate and Laura had chosen this area when they had first been looking for somewhere to settle.

Somewhere to hide.

There were never any passers-by, but if there had been, they would almost certainly have been startled by the gunshot that rang out from the house that morning, echoing across the flat, wet earth and sending a cloud of parakeets rising up from the nearby trees.

4

"**D**o I swing from the trees? Do you see me eating bananas? Do I *look* like a monkey?!"

A polite laugh fluttered across the audience. Indeed, most of them had never seen anyone who looked *less* like a monkey than the man who stood before them on a rickety stage, beneath a banner that read:

CHURCH OF THE TRIPLE WHEEL

Pastor Ezekiel Crane looked down over the few hundred or so of his flock, gathered together in a clapboard chapel on the outskirts of a small Midwest American town. His face was very pink on the shiny forehead, and his cheekbones looked as if they had been pumped up from inside. His full lips were a darker pink still and his square chin was divided by a deep dimple. His hair was blond and thick, and his teeth were Hollywood perfect.

Less charitable observers might have said that Ezekiel Crane's appearance was the result of dozens of cosmetic surgical procedures, each paid for with the funds that his followers donated at every meeting. Some said that he wore a wig and false teeth. Others spread more outlandish stories, suggesting that he never slept, was given daily blood transfusions and ate live chickens for breakfast.

There was no shortage of rumours…

Crane surveyed his audience, trying to catch the eye of as many individuals as possible, eager as always to make contacts and converts. This was a typical audience for him: hard-working nuclear families – mom, dad and two kids – the pillars of Middle America. Crane had been surprised by this at first. He had expected more followers from the fringes of society, the hippies and New Agers, but his message seemed to resonate with the most conformist of people. Those who appeared to be the most certain about life had turned out to be the most uncertain of all. Crane was pleased. His disciples were not only respectable, but also well-behaved and loyal.

And they had money. Money they were falling over themselves to donate to Crane's movement.

"Evolutionists would have us believe that we are descended from the great apes," Crane continued. "And their theory has always been a convincing one … until now." He turned to an easel by his side and flipped over a sheet of paper. On the other side were pictures of a chimpanzee, an orang-utan, a gorilla and a human. Next to the pictures were numbers.

"Now, if we were related to these guys, you would expect some genetic similarities ... and there are *some*. But it's not the similarities that are important; it's the *differences*. If we were descended from the apes, then we would have the same number of chromosomes, right?"

He tapped the board with a pointer.

"Well, if we look at the figures here, we can see that the apes all have forty-eight chromosomes, that's twenty-four pairs. Now, if you look here" – Crane pointed at the idealized human figure silhouetted on the sheet – "humans have only forty-six chromosomes, twenty-*three* pairs. Which means that we have a pair of chromosomes missing." He stared out at the crowd, shaking his head. "Now, I'm no scientist, but chromosomes don't just disappear, do they? So where have they gone?"

There were murmurs from the crowd. Crane took a couple of steps forward, speaking more intimately, fixing the faithful with his eyes.

"What I believe, my friends ... what I *know* ... is that we are a completely *different* species. One that has existed from the beginning of time. Ape*like* maybe, but different. And what changed us from our primitive form into what we are now is a genetic input from *elsewhere*. A genetic input that fused our chromosomes and made us *men!*" Crane brought his hand down on the lectern in front of him for emphasis.

He heard a collective intake of breath from his audience. It always happened at this point in his speech, as if this were the moment when he was going to unlock the secret of mankind for them.

This was the point at which he knew he had them in the palm of his hand.

"Now, if you turn to page fifteen in your books, we'll read together the words of Ezekiel, the great prophet I am named after. Then we'll see the truth together."

The audience shuffled and opened their copies of *The Triple Wheel*. Ezekiel Crane had edited parts of the Bible and other sacred writings that appeared to reinforce his theory and dotted them throughout his book, which, along with the accompanying CDs and DVDs, were selling in increasingly large numbers. Some of those in the audience had read it already, of course, but they were happy to listen again and have their faith in Pastor Crane renewed and strengthened.

Crane began to lead them in the reading:

"Now it came about in the thirtieth year,
On the fifth day of the fourth month
While I was by the River Chebar amongst the exiles,
The heavens were opened and I saw a vision...

"As I looked, behold, a whirlwind
Was coming from the North, a great cloud
With fire flashing forth continually

And a bright light around it, and

Something like glowing metal in the midst of the fire.

Within it there were figures resembling four living beings

And this was their appearance: they had human form."

"Great sermon, Pastor Crane," Brother Jedediah said. He passed Ezekiel Crane a cold Dr Pepper and smoothed a hand over his thinning scalp, as if trying to make himself smart for his boss.

Crane put his white shoes up on the dressing-room table and cracked open the can with a hiss. "Thank you, Brother Jedediah. I thought we'd never get rid of them."

Crane had given a two-hour sermon with readings and songs. He had then spent another hour blessing children, and signing books and CDs while the collection buckets were passed around. He had encouraged his followers to go home and listen to the CDs whenever they could – in the car, in bed, at any time, night or day – so they could learn and spread "the good news".

"Don't know where you get your energy from," Brother Jedediah said.

"From above," the pastor said. He smiled and tipped his Dr Pepper at the little man in a "cheers" gesture.

It was true that Crane did not look particularly tired. His creaseless face betrayed no fatigue and only the dark circles of sweat under the arms of his suit gave away the fact that he had been working hard. Crane swigged down the last of the cold drink and crushed the can in his hand.

"I got a good feeling, Jed," he said, smacking his lips. "I can feel it in my bones. I've got them buzzing, and now them worker bees are all coming round to my way of thinking."

"Hallelujah to that," Brother Jedediah said. He placed a hand on his sweaty black satin shirt over his heart. "Hallelujah and amen."

5

The sun made the landscape shimmer, and Rachel imagined she could see patches of water on the rough track ahead. The Great Central Road stretched in front of them into infinity. Rachel had thought it would be a major highway, but in reality, it was little more than a rough track used by only a few thousand intrepid vehicles a year.

Over dinner at a small motel the night before, Levi had revealed where their journey would take them. Rachel and Adam were excited. It was the most famous landmark in the country, but they had never been there. In fact, during their two years in Australia, they had rarely gone further than their local beach.

"Do you think we have enough food for the journey?" Adam asked, concerned as always about his stomach.

"There's plenty of food out there," Levi said, gesturing at the landscape around them. "If you know what you're looking for…"

They spent the first hour in silence, taking in their surroundings. With every step, the horizon seemed to get further away and both Rachel and Adam began to worry about exactly how far they were going to have to walk.

"Don't worry," Levi said, reading their thoughts. "After the first hundred kilometres or so it all goes much quicker." He grinned at their astonished faces. They had assumed they were already within striking distance of their destination.

"So how far are we going altogether?" Adam asked.

"About a thousand kilometres," Levi said. "But who's counting? It's easier if you don't think of it in terms of miles or kilometres. If you just think of it as a distance that needs covering, it becomes longer or shorter, depending on your state of mind. Kind of like time."

Rachel knew what Levi meant. Although a hundred years was obviously way out of her own life experience, sometimes ancient history could feel as if it had only happened yesterday. She walked on, losing herself in thoughts about the past, and the track seemed to melt away under her feet...

Laura had made it no further than Kalgoorlie the night before. Five hundred kilometres had been the most she had been able to manage and she had checked into the Nelson Hotel at nine, exhausted and in need of a drink. Laura always stayed at the Nelson when she passed through Kalgoorlie, partly because it was quiet and private, but mainly because she and Kate had made a pact that, should anything happen to them, this hotel was to be their emergency refuge. It would be a meeting point and somewhere they could lie low for a few days. Being a mining town, plenty of people came and went in Kalgoorlie, and it had a reputation for turning a blind eye to people's indiscretions.

It was a good place to hide.

Laura now wished that she and Kate had told Rachel and Adam about their back-up plan, but they had always assumed that they would be with the kids if anything ever happened. Besides, they hadn't wanted to burden the twins with the fear that they might be under any kind of threat.

She had tried calling Kate again that morning to let her know where she was, but the tone had told her that the phone had been disconnected, and that had made her anxious.

Laura revved the engine of the old Jeep and headed out on the road from Kalgoorlie. As she drove, she willed herself to see a pair of twins and an Aboriginal boy on the road, repeating the words "Rachel" and "Adam" over and over to herself, as if by speaking their names she might summon them into existence.

She turned on to the Great Central Road that ran east towards Uluru, Australia's best-known natural landmark. As a child, Laura had become obsessed by the isolated mountain. She had been fascinated by the way it stood alone in the desert, squarely in the middle of the continent. It was as if someone looking down from outer space had stuck a pin at the exact spot that marked out the centre of Australia.

She still loved the mysterious way that the rock changed colour with the climate and the light. It could be silver-grey in the rain – streaked with black where algae grew in the damp crevasses. It could glow red at sunset, partly from the light and partly from the iron oxide particles rusting among the sandstone. At dawn it could appear violet as the early light caught the quartz that made up twenty-five per cent of its composition.

But it was not just the unique structure of the giant rock that had captivated Laura's imagination, or the fact that three-quarters of it was underground – iceberg-like – a piece of information which had made early geologists think it was a meteor. For Laura, it was more to do with the primal feeling she got every time she looked at the mountain. She could never suppress a flutter of excitement at its great age and the myths that surrounded it.

The legend of the Anangu, the Aboriginals who traditionally owned the area, said that before the world was fully formed, two creator beings – brothers – had fought in the wet mud, creating the table-topped mountain. The Aboriginal belief was that the spirits of these warring brothers still inhabited Anangu land.

Given her research credentials and the special relationship she had built up over many years with the local tribes, the Anangu had given Laura almost total freedom to continue her study of the monolith. She knew where the Dreamtime tracks ran. She knew the sacred areas that could not be photographed and she respected the traditions.

And she knew the perfect spot to hide something very valuable.

The most obvious place in Australia.

6

Some time must have passed before Levi spoke again, because as he did so Rachel and Adam suddenly became aware of their surroundings again, as if awakened from a daydream. Looking behind them, they could see that they had already walked a very long way. It was like they had been mesmerized by the heat and the sunlight and the soporific buzzing of the insects.

"How far have we walked?" Adam asked.

"Why do you need to keep counting?" Levi laughed. "Let's just say a fair way."

Rachel could tell by the position of the sun in the sky that they must have walked for three or four hours at least.

"This is where we turn off," Levi said. He checked some stones at the side of the road and looked across the plain to an area of sparse shrub land. "We should get off the road, because if anyone's on our trail, this is the only way they can come. We also need somewhere to sleep tonight and some food."

Adam looked around and, seeing no sign of a town or even a roadside motel, began to fear the worst.

"We're sleeping outside?" he said.

Half an hour later Levi led them into a small clearing surrounded by scrubby trees and bushes. He surveyed it and spread his arms out as if he were leading Adam and Rachel into the lobby of a five-star hotel.

"The Garden of Eden," he said, grinning.

The irony was not lost on Adam. "You can be Eve," he said to Rachel.

They lay their bags down on a soft, sandy area, and almost immediately, Levi began scratching around in the earth with his hands. Within seconds he had uncovered a large, brown-skinned ball, the size of a large potato.

"Desert yam," he said, pulling the stalks off the tuber and brushing the sandy earth away with his hand. "Great to eat. Can you find some more, Adam?"

Levi took Rachel to the line of tall stems that grew along one side of the clearing. He snapped one off at the base and showed her where dried sap had formed into waxy chunks of resin near the roots.

"Can you collect some of this, Rachel?" he asked. "And when you've done that, we could do with some firewood."

"Sir, yessir!" Rachel said, mockingly.

Levi studied the long, straight stem he had snapped off and began shaving its tip with a stone, weighing it in his hand as if it were a spear. Then, when he was satisfied, he turned and walked away from the clearing.

Twenty minutes later Adam had collected a dozen or so yams, while Rachel had amassed a small pile of resin and enough twigs and small branches for a decent fire. Levi reappeared then, having crept soundlessly up behind them. He held up a dead lizard. It was more than sixty centimetres long, with a hole in its neck where Levi had speared it.

"Goanna," he said, smiling. "Now we can eat."

"Oh. My. God," Rachel cried.

Levi knelt down and laid the pieces of resin among the dried wood. "It's like a natural firelighter," he said.

Adam picked up two short sticks. "Do I rub these together or something?"

Levi grinned. "Well you *can*," he said; "but seeing as we've got a lighter in the bag…"

Adam tossed the sticks away. "I thought you could set fire to pretty much whatever you liked," he said. He was remembering the newspaper on the bus. "Whenever you feel like it."

Levi looked up at him, his eyes suddenly hard. "I can only do that when I'm *really* mad."

Once the fire had been going for a while, Levi washed and gutted the goanna and placed it on its back in the hot embers. Its head looked scaly and devilish, its tongue lolling out from between sharp teeth. Rachel stared at it with disgust.

"You'll eat it if you're hungry enough," Levi said, reading her thoughts.

"I'll try anything once," Adam said. "Besides, I'm so hungry I could eat my own foot."

"That's the idea, Adam, but hopefully it won't come to that." Levi prodded at the goanna. "This is part of your education. The tribes round here weren't too good at looking after themselves, either, until the ancestors came from the sky and showed them how. The tribes were pretty primitive then, back in the Dreamtime, and the ancestors taught them how to hunt and fish. They taught them how to make fire and how to cook what they killed." He grinned at the twins. "Some people *still* need to be taught…"

He lifted the lizard from the fire and peeled off its skin like it was a baked banana. He pulled the flesh from the bones with expert fingers and laid it out in strips on a large leaf. Then he dug the yams out of the ashes and split them with a penknife.

Rachel and Adam tucked into the hot yams, which tasted like sweet potatoes and were all the better for being eaten in the open air. Levi offered them the meat. Adam took a strip and chewed it, his face registering at first squeamishness, then pleasure.

"Eat some, Rachel." Levi offered her the leaf. "Think of it as chicken. It's kind of related to a chook, if you go back far enough."

Rachel took a deep breath. It did *look* like chicken. She picked up a small piece of the roasted lizard and put it in her mouth. It was better than the best chicken she had ever tasted: tender and smoky from the fire. Delicious.

Once the leaf was stripped of goanna meat and all the yams had been eaten, Rachel, Adam and Levi licked their lips in satisfaction.

"Tempt you to an apple…?" Levi pulled half a dozen small apples from his pocket and passed them round.

The apples were cool and sweet and cut through the greasiness left by the meat. Rachel rested her head on her backpack, her stomach full and contented. She looked up at the stars, clear in the blue-black sky above. She could feel the warmth of the embers on her cheek and, while Levi hummed a faint tune, she fell fast asleep.

7

The sky is unnaturally blue: turquoise and glowing with a new light. Tall eucalyptus trees dot the landscape, their thin trunks skin-smooth, their sparse branches reaching up, fluttering long fingers, towards the sky.

The girl looks up at what appears to be the sun, but it is a sun that is coming closer. As it approaches, she sees that it is spherical: an orb created from spinning wheels of light. She should run, but she does not. She is hypnotized by the spinning wheels that intersect one another and come closer until she can almost see flames flickering across their surface. She shuts her eyes, momentarily blinded by the white light, and when she opens them again, she sees something else, something within the ball of light.

It is a figure, man-like, silhouetted within the wheels.

She is frightened. She is about to run, but there is no time – just before the orb crashes into the desert, it explodes, flattening her to the ground.

The explosion makes no sound. Thousands of smaller orbs

are dispersed into the sky. They explode, filling the air with glittering fragments that tumble to earth like tiny stars. When she raises her head, the sky is black and thick with buzzing insects. They swarm around her head, crawling into her ears, her mouth, her nose.

Bees...

But they do not sting. She spits them out and brushes them off with her hands. Getting to her feet, still covered head to toe in bees, she starts to run. As she flees, fat drops of rain begin to fall, cold on her skin. The drops quicken and fall harder until she is soaked by the pouring rain.

She runs.

The dry desert floor becomes wet and slippery, then disappears under her feet as if she is flying several centimetres above the ground. She moves faster, not feeling her feet, the landscape flashing by in fast forward, bees flying off and trailing after her.

Then, she stops.

A huge parakeet squawks overhead, before swooping down and drawing her attention to something on the ground.

The creature is long and fat, like a catfish. She cannot see whether it has feet like a lizard or is more like a snake – but as it slithers along, it leaves a deep groove in the earth, slick with slime. She knows she should not go near it, but she is transfixed by the swirling pattern on its bronze-coloured skin. She knows she should not touch it, but it moves so slowly that it will not be able to escape, and she cannot resist it.

She kneels down and her arm moves involuntarily towards the creature's slippery skin. The head rears back fast, revealing a silvery underbelly and tiny eyes that glint on either side of its head. The mouth is no more than a hole surrounded by small barbs that latch on to her arm. Sinking in and locking on to her flesh, it begins to suck…

Rachel woke up and a spasm of shock ran through her body. She checked her arm. There was a small bump. A mosquito bite, maybe.

"You OK, Rach?"

Rachel looked over to the other side of the campfire where Adam had been sleeping. He still looked a little sleepy, but his eyes were wide and slightly panicked.

"Bad dream… Did you…?" Rachel asked.

A nod. "With that … thing, whatever it was." Adam shuddered at the memory.

"Guess eating lizard doesn't agree with me."

"Won't be the goanna that gave you dreams," Levi said. "We're right on a Songline here. That'll be where your dreams came from, telling you stuff about the history of this place from millions of years ago."

"Do you know what we dreamed about, then?" Rachel asked.

"Probably. You see, that stuff is literally set in stone. The earth keeps memories, and when you're on a Songline, they come back to you." Levi kicked dirt across the cold ashes to hide them. "That's why I brought you this way – to bring you up to speed. It's part of *your* history too."

Rachel felt uneasy. What had seemed like a simple and beautiful landscape of sun and eucalyptus trees suddenly gave her a sinking feeling. She felt that something else, something frightening and dark, lurked just beneath the surface.

As if to confirm her worst fears, two figures were beginning to appear out of the shimmering heat haze on the horizon. They were upright and humanoid; their bodies were spindly and marked with white shapes, as if their skeletons were visible through their skin.

"What shall we do?" Rachel looked nervously at Levi, whose face was impassive.

"Wait," he said.

They stood frozen as the figures came nearer, each one carrying a tall spear. Rachel could see that they were men, not unlike Levi himself, and very dark-skinned. What had appeared to be bones from a distance were in fact chalky-white markings painted all over their bodies.

The men eyed the twins without emotion, then stepped forward. They mumbled something and made what Rachel took to be signs of deference to Levi. The boy made similar signs back and then a grin spread across his face. The formalities clearly over, the two men grinned back, and all three fell into a hug, patting one another's backs and chuckling.

Levi pulled away and dragged the two men across to Rachel and Adam. "Rachel, Adam," he said, "meet Clifford and Charlie Possum."

Rachel and Adam said hello.

"These guys are Anangu," Levi continued. "They're the traditional custodians of the rock. The government handed control back to them a few years ago."

"So, we can be your guides," Clifford Possum said. He reached into a small leather pouch and offered them damper, a kind of floury bread with a lump of dark golden honeycomb in the centre.

"You keep bees?" Rachel asked.

"We don't *keep* them," Clifford said. "They're wild. We harvest the honey from the colonies out in the bush."

"The Anangu were the world's first bee-harvesters," Charlie said. "Story is that the bees came from the sky with the ancestors, so they could pollinate all the plants and help us develop our crops."

Rachel blinked, remembering her dream: the insects that had scattered like pin-pricks of light when the orb had crashed to earth.

"Without the bees we couldn't survive," Clifford said. "And we know every single colony from here to Uluru."

"How far is Uluru from here, then?" Adam asked.

Clifford Possum screwed up his brow. Distances were clearly as irrelevant to him as they were to Levi. "Dunno," he said. "Guess about four hundred kilometres."

Rachel was both amazed to hear how far they had come in a few hours and alarmed to discover that they still had such a long way to go. Adam clearly felt the same.

"Four hundred? Are we going to walk the rest of the way?" he said.

Clifford chuckled. "I think you've done enough walking."

Rachel began to wonder how they would get to Uluru. There were clearly no horses or cars. "Are we going to travel along the Songlines?" she asked.

Clifford and Charlie Possum seemed to find this idea funny and roared with laughter. "No, you crazy girl," Charlie said. "*We're* not walking all that way."

Clifford grinned. "We're going to fly, like the bees!"

8

Down towards the end of Broadway, beyond the fashionable areas of SoHo and Tribeca, lies the financial district of Manhattan. Among the steel and glass office blocks that thrust into the New York sky and drive the money markets of the world are the headquarters of a very different kind of organization: the Flight Trust.

The Flight Trust was founded in the early twentieth century by a group of upstate philanthropists who had benefited from the boom times and hoped to give something back to America other than their taxes. One original trustee with a passion for man-powered flight had backed the Wright brothers in their pursuit of conquering the air. The enterprise had made little money – but it had given the trust its name.

The Flight Trust had continued to sponsor pilots and explorers, such as Charles Lindbergh and Amelia Earhart. It had also invested in providing new technology for the air force in the First and Second World Wars: invaluable research that the Trust had traded for government bonds, making it a very rich organization indeed.

The Trust's headquarters had been housed on the same spot for as long as anybody could remember. The original brownstone had long since been demolished and replaced with a modern mirrored-glass block that towered above all the buildings around it. It was an iconic part of the New York skyline and its elegant tower rushed skyward from the street, a vast pair of aluminium wings opening from its summit.

Locals called it the Flight Building.

Since the Second World War, aircraft technology had become a matter of state secrecy and the Flight Trust was now very low-key, operating on a more "hush-hush" basis. To the public, it was ostensibly a charitable organization whose interests were in curing diseases, ending famine and saving the rainforests.

The truth was rather different.

The Trust had set up a secret offshoot in 1950 to continue its research into manned flight and specifically into the space programme. Neil Armstrong had worn a discreetly embroidered "FT" on his spacesuit when he had walked on the moon. This new top-secret organization had within it an even more shadowy department that exclusively investigated extra-terrestrial activity and UFO sightings. It had been especially active during the 1950s, when there had been a rash of sightings across America and even rumours of a landing in New Mexico.

This department was called the Hope Project…

* * *

The current director of the Hope Project swung round in his chair and looked out across the river. From his vantage point behind a glass desk on the sixtieth floor of the Flight Building, he could see everything in miniature, including the old ferries chugging in and out of the shabby docks as they had done for years.

Many thousands of those who now made up New York's cosmopolitan population had come in through those ports. Gasping for air and jostling for space, they would have been unable to believe that they had finally escaped whatever horrors they were running from: poverty, famine, genocide.

The director was grateful that it had happened to his grandparents and not to him. He was one of the lucky generation who had missed out on major wars and persecution, and had lived in relative comfort in the brave new world of post-war America.

He was not an old man, but the efforts of the past couple of years had made him tired. His thick black hair was grey at the temples and he had permanent dark rings under his eyes. Things had been coming together for the Project, but every time he had thought he was getting somewhere, there had been another major hiccup.

He could not afford to let it happen again.

His assistant came in, bringing him his sixth cup of coffee of the day and smiling tightly. The director didn't really want the coffee, but knew that the cup and the smile were to let him know that they had no further news.

He asked anyway: "Any word from the Australian operatives?"

His assistant shook her head, still smiling, hoping to divert one of the director's legendary explosions.

"Thanks, Meredith," he said.

Meredith left, grateful that her boss's temper had held.

He picked up a pencil and doodled round the edge of the map of Australia that was laid out in front of him. A red circle had been drawn around Perth. No further information. He stared at the map, hoping it would yield something, but all he could see were vast swathes of desert. The place was so featureless that it really could swallow people up.

They could just disappear.

If only they were in New York, he thought. Here he had all the resources to pick them up: CCTV, trackers, street teams, people in the field, phone signals. It would be easy. But they weren't here, so he had no option but to be patient. He had been waiting for more than two years now and in that time the Hope Project had scoured the globe in search of the Newman twins. A "no questions asked" reward of one million dollars had been offered for information regarding their whereabouts. The details had been posted on a thousand different websites – but as yet the money had gone unclaimed.

He leaned back in his chair and rolled his head around.

It did not matter any more. Thanks to the new leads the Australian operatives were following, soon the children would be exactly where he wanted them...

He picked up the remote on his desk and turned up the volume on one of the hundred screens that took up one huge wall of his office. Stock prices were falling again. He did not want to know and turned up the volume on another screen, where an orange-faced girl in a blue suit was saying that it would be sunny upstate tomorrow.

The next screen got his attention.

The man on the TV looked freakish, but his delivery was mesmerizing. The blond hair and teeth were obviously fake, and he had had plenty of work done to his face, but there was just something about him. The TV picture widened to reveal his audience – a thousand or more people, cars parked in dozens of lines behind them.

The man strode across the stage to a microphone, his long legs covering the distance in three paces. Behind him fluttered a banner: something about a "Triple Wheel". The director was impressed by the way the man held his audience in the palm of his hand, fixing them with his eyes and a pointed finger. And they didn't look like the regular congregation of trailer-trash and hillbillies either. They looked normal.

A strapline under the image of the man read: PASTOR EZEKIEL CRANE PREACHING AT THE BALLOON FESTIVAL, ALBUQUERQUE.

The camera cut wider still to show hundreds of hot-air balloons being released into the air and floating over the huge parking lot where Pastor Crane was preaching. The director turned up the volume to hear what the man was saying.

His voice boomed out across the arena:

"And Ezekiel said:

'And this was their appearance: they had human form.

'And in the midst of the beings,
There was something that looked like burning coals of fire,
Like torches darting back and forth among the living beings.
The fire was bright,
And lightning was flashing from the fire...'"

The man on the screen paused and nodded knowingly at the crowd. "What *was* Ezekiel seeing all those years ago? I'll *tell* you what he was seeing. He was seeing jets and flaming rocket fuel. He was seeing technology thousands of years in his future."

The director could not take his eyes off the screen; off this man whose face was so strange, and yet so compelling.

The man continued to preach, his voice getting louder, the pitch and passion soaring as the balloons rose up into the sky all around him. "A technology thousands of years in *our* future. What Ezekiel was seeing was a stargate that was his portal to the Promised Land." He raised both hands skywards and closed his eyes. "Ezekiel One, Brothers and Sisters. Amen."

The crowd went wild. They clapped and whooped, and somewhere in the back of the director's mind, a loud alarm bell began to ring.

9

Clifford Possum nudged the joystick and the small crop-sprayer banked left. Rachel and Adam were squeezed in on either side of Levi in the back, the small seats of the aircraft not really having been built for three passengers.

Levi was clearly a nervous flyer and had said very little in the past hour. His eyes darted around the cabin and when he looked at Rachel, his smile was sickly.

Charlie Possum pointed to the arid ground a thousand metres below them. "Look," he said, his voice barely audible above the roar of the engine. "Can you see the carving?"

Rachel craned her neck and peered out of the small window. It looked like a scale model of a desert, the sparse clumps of green like the sprigs of parsley used to denote foliage on a model railway. Rachel looked around to see what Charlie was trying to show her and then, just as her eyes adjusted to the monotony of the landscape, she saw something that stuck out:

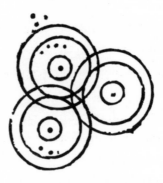

They looked like crop circles, but Rachel soon realized that they must have been carved *into* the sandstone. At first, she saw it as a face – maybe a monkey or a possum – with two eyes and a mouth. It looked quite similar to those animal faces Rachel had seen the Aboriginals paint. She blinked and looked again, and suddenly it was not an animal face but three wheels. Her gaze began to follow each line; the shape drew her eyes hypnotically faster and faster round the carved wheels until another shape revealed itself where the circles intersected…

Rachel felt the hairs on her neck tingle and goose bumps prickle her arms. She glanced at Levi, who was already looking down at the circles in the desert and smiling weakly.

"Adam!" Rachel shouted across at him. "Can you see this?"

Adam strained to see through the cabin window and down on to the landscape below. Initially, he looked confused and then, exactly as it had happened to Rachel, the shape became evident to him. His nervous glance told Rachel that he knew what it was too.

It was a sign that they had not seen for some time.

The plane hit the ground with a bump, churning up dust and skidding for a hundred metres or so before coming to a stop.

Rachel clambered out of the cockpit and stretched her legs. The mountain had looked so close when they were coming in to land, but it was still a kilometre away. It was so immense that it was hard to get a sense of its scale even from this distance.

"It's quiet," Adam said. "I thought this was a big tourist destination."

"It is," Charlie Possum said. "But most of the tourists come from the road, which is round the other side."

"Which is where we *don't* want to be," Clifford confirmed. "Shall we get going?"

Levi nodded, and they began to walk towards the base of Uluru.

Clifford and Charlie studied the plants around the rock, as if each change in the direction the stems were pointing gave them a more and more precise idea of where they were headed. Eventually, after foraging for an hour around the lower slopes of the monolith, Clifford announced that he had found the right path.

Looking up, Rachel could see a narrow track. Grey streaks ran like veins through the reddish stone of the mountain, and within the streaks tiny fragments of quartz glittered, making the rock look somehow alive. Rachel began to feel a strange pull, almost a magnetic force, drawing her to the mountain. She looked around to see if Adam felt the same, but he was already on his way up the path, following closely behind the Aboriginal brothers.

They climbed for another hour and then Charlie Possum stopped and pointed. "It's up there."

"OK, let's go," Adam said, striding on.

"This is where we stop," Clifford said. "We'll meet you back at the plane."

"Why?" Rachel asked.

"It's a sacred site," Charlie said.

"We're forbidden to see it," confirmed Clifford.

Adam looked confused. "But *we* can see it?"

Charlie and Clifford Possum looked at Levi.

"Yes, you can," Levi said to Adam. "You *need* to see it."

Rachel wondered why she and her brother had been singled out for such a privilege. Somehow being given special permission did not make her feel any easier.

The three of them clambered on, the path getting narrower and steeper until it appeared to go no further.

"You sure this is the right path?" Adam asked.

"Positive," Rachel said. Out of nowhere an image had began to form in her mind: bright sunlight, a woman with red hair tied back, climbing round the folds in the rock.

"Laura's been here," she said.

Adam looked up at his sister, who was now several steps ahead of him. Before he could ask her how she knew, Rachel appeared to vanish into the red rock. He ran up the last few steps to see what had happened to her, and in doing so, stumbled across the slit-like entrance to a cave, concealed in the body of the mountain.

Adam went in and Levi followed.

As their eyes adjusted to the darkness, Rachel and Adam were alarmed to see four figures, the size of small humans, square-shouldered, with large, domed heads, painted on the walls around them. Lash-like lines radiated from their eyes, and a similar halo of rays was painted in bright orange around their heads.

They looked like four guardsmen, protecting the cave.

"Wandjina," Levi said. "Ancestors."

The twins blinked and tried to focus on the paintings. Orbs of golden light seemed to swim in front of their eyes. Rachel thought it must have been the image of the strong sun still imprinted on their retinas – but how ever much she blinked, the orbs still circled around the inside of the cave.

"Can you see the blobs, Adam?" she asked, rubbing her eyes.

"Not just me, then," Adam replied. "What are they?"

"I guess 'energy' is the best answer," Levi said. "Look, you know when beings die—"

"You mean they're ghosts?" Adam gasped.

"It's not that simple," Levi said. "When beings die, the body is finished with. It was just a home for the ... energy that drove it along. That energy has to go somewhere."

"Are you saying that these orbs are people's souls?" Rachel hazarded.

Levi sighed. "You two always want everything to be so precise. Can't you just live with the idea that these are orbs of energy harnessed from the world around you?"

Rachel didn't want to live with the idea. She wanted answers, but she guessed she would have to live with it for the time being.

"And if you're tuned in – which you two *are* – then this energy will help you," Levi continued.

Rachel held her hand out to try to touch one of the orbs, but her fingers went straight through it. She got close enough to see that inside the ball of pale golden light, other things moved around. They looked phosphorescent, like the inner workings of a jellyfish. As she stared, the luminous strands started to reform and brighten, as if they were filaments in a bulb.

"Look, Adam," she said.

Adam was already looking. The lights began to revolve and separate – spinning and rotating until there were three small wheels of light intersecting gyroscopically within each orb. All the orbs were becoming brighter. They spun and grouped together until they became a swarm – creating a vortex that reached up into a corner of the narrow cave. In the brighter light, the paintings of the Wandjina seemed to throb with life.

"Go and look," Levi said. He pointed at the corner of the cave where the orbs had gathered. "Climb up!"

For the first time since they had known him, Levi was showing excitement – the look in his eye so unfamiliar that Rachel was slightly unnerved. But before she could express any doubt, Adam was climbing the wall. He quickly found a foothold and began pulling at lichen near where the activity of the orbs was focused. He rapidly scraped away a hole in the wall, pulling at the rocks that filled it and dropping them to the floor of the cave below.

In minutes Adam was clambering back down with a metal box the size of a biscuit tin in his grimy hands.

"Open it," Levi encouraged. "We need to move fast."

Adam and Rachel knelt down and peeled away the tape that was sealing the lid. Inside was a package of newspaper. Adam lifted it out and began to unwrap it.

Rachel could feel excitement fizzing up inside her – although she had no idea what she expected them to find. Adam had unrolled the newspaper to find a cloth beneath it. His hands shook as he unfolded it. The activity of the orbs became suddenly frenzied, bouncing around the walls of the cave. Levi bent down beside them, his eyes bright as Adam undid the last layer of cloth.

Triskellions.

Two of them. Gold and beginning to shine.

"Take one each," Levi said; "then hold hands."

Rachel and Adam each picked up a Triskellion and joined hands, and as they did so, the cave lit up, bright and white, the orbs glowing with the ferocity of halogen bulbs.

Energy surged between the twins. Their hands shook and their minds raced with the images flashing before them: a chalk circle, a burial, a knight and a maiden, a saint and a burning, twins, bees, darkness...

It was as if the software of Rachel and Adam's life was being reinstalled; as if they were being rebooted from the state of inertia that had held them and kept them dormant for the past two years.

Their joint memories refilled their brains, and the twins opened their eyes and looked about the bright cave. The figures of the Wandjina surrounded them, looking down on them like benign relatives at a baptism. Rachel and Adam stared at Levi in amazement. Layer upon layer of his flesh was beginning to peel away, revealing a face more angular, more familiar...

It was as if Levi's face had been an illusion they had wished to believe. A disguise that had made him acceptable to them.

Rachel found it hard to catch her breath. Something leapt in her stomach as she saw the face of Gabriel.

10

The plane's engines were already running by the time they got back to the base of the rock. A heat-haze shimmered across its wings. The cockpit's small window opened and Clifford Possum leaned his head out. "Come on, you guys; hop on board…"

Rachel, Adam and Gabriel ran, ducking beneath the wing and turning towards the cockpit.

"Where's Charlie?" Gabriel asked.

Clifford peered back over his shoulder into the plane. "Oh, he's around here somewhere. Probably taking a leak."

"I'm here."

Rachel, Gabriel and Adam froze as Charlie Possum walked round from the other side of the plane.

He was pointing a shotgun at them. "Get your hands up and don't do anything stupid," he said.

From the cockpit, Clifford Possum stared down, open-mouthed, at his brother. "What the hell d'you think you're doing?"

Charlie shouted up at him without taking his eyes off Gabriel and the twins, and he kept the gun pointed at them. "*One million dollars*, bro. That's the reward for these kids. You any idea what we could *do* with that kind of money?"

The next time Clifford Possum spoke was as he was jumping down from the cockpit and walking slowly towards his brother. "It's not right, Charlie. You know that."

Charlie grunted and shook his head.

"Put the gun down, Charlie," Clifford said.

Charlie said nothing. Keeping one eye on Gabriel and the other on his brother, who was getting closer with every step, he raised an arm to wipe away the sweat that was running down his face.

"Why don't you *do* something?" Rachel hissed at Gabriel.

"I don't have to," he said. "Watch…"

Charlie Possum was shaking, the shotgun veering back and forth between the children and Clifford, who was now no more than a metre away from him.

"You know this is wrong," Clifford said.

Charlie shook his head vehemently. "Don't make me shoot you too."

"You wouldn't," Clifford said, taking another step towards his brother.

"Stop!" Charlie cried, waving the gun.

But Clifford kept going. He lunged forward at the last second – just as Charlie raised the weapon – and made a grab for the gun.

The shots were deafening.

As Rachel, Adam and Gabriel backed away, they could see that the fuselage was peppered with bullet holes, and fuel was beginning to pour from one of the engines.

Oblivious to the danger, the two brothers wrestled over the gun, their screams of anger and frustration echoing off the rock that towered high above them.

"Can't you stop them?" Adam asked.

Gabriel shook his head and dragged the twins back, pulling them away from the plane until they were a safe distance from the explosion that he knew was coming.

The force of it knocked the three of them off their feet. By the time Rachel had managed to stand up again and wipe the sand from her eyes, the plane was already engulfed in flames. She stared into the inferno, trying to make out the figures of Charlie and Clifford Possum. She knew there was no way they could have survived the blast, but just for a second she imagined she saw them: two dark figures, twisting together against a wall of flames.

The spirits of two warring brothers.

Rachel watched Gabriel turn and saunter away and was gripped by panic. It was as if they were suddenly out of control on a terrible rollercoaster ride. She took hold of her brother's arm, which was trembling. Their heads spun with images, memories, feelings; few of them good. Since holding the Triskellions, they had returned to a shocking reality; one in which they remembered the traumatic adventures that had brought them to this continent in the first place.

And now they were out of immediate danger, the full realization hit them both in the stomach like a low punch.

Rachel began to cry and she could clearly see the distress on her brother's face; could feel it in her mind. She turned away from the terrible heat of the fire and saw Gabriel sitting on a rock. He was holding the Triskellions and smiling.

"We were happy, and safe!" Rachel screamed at him. "Then you come along and … start all *this* again."

"You weren't safe," Gabriel said.

"And we are now?" Adam snapped.

Gabriel shrugged and stood up. "We need to go."

"I'm not going anywhere!" Rachel said. "I want to go back and see Mom. Make sure she's OK."

Gabriel said nothing.

"I'm with Rachel." Adam's voice quavered with fear and panic. "Whenever we've followed you, it's ended in disaster."

"But that's just it" – Gabriel rested a hand on his shoulder – "it hasn't ended yet, and it can't end without your help."

"I want it to end," Adam said.

"Good. Then let's make it happen. Aren't you both sick of running? Of hiding?"

Rachel could read her brother's thoughts and knew the answer.

Gabriel had remained so calm and seemed so unmoved by Rachel and Adam's pleas that it was clear there was only one possible way to go.

His way.

"So how do we help you?" Rachel asked.

"There's another one," Gabriel said; "another Triskellion."

"And what happens when we find it?" Rachel asked. "*If* we find it?"

"We need to bring the three together," he said. "That will be the end of it. And yes, we will find it. You already know where it is."

Rachel had a sudden hunch. "It's in the United States, isn't it."

Gabriel nodded.

"Home," Adam said.

They turned at the sudden scream of sirens. A fire engine from the visitors' centre was racing across the scrub towards the burning plane.

"We need to move," Gabriel said. "They mustn't find us here."

They dodged through the undergrowth and skirted round the base of the mountain until they could see the visitors' centre in the distance. Adam went in and bought some water, and Rachel said she needed the toilet. She checked her purse; she still had some money.

After buying something to eat, she found a payphone and dialled the number of the house they had left some days before. There was no answer. Just a piercing continuous disconnected tone.

Rachel had not expected her mother to be there, but having it confirmed only added to her panic.

She thought for a moment; she really needed to speak to someone. She looked around. No one was waiting for the phone.

She dialled another number…

11

"Mel Campbell…"

Laura had barely been able to hear the ringtone of her phone over the grumble of the Jeep's tired engine and had only just remembered in time to use her alias.

"No names," the girl said. "It's me."

Laura slowed down and pulled over. "Are you OK?" she asked. Her heart leapt at the sound of Rachel's voice on the line.

"Sort of," Rachel said. "It's all come back to us, though… Who we are; what we've been through."

Laura sighed and felt a pang of guilt. The worst had happened, and yet the scientist in Laura Sullivan felt a nagging urge to know what would happen next. "Are you safe?"

A brief snort came down the phone. "Guess not. *He's* come back."

"Who?" Laura asked, knowing full well who Rachel meant, but needing it confirmed.

"Think. The boy."

"Where are you?" Laura asked. "I'll come and find you; I'll try to protect you."

"You can't," Rachel said. "Protect Mom."

"I'll do my best." Laura felt herself flush, knowing that her protection had already been inadequate.

"I tried her at the house, but the phone's been cut off. Where is she?"

Laura didn't know what to say. "Just tell me where you are," she urged.

"It's best that you don't know. We're leaving now, anyhow."

"I think I know where you are," Laura said. "Did you find them? In the biscuit tin?"

There was a pause on the other end of the line.

"Yeah," Rachel said. "We did."

"Just tell me where you're going," Laura pleaded.

"No," Rachel said, and then her voice softened a little. "We're going to finish this."

"Please let me come with you…"

"Gotta go."

"Love you…" Laura said.

But Rachel had already gone.

Laura grabbed a crumpled Kleenex from the dashboard, blew her nose loudly and wiped the tears away with the back of her hand. She knew now that they were way ahead of her; she had no chance of catching them.

Deep down, she had always known.

She shrugged, defeated, and her mind flashed back to the cave on the North African coast where they had discovered the second Triskellion. There, she had seen the twins' arrival from New York, their stay in England, the trek across Europe and finally the time they'd spent in Australia, all detailed in a mural painted thousands of years before.

Laura could not bring herself to think of the last series of images: the ones only she had seen that showed an alarming future that had not happened.

At least, not yet.

Laura arrived back in Kalgoorlie early the next afternoon. She had driven all night, keeping herself awake with coffee as soon as she had reached the first signs of civilization.

She checked back into the Nelson Hotel. The room was hot and, although her body ached from hours and hours of bumping over rough terrain, she slept fitfully – bad dreams and anxious thoughts never far from the surface.

She was finally woken by a knock on her door.

"Hello?" she said, nervously.

Another knock.

Laura swung her legs out of bed and pulled on her jeans. She fumbled in her bag and slipped a folding knife into her pocket, then, thinking better of it, opened it and held it concealed in her hand. She crept up to the door and listened, sensing someone still outside.

"Hello?" she said again.

"Laura?" The voice was quiet, close to the door.

Laura fumbled with the catch and swung the door wide open. Standing in the hall, looking drained and frightened was Kate Newman.

Laura bundled her into the room. She caught sight of the haunted expression on Kate's face and hugged her. "You OK?" she asked. She could see that Kate was anything but OK.

"Not really," Kate said weakly. "I'm wanted. For murder."

12

Laura sat Kate down on the bed and made them both coffee. "What are you talking about?" she said, handing Kate a cup. "What murder?"

Kate began to talk…

She had not been nearly strong enough to resist the man who had forced his way into her house. The American had nearly wrenched the door from its hinges, and Kate had fallen back into the room. He had followed coolly behind and closed the door quietly, locking it with the key.

Kate had held the back of a chair, her knees trembling and her heart beating so hard she thought it might burst through her chest.

The American had sat down at the kitchen table without taking off his sunglasses. "Where are they?" he'd asked.

"I don't know."

He'd pushed his glasses up on to his head and pinched the bridge of his nose between his fingers, as if he had already become tired of waiting. "You're their mother, Kate.

You must know where they are."

"I honestly don't," she had said. "They left in the night."

"By themselves?"

"Yes," Kate had lied, thinking that if there was any chance of them escaping, the boy they had left with would provide it.

"Tell me what you know about your kids." The American had looked straight into her eyes.

"They're just a pair of normal kids who happen to be twins."

"Nothing … *special* about them, then?" he had asked.

The maternal instinct had risen up, strong. "Of course they're special. They're my kids."

"We know *that*. But what about special powers? Mind-reading? ESP? Hypnosis?"

"They're just kids," Kate had said. "Leave them alone."

"What do you know about the Hope Project, Kate?"

"Never heard of it."

"Now I *know* you're lying," he'd said, any inflection of warmth gone from his voice. "Apparently, you were a guest of the Project in England for some time a couple of years ago. This is a nice way to repay our hospitality."

He had got up and walked towards her, cracking his knuckles. Kate had steadied herself against the chair. She'd known she was in a corner now and didn't like to think what might happen if she didn't co-operate.

"W-w-wait…" she'd stammered. "I'll tell you what I know.

Just promise me you won't harm them."

"Come on, then." The American had smiled faintly. "Talk."

"OK. I know that they're different; that they have different genes to the rest of us."

"Now we're getting somewhere," the American had said. "And have you heard of Triskellion?"

Kate had nodded. "It was the place where I grew up."

"And what about the artefact that has the same name? Have you ever seen one?"

Kate had known she would have one chance at this, and she had to get it right. She'd hesitated for what had felt like the right amount of time.

"Well?" the American had pressed.

"Yes," she'd replied. "My kids have two of them."

"And do you know where the Triskellions are?"

"Yes. If I show you where they are, will you leave us alone?"

The American had nodded. The excitement had been written clearly across his face.

Kate had taken timid steps over to the cupboard concealed under the stairs by the tongue-and-groove planks.

"Secret cupboard?" the man had joked.

She had run her fingernails along the side of one of the planks. The cupboard had swung open, and with her body she had masked the shotgun that Laura had put there a few days before. She had known she would have to be quick.

In one move she had unhooked the gun and swung it back round into the room, noting in a millisecond the look of panic on the American's face.

"I killed him." Kate's face was blank, traumatized.

Laura shook her head in disbelief.

"He was from Hope," Kate said. "He had a list. He knew who we were. He knew the kids' names!" She took a sip of her drink with a trembling hand.

Laura felt a flutter of panic. "Which names?"

"Their real names," Kate said. "*Our* names."

"We need to get away from here, pronto," Laura said. "How did you leave the place?"

Kate barely heard her. Her mind had flashed back to the moment when the American had tried to wrestle the shotgun from her: how she had accidentally pulled the trigger. He had flown backwards, his black shirt blown to tatters and wet with blood. "There was a struggle…" she murmured. "The gun went off."

"Kate?" Laura said, bringing her back. "How did you leave the house?"

Kate looked at Laura's horrified face.

"I burned it down," she said. "I didn't know what to do… I wanted to destroy everything … the evidence. Now, where are my kids?"

13

The Boeing 747 began its descent from the clear blue.

Rachel shaded her eyes as she watched the wing tips tremble; wisps of cloud and invisible air currents skimmed across the plane, forcing it down towards the earth. Rachel had no clear idea just how these things stayed in the sky. She vaguely knew the physics – the combination of forward thrust and air resistance and so on – but the fact that it stayed up still seemed like a minor miracle.

It appeared that Gabriel also had little confidence in the aeroplane staying in the sky. He had looked sick and nervous for every minute of the past thirty or so hours, and had only rallied a little when the flight had touched down in Chicago and let some passengers off before continuing on to New York. For the past hour his eyes had kept darting nervously to the overhead locker where the Triskellions were wrapped up tightly in Rachel and Adam's backpacks.

The thirty hours of travelling had given the twins time

to get used to the memories that had come back to them. Their childhood in Manhattan. The home they had grown up in. The years spent with the father they would now try to re-establish contact with.

They were both trying not to think what the next leg of their adventure would reveal. Gabriel was giving no clues away. In fact, he had barely spoken to them at all.

Rachel held Gabriel's hand as they continued their descent, feeling for once that she was more in charge of the situation than he was.

The plane banked, and New York stretched out below them: a collection of small islands and peninsulas. As they got closer still, the spires and mirrored towers of Manhattan came into view and sparkled – as shiny and magical as the Emerald City in *The Wizard of Oz*.

The plane dropped further and Rachel recognized the East River below, and just beyond, the runway of LaGuardia Airport. After the bright light of Australia and beneath the cloud canopy, the world looked greyer – and more familiar.

Home.

They queued at passport control. The immigration officer looked Rachel and Adam up and down, studied their passports for a moment and then called a colleague. The two officers then looked through the twins' passports and at the stamps on the pages. They typed in an address on a computer terminal.

The first officer looked up, and Rachel managed to catch his eye.

"We've been to see our grandma," she said, and smiled.

The other officer looked at Adam, who also smiled and nodded in agreement.

"Welcome home." The officers spoke in unison, and waved them through, the first man tipping his cap at Rachel.

They left the terminal building and walked across to where the buses stopped to rejoin Gabriel, who had somehow slipped through customs unnoticed. Adam had seen a payphone and went inside to try to make contact with their father.

Across the concourse, a small group of men in grey suits and women in pink and blue twinsets had gathered. The women were handing out leaflets, and one of the men was talking through a megaphone: "Come and join us at the Church of the Triple Wheel. Ezekiel One will soon be upon us. Become a Triple Wheeler today and be ready for the Gathering…"

A lady in a pink cardigan stepped forward with a beaming smile and gave Rachel a leaflet. "Spread the good news, young lady. Prepare for the Gathering."

Rachel took the leaflet while Gabriel waved away the advance of a young man with a CD.

"Prepare," the man said. "Listen to Pastor Crane in your own home."

Rachel looked at the leaflet. It read:

EZEKIEL ONE. THE TIME IS NOW!

She looked at the picture of a man with a plastic-looking face and blond wig addressing a rally somewhere; his eyes were bright and full of what she took to be religious fervour.

"What's Ezekiel One?" she asked.

Gabriel leaned across. "Let me see," he said, taking the leaflet. "What did you say he was called?"

As Gabriel stared at the leaflet, Adam rejoined them. Rachel saw the look on his face. "Did you speak to Dad?" she asked.

Adam was pale. He shook his head.

"What?" Rachel asked.

"I called his cell phone," Adam replied. "It's been disconnected."

"OK, well—"

"Then I called the university… I got through to Dad's head of department." Adam stopped, opening his mouth and then closing it again. After a second or two he found the words: "They've never *heard* of him. I thought it was just a stupid mistake, you know. Made sure they were spelling 'Newman' right, whatever…"

"So…?"

"No mistake."

"I don't understand," Rachel said.

"They told me Ralph Newman's never worked there," Adam said. "It's like Dad never existed…"

"There's probably a perfectly simple explanation," Gabriel said.

Rachel nodded. "Right."

"Or a perfectly terrifying one," Adam said. "What if they've got him? Those freaks from the Hope Project. What if they're using Dad to try and get to us?"

Rachel looked at Gabriel. She could tell straight away he was thinking that it was a possibility.

"Let's not panic," she said. "Let's just get on a bus and get ourselves into Manhattan."

Adam half smiled. It sounded like a good plan. "OK," he said. "Let's go check out the old apartment."

A few states away, Pastor Ezekiel Crane sat in his Winnebago picking out a tune on his guitar. He had spent the morning addressing a crowd at an out-of-town shopping mall: a vast temple to TJ Maxx, Starbucks and Timberland. It had been mainly his usual crowd – straight, law-abiding families with 2.4 children. Although, recently he had noticed a new element creeping in. On the fringes of the crowd at his rallies, he had begun to see blue-collar workers: truck drivers in baseball caps and plaid shirts who took their hats off out of respect when he spoke. There were also shop girls, mall-workers, security guards and people of diverse origin who kept the pavements swept and washed.

"Beginning to see some new faces, Jed," he said. He tipped a white-filtered cigarette from a paper pack and put it into his mouth before dropping the pack on to the counter top, next to his ever-present can of Dr Pepper.

"Yes, sir, Pastor Crane. New faces. The good news is spreading and the people are listening. Hallelujah." Brother Jedediah fumbled in the deep pockets of his black slacks and found a lighter. He lit Crane's cigarette with a flourish as if he were trying to impress a lady.

Crane took a long drag and blew the smoke from his smooth nostrils.

Brother Jed looked pleased with himself and hitched his trousers up over his big stomach. "They're all preparing for the Gathering," he said. "Yes, sir, and amen!"

A bee crawled over the counter top to feast on the sticky drops of Dr Pepper that had spilled from the can. Ezekiel Crane watched the insect drink, then, gently picking it up between finger and thumb, he enclosed it, without crushing it, in his fist. He shook his hand a little to make the bee defensive, then appeared to enjoy the little jolt of pain as it plunged its sting into the palm of his hand.

His eyes began to widen and glaze over. In his mind, he saw a plane touching down and watched as three figures he knew all too well disembarked and moved towards the city.

Crane looked up at his sweaty assistant through narrowed eyes. He stared at the TRIPLE WHEEL badge pinned to the man's lapel and took another deep drag on his cigarette. "Brother Jedediah," he said, "I have a stirring in my bones; I sense it in my waters ... I can feel it in my soul." Crane opened his hand and let the dead bee fall to the floor.

"You can, Pastor?" Brother Jedediah was hanging on his master's every word, panting like an eager dog.

"Yes, I can. Shall I tell you what I'm feeling, Jed? I'm feeling that the drones are getting ready to swarm. I'm feeling that the Gathering may have already begun."

14

The subway thundered along past names that were old friends to Rachel and Adam: Canal Street, Spring, Bleecker. The train rattled and screeched through stations almost completely tattooed with graffiti, while the yellow light in the carriage made everyone look pale and ill. Gabriel looked as much a fish out of water as he had on the plane.

Although she felt better being on her home turf, Rachel was unnerved by the lack of confidence Gabriel was showing. Before, he had been so much more in charge.

In control.

In the ancient English countryside, on the prehistoric coast of Morocco, in Europe even, Gabriel had seemed more grounded. Even as Levi in Australia, he had seemed completely at home in the barren desert. But somehow the hustle and bustle of New York seemed to diminish him.

They got out at Astor Place and Gabriel flinched at the four lanes of yellow taxis and assorted vehicles that honked and jostled their way down the wide street outside. Rachel took his arm and Adam slapped him on the shoulder. "Welcome to the Big Apple," he said.

They walked across the square and down into the smaller leafier streets that led to the East Village, where they had lived until two years before. Gabriel relaxed a little as the streets became smaller, the buildings lower, the cars fewer and the trees greener.

Rachel began to feel happy and in doing so, realized how little happiness she had felt since she was last here.

"You don't seem too impressed by the city," Adam said. He watched Gabriel looking across the street at an old homeless white man, apparently drunk, shouting at an equally drunk and equally old homeless black man.

"I think it's hell," Gabriel said.

"A little harsh." Rachel almost laughed. "You've only been here five minutes."

"Sorry." Gabriel smiled. "Maybe I used the wrong word – but I'm usually right."

Rachel felt a little prickly in defence of her own town. Gabriel had only been on the bus and the subway and two blocks later he was an authority on the place. To be fair, she hadn't seen too much of the rough side of the city herself. She had come from a reasonably prosperous family and had kept to the safer parts of town. Their father had – at least she'd *thought* he'd had – a good research position at the university. They'd owned a large apartment. Her mom had …

well, she didn't want to think about where her mother was or what her mother was doing. As soon as they found their dad, they could start looking for their mom. Try to get her home.

"I think you're jumping to conclusions," Rachel said.

"OK," Gabriel said. "All I'm saying is that living in a city this size means people lose a lot of what makes the world worth living in. The ground under our feet was once as wild as the outback of Australia."

Rachel had forgotten that the city had once been a wilderness, but now she had a sudden image of a series of islands, lush and fertile, connected by waterways, with the ocean beyond. Natives as old as the Aboriginals had populated and cultivated the area; had given the central part of the city its name: Manhattan.

"Get outta the goddam way!" A harsh Brooklyn accent jolted Rachel from her thoughts. A taxi driver had almost clipped her with his wing mirror as she'd stepped dreamily off the kerb.

Adam grabbed her by the arm and shouted his own choice words at the driver, who raised a single finger at them out of the window of his battered yellow cab.

Gabriel raised an eyebrow. "Welcome home," he said.

They walked on a few blocks further, past shops, galleries and restaurants – all of them new since Rachel had last been here.

"It's all changed," she said.

"Neighbourhood's coming up," Adam said, grinning.

Rachel felt that the changes to the familiar streets were an imposition. She had wanted everything to be exactly the same as she remembered. She was pleased to see that her favourite vintage store was still there: a pretty seventies print dress displayed on a mannequin in the window. Rachel stopped and looked at it, then glanced down at her worn jeans, scuffed sneakers and baggy T-shirt. She was a mess. She couldn't remember the last time she'd had new clothes. Adam and Gabriel looked back to see what she was doing. They looked pretty scruffy, too. Neither of them would have looked out of place in a skate-park. But it was different for boys…

Five minutes later Rachel re-emerged on to the street with the dress and a brand-new pair of white Converse in a bag.

"C'mon, Rach," Adam said, shrugging at Gabriel.

They turned into East 11th Street, and Rachel's heart lurched as they neared their old home. She could tell Adam felt the same because he looked at her and crossed his fingers.

The brownstone building looked as if it might have been cleaned and repainted. The familiar steel fire escape zig-zagged up the apartment block and the arched windows on the third floor looked homely, like benign eyes looking out across the street.

Rachel stopped Gabriel. "This is where we live," she said.

In all her travels Rachel had managed to hold on to one thing from her past: her key ring. She made a nervous check in her pocket to make sure it was there. It was, and she put the front-door key in the lock.

They went inside. Rachel had not realized how strong the feeling in her gut would be as she walked down the familiar hallway. The building was not just a building; it was a repository for nearly all their childhood memories.

"Do you feel it too?" she asked Adam.

He nodded. "Hmm."

It was in everything: the light in the entrance hall, the thick layers of paint around the doorframe. The worn front steps reminded them of coming and going, first to kindergarten, then to middle school. Their Christmases had been here, as had all their birthdays until the age of fourteen.

Home.

They went up the stairs to the third floor. The corridor was brighter than when they had last been here and the smell of fresh paint was stronger than the floor polish and disinfectant that the twins remembered. With their sensory memory thrown off a little, they realized that although they knew every nook and cranny of the building, the old patina was gone. It was as if their layer had been erased.

In her heart of hearts, Rachel knew that her dad would not be in the apartment. Not hearing from your father for two years was unusual even after the most acrimonious of divorces, and she hoped that the apartment might at least yield some clue as to his whereabouts.

Taking a deep breath, she pulled the key ring out of her pocket again. The key would not go in the lock. She tried again, but it was too big for the slot.

"Must've changed it," Adam said.

The rattling of Rachel's key had clearly alerted someone inside; they could hear steps coming towards the door. "Who is it?" A woman's voice came from inside.

A security chain rattled and a bolt was thrown. The apartment door opened a crack.

"Rachel and Adam Newman," Rachel said.

The door opened a bit wider, and a woman's face poked through. She was youngish, about thirty, with streaked blonde hair and a pleasant freckled face. They could hear a child in the background.

"Yeah?" she said.

"Hi," Rachel said, smiling her friendliest smile.

"Hi," Adam said.

"We … er … used to live here," Rachel stammered. "We thought our dad might still be here. Do you know him? He's called Ralph Newman."

The woman looked from Rachel to Adam and then at Gabriel. "No, I'm sorry. I've never heard of a Ralph Newman."

"Oh, but … don't you rent this place from him?" Rachel asked. She peered past the woman, trying to see into the apartment. It certainly looked different. The hallway had been painted a pale yellow.

"No. Me and my husband bought the apartment from the co-operative who own the building nearly two years ago." She was starting to look a little suspicious. "I've never heard of anyone with that name living here."

"*We* used to live here!" Adam insisted.

"I don't think so," the woman said.

The idea that their father had sold their home was a blow that Rachel and Adam felt simultaneously. They couldn't believe he would have done anything so heartless. They heard the child call out in the room beyond.

"You'll have to excuse me," the woman said, closing the door on them.

15

Many blocks downtown, the director of the Hope Project looked as if he was about to murder someone. His assistant, Meredith, was sheepish as he read the printout she had just handed him.

"Send Crow in," he snapped. "Now."

Meredith, relieved that his temper was going to be vented on someone else, turned to leave. "Coffee, sir?" she asked on her way out.

The director made no answer.

Moments later a compact muscular man with a broken nose entered the office. He was nervous and was trying to disguise it with a grimly set jaw.

"Sit down, Crow."

The man tugged at the creases in his trousers and sat down opposite the director. He rubbed a hand over his blond buzz-cut and cleared his throat.

"How do you explain this?" The director waved the piece of paper at Crow and read the bullet points aloud: the body of a Hope operative had been found in a burnt-out house in Western Australia. He had been shot before being burned.

"I don't know, sir, is the truth. We picked up the message from the Australian police yesterday."

"Let me get this right, Crow," the director said; "we're one of the world's most secretive and powerful intelligence services and now we're letting hick Australian policemen from Woola-Woola do our investigating for us?"

"No, sir," Crow protested. "I thought our agent had it under control. He'd found the house and had it watched by the local operative there."

The director stared at the map of Australia on his desk, then he took a pen and drew a line through the circle around Perth up to the area where the dead man had been found.

"Our agent assured me it would be easy once they'd found the house," Crow continued. "He didn't expect any resistance; it was just two women and two kids."

"Are you out of your mind, Crow? Have you forgotten what the Hope Project is about? Have you forgotten where these kids are from and what they are capable of?"

Crow looked at the desk and ground his teeth. "No, sir."

"At best you are irresponsible, letting our agent go there alone. At worst, you are incompetent."

Crow went to speak; the director held up his hand to silence him. "I don't want to hear any more. It was you who persuaded me that Van der Zee's idea to let those kids loose in the first place was the right thing to do. If I'd taken my own advice, we'd have them sliced up and bottled in specimen jars – where they belong – by now. And Van der Zee would still be alive, and so would one of our best agents. *And* we might have some conclusive research results!"

"I think the agent wanted the glory of bringing them in alone," Crow said, attempting to defend himself.

"This isn't about glory. He was your responsibility, Crow."

As the director tidied the papers on his desk, Crow felt that his dressing-down was coming to an end. "I'm going to recommend you for a transfer," the director said, looking up at Crow, who appeared to be holding his breath. "To Alamogordo."

Crow was horrified. There were some postings that might have suited him, but being sent to the most secretive Hope Project centre of all, in the middle of the New Mexico desert, was like a death sentence. Once you went to Alamogordo, you never came back from the wilderness. Crow couldn't speak. He rose from his chair.

"With immediate effect, Crow," the director added. "Clear your desk."

Crow slunk out of the office, his head hung low.

"Hey, Crow," the director called after him. Crow turned back, a look on his face that said he expected his boss to reveal it was all a big joke and that he still had his job in New York.

"Yes, sir?" he said.

"Alamogordo's not so bad." The director smiled. "I sort of grew up there. So long…"

Rachel was not satisfied. She could not believe that the apartment was no longer theirs. "I'm going in," she said.

"You sure?" Adam asked. But Rachel was already rapping on the door.

The young woman opened it again, looking exasperated. "What?" she said. "I told you I couldn't help you."

Rachel held the door open and fixed the woman with her eyes, holding her gaze, waiting until she had control. "I know. I'm really sorry," she said, "but I'm sure you wouldn't mind if we just looked around."

The expression on the woman's face softened and she began to smile. "Sure," she said, as if they were old friends. "Come in." She opened the door wider and the three of them walked in.

"I'm Rachel, and this is Adam … and Gabriel," Rachel said.

"I'm Holly," the woman said, shaking hands. "And this is Ben." She pointed to a toddler, who was sitting on the floor, surrounded by toys and building bricks, watching *Sesame Street* – just as Rachel and Adam had in this room ten years or so before.

"Hi, Ben," Rachel said.

"Say hello, Ben," his mother said. "Sorry, he doesn't really speak much yet. He's only just turned two."

Ben looked at them, but said nothing.

Holly led them through the living room and into the kitchen. Rachel's eyes flicked around, taking in the differences and the similarities. They were certainly the same rooms, but now they were filled with someone else's taste and furniture. Everything looked so different. The kitchen was the only thing that had remained the same; the industrial cooker and the steel worktops on which they had last eaten their breakfast more than two years before had not changed.

"Love your kitchen," Rachel said.

"Thanks," Holly said, wiping the surface with her hand. "We left it just as it was when we moved in. We decorated everywhere else."

"You don't have any old letters or bills and stuff from the previous owners, do you?" Adam asked.

"I don't think so," Holly said. "I'll have a look, though."

She went to a cupboard and pulled out a few letters and handed them to Adam. He flicked through the pile; it was mostly free offers for people whose names meant nothing to him.

"Thanks," he said, handing them back.

"Can I get you guys a drink?" Holly asked.

Although she would have loved one, Rachel felt it was time to go. The apartment was no longer theirs.

The twins followed Holly back into the sitting room, where they had left Gabriel watching TV and playing with

Ben. In the middle of the floor was a building of astonishing complexity made of Lego bricks, drinking straws, cocktail sticks and anything else that had been to hand.

Holly gasped at the spires, the swooping walkways, the buttresses and the windows made of marbles and ice cubes that were beginning to melt, all lit from inside by a lava lamp and torch.

"Oh my God," she said. "That's so beautiful."

Ben looked up at his mother and smiled. "Gabriel showed me how."

Holly's jaw dropped even further. Not only had her two-year-old son built an amazing construction from scratch, but he had also just put his first sentence together.

"I just helped him along a little," Gabriel said, grinning.

Looking at him, Rachel realized suddenly how much she had missed that smile. Seeing Gabriel standing there in her old home, seeing the beauty of what he had accomplished and the joy he had brought to the child and his mother, she felt a rush of warmth towards him. But she also sensed that given their circumstances, such moments as these would be rare and brief. "We need to go," she said. "Great to meet you."

The young mother was still staring at the cathedral her child had built as they let themselves out of the apartment.

16

Rachel was disappointed. She had expected the apartment to yield at least some small intimation of their former life. Some clue as to their father's whereabouts. Only the kitchen remained as proof that the place had ever been their home – all other evidence of their existence had long since been wiped away. They walked down the staircase in silence, past all the other anonymous apartment doors that concealed other people's lives.

Back in the entrance hall they could hear hammering. The noise was coming from an open service door. Inside, a bulkhead light lit up a flight of stairs leading down to the basement.

Adam paused a moment and looked down.

Rachel read his thoughts: "Mr Hoffman?"

Adam nodded. The janitor of the block might still be the same one who had been here since they were small.

Adam and Rachel ventured downstairs towards the source of the banging, while Gabriel waited in the hall.

The basement was concrete and brick: warm and dusty with thick pipes that provided the block with heat. In the corner, a man in a brown duster coat was attacking a heating pipe with a wrench.

"Mr Hoffman?" Rachel called.

The man could not hear her above the clanging. Rachel went over and touched him on the shoulder. He jumped and let out an involuntary cry. "What the…?"

As he turned, Rachel saw that it *was* Mr Hoffman, a little greyer and a touch heavier, but still the same man who had looked after the building for as long as they could remember.

"You tryin' to gimme a heart attack? Whadda you want?" He gripped the wrench in his hand as if he might be about to fend them off with it. He looked from one twin to the other, not recognizing either of them.

"Sorry, Mr Hoffman we didn't mean to alarm you. We're Rachel and Adam Newman."

"Congratulations," Mr Hoffman said in a gruff voice. "Now if that's all you came to tell me, can you leave me to get on with fixing this pipe?"

Rachel persevered. "Sorry, no. I mean we're Rachel and Adam Newman who used to live in apartment three zero one."

Mr Hoffman looked a little closer. "Lotta people come and gone recently. I can't remember them all."

"Our mother was … *is* Kate Newman. The English woman?"

"Sure. I remember Kate Newman. She was always polite to me. Good manners. Her husband was a schmuck, though. How could he leave a good woman like that and throw her out of house and home?"

"That was our mom and dad," Adam said.

"Kate Newman had young kids," Hoffman said. "Twins."

Rachel pointed to herself and Adam. "That's us," she said. "We've grown a bit. It's been two years, at least."

Mr Hoffman looked at them closely again, a glimmer of recognition creeping across his face, followed by a smile. "You were the kid who fell off the fire escape?" He prodded Adam gently in the chest.

Adam nodded. He remembered the incident well. He had fallen from the first floor, nearly breaking his neck, but escaping miraculously with only cuts and bruises.

"You gave me quite a scare," Mr Hoffman said, rubbing his chin. "Why, I knew you two when you were just babies. Cute little twins in pink and blue."

Adam chuckled, embarrassed.

"You taking a trip down memory lane?"

"I suppose we are, in a way," Rachel said. "We were just looking for any stuff of ours that might have been left here. You know, letters or anything like that. You see we can't find our dad."

Mr Hoffman gave them a look that said as far as he was concerned finding him would be no good thing, but aloud he told them to "Come into the office."

They went into a small bleak room on the other side of the basement. Mr Hoffman had furnished it with a cushioned office chair. Padding exploded from the splits in its worn plastic upholstery and a scrawny-looking black and white cat lay curled up in one corner.

"That's Bilko," Hoffman said. "Meanest cat you ever saw."

The cat opened its one eye, studied the children for a few seconds, then went back to sleep.

Besides the cat and chair, there were a kettle, some stained coffee mugs and an electric fire that was not needed in the stuffy underground air. On one wall, Mr Hoffman's tools were arranged on a board, their shapes outlined in marker pen – where a tool had been lost or misplaced, its ghost remained, silhouetted by the outline. On the other side of the room was a battered filing cabinet and a desk, stacked up with papers, pens, half-smoked cigars, bits of junk in various shapes and sizes.

Mr Hoffman made a cursory attempt to tidy the surface of the desk, muttering all the while: "Newman … Newman. Apartment…"

"Three zero one," Rachel prompted.

He looked in pigeon holes above the desk that were stuffed with papers and receipts and the odd fast-food carton.

"Newman. Newman…"

He climbed up on his chair and looked at wads of envelopes, held together by rubber bands and piled up on top of the pigeon holes.

"Newman. Newman…"

He climbed down again and looked in the drawer of the desk. It revealed cigar boxes, tins of cough sweets, tubs of oil and a variety of nuts, bolts and tubes of glue. Mr Hoffman stopped momentarily and scratched his head. He turned to see Rachel and Adam looking expectantly at him, watching his every move.

"What was that number again?"

"Three zero one," Adam said.

Mr Hoffman opened the top drawer of the grey steel filing cabinet and flicked through the files suspended in the drawer. "Just give me a second…"

He slammed the top drawer shut and opened the middle one. He ran thick fingers, clearly not designed for administrative work, across the files. Then his fingers stopped. "Newman. Got it!"

He lifted a file from the cabinet and placed it on top of the other papers on his desk. He opened the folder and Rachel could see there were several letters inside. Mr Hoffman looked at the twins and tapped his head with his forefinger. "Knew there was something somewhere for Newman."

Rachel's stomach fluttered with excitement as she rifled through the letters. One stood out from the statements and utility bills. It was a thick white package with an English stamp showing the head of the Queen. It was addressed to RACHEL AND ADAM NEWMAN in a spidery handwriting that she recognized.

"It's from our grandmother," Rachel said, staring at the postmark.

The letter was stamped TRISKELLION and dated a little over two years earlier.

They found a booth in a diner two blocks away and ordered Cokes and all-day breakfasts.

"Open it," Adam said.

Rachel looked around nervously. No one was paying them any attention. She glanced at Gabriel, who looked as eager as Adam to see the contents of the package.

It was thick and fastened with Sellotape. Rachel used a knife to slice it open and slid the contents out: a letter and a black and white photograph.

The photo was of three people: a man and two women, one of whom was in an air force uniform, with a large aeroplane on a runway behind them. The woman in the uniform was glamorous and curvaceous. Rachel knew from the hairstyle and the lipstick that this was her grandmother, Celia Root. The other woman was also striking, but taller and more stern-looking. Rachel did not recognize her. The man was handsome with a strong jaw and nose.

"That's Commodore Wing," Adam said.

"Our grandfather," Rachel said, as much to remind herself as Adam.

In front of the three adults were two young boys. One was smaller and wearing shorts, the other was a more all-American kid: taller, with a flat-top and long trousers. Both boys were staring intensely into the camera, their faces unsmiling.

Rachel unfolded the letter. It was dated August two years previously. It had been written while they were still in Triskellion.

Clutching the photograph, Rachel began to read. The opening lines of her grandmother's letter made her heart thump against her ribs and filled her mind with vivid sights and sounds which grew in detail and colour, until they felt as real as her own memories…

My darlings, Rachel and Adam,

In order to understand everything that has happened to you, you will need to go back to where it all began. I enclose a photograph of myself in my younger days in the 1950s and I know that this will help you see the truth. I am so sorry that I will not be there to help you, because if you are reading this then I am almost certainly dead…

part two:
the homecoming

17

C elia Root crossed the hot airstrip of Alamogordo Air Force Base and took the last few steps towards the house of her old sweetheart, Gerald Wing.

The day was getting hotter still and Celia's blue service tunic felt rough against her clammy neck as she walked across the neatly cropped dried-out lawn to the house with the big blue Packard parked outside. She took a deep breath and walked up to the door. She rapped decisively, so that she knew there would be no turning back.

The door was opened by a woman wearing civilian clothes. "Hello?" she said. She was American.

Was she Gerry's housekeeper? Celia wondered. His secretary?

"I'm so sorry to disturb you," Celia said. "I was looking for Squadron Leader Wing."

The woman smiled at the formality of Celia's request. "I'm afraid the squadron leader isn't here right now," she said. "But he'll be back soon. Do you want to come in and wait?"

"Thank you," Celia said. "I'm Airwoman Celia Root."

The woman smiled again and held out her hand. "How do you do. I'm Eleanor Wing."

Celia fought to recover her breath, and tried her best to smile at the woman she now knew to be Gerald's wife.

The house was modern inside, with spindly furniture in brightly coloured upholstery and lamps that looked like parts of a spacecraft. Celia followed Eleanor into an open-plan living room and sat down on a long red sofa. She was still in a daze, trying to come to terms with the fact that Gerald Wing had married.

"Have you been at the base long?" Eleanor said. "I think I would have remembered you."

"I only arrived today," Celia said. "From England."

"So are you here to see Gerald on air force business?"

"Not really. I mean to say, I am in Alamogordo on RAF business, but I know Gerald from back in England. We come from the same village."

"How delightful," Eleanor said, sounding genuinely pleased. "Gerry will be so thrilled to see you."

Suddenly Celia was not sure that Gerald would be thrilled to see her at all, but before she could say anything else, two boys came running into the room.

"Mommy," the smaller boy squealed, "Rudolph's hitting me and pinching me." The boy was wearing shorts and a grey jumper. He had tears in his eyes and held his forearm out to show his mother the pinch mark.

"He did it to himself," the bigger boy whined. He was a

couple of years older, and to Celia looked somehow more American, with long trousers, a plaid shirt and his hair cut in a military style called a flat-top. "He's just trying to get me in trouble again."

"Is this true, Hilary?" Eleanor looked sternly at her younger son. The small boy fixed his mother with bright blue eyes.

"He's lying, Mommy. He hurt me."

"I'll talk to you both about this later," Eleanor said. "Now go to your rooms. Your father will be home in a minute and he will not be pleased."

Both boys turned and left the room. Hilary glanced back at Celia as he went and poked out his tongue.

"I'm sorry about that," Eleanor said. "I'm afraid an air force base is not the best place to bring up children."

"Have you been married to Gerry long?" Celia coloured, suddenly feeling she was becoming a little too personal, but Eleanor's face registered no surprise.

"Oh, just over seven years," she said. "Rudi's my son from my first marriage."

Seven years, Celia thought. Just about the length of time since Gerry had last written to her. "I'm sorry," she said. "Rude of me to pry."

Eleanor went up to the window and pulled a curtain aside. A military Jeep had rumbled up to the front of the house and Celia heard a door slam.

"Speaking of Gerry," Eleanor said, "here he is now... Keep quiet; this will be such a surprise!"

* * *

Surprise was not the word Celia would have chosen to describe the look on Gerald Wing's face when he saw her standing in the middle of his sitting room. Horror, perhaps, or confusion. Rage, even.

"Celia?" he said.

"Hello, Gerry." She could see that he was trying to contain himself, to conceal from his wife whatever emotion he was going through.

"Let me fix some drinks," Eleanor said, walking towards the kitchen.

As soon as his wife had left the room, Wing turned on Celia. "What the devil are you doing here?" he whispered hoarsely. "Are you mad?"

"I thought you'd be pleased. I didn't know you were married."

"Well, I am," Wing said. "And that's that."

"Why did you stop writing?" Celia's voice was beginning to crack.

"How could I write?" he said. "I was married! Besides the authorities wouldn't allow it. No contact with home was permitted."

"Do you love her?" Celia blurted out. She didn't care about the authorities – or his work.

Wing's head dropped, and when he raised it again to look at her, the anger had gone from his eyes. "You know you and I could never have married, Celia … and you know why."

Against her better instincts, tears began to prick at Celia's eyes. Wing looked away and saw his stepson eavesdropping at the bottom of the staircase. The boy darted back upstairs.

Wing handed Celia a large handkerchief. His voice softened. "Chin up, old girl. Eleanor will be in with the drinks in a moment and I don't want her thinking I've made you cry."

But the softening of Wing's voice did exactly that and, mumbling an apology, Celia rushed to the front door and stumbled into the street. Gerald followed and pulled her back, and there was no more than a momentary resistance before she was in his arms and they were kissing each other.

Lost in their embrace, neither saw the two boys watching them from the upstairs windows...

18

It had begun to get dark and Gabriel suggested that they find somewhere to spend the night. Somewhere to relax and work out what their next move would be.

"Let's go stay at some swanky hotel," Adam had suggested.

Rachel had agreed, as desperate as her brother for a hot shower and the space to relax and take in what they had read and "seen" of their grandmother's past.

They had checked in to the Waldorf Astoria. The twins' powers of "persuasion" meant that money was no object.

Now, while Gabriel sat centimetres away from the vast television set in the corner of their suite, happily flicking from channel to channel, Rachel and Adam lay sprawled on the bed, both wrapped in white towelling robes.

Rachel looked over at her brother. She knew without asking that he was thinking the same thing as her and had been since the visit to their old apartment – although neither of them had been brave enough to say it out loud.

"You think they've got Dad?" Rachel said.

"Who?"

Rachel knew that Adam understood exactly who she was talking about, but equally she knew that it was not the easiest thing to talk about. "The Hope Project. Van der Zee's cronies," she prompted.

Even saying the name made her shudder. Clay Van der Zee had been the American doctor who had kept the two of them captive in a secret research laboratory in the English countryside; who had given the instruction to have them killed. Under his orders Rachel and Adam had been chased across Europe until he had finally perished when one of his own attack helicopters had crashed into his boat off the coast of Morocco.

Just after they had found the second Triskellion.

"They must have taken him," Adam said. "Why else wouldn't he be around? They must have got to the people he works with at the university, too … made them pretend they'd never heard of him. It's like he just … never existed."

"They'll try and use him to get to us," Rachel said. "Just like they did with Mom."

"But he doesn't know anything."

"*They* don't know that."

Adam nodded grimly, fighting to dispel the image of his father suffering simply because of them.

Being tortured for information he didn't have.

"Dad's pretty tough," he said, tears pricking at the corners of his eyes. "Isn't he…?"

On the other side of the room, Gabriel was still channel-surfing, fascinated by the bizarre array of contrasting images that flashed in front of his eyes every few seconds. Cartoons, sports and adverts. Lots of adverts. He stopped flicking when he saw a face he recognized, heard a lilting voice. A caption appeared on the screen: THE GATHERING IS ONLY DAYS AWAY!

He turned towards the twins. "Hey, it's those people we saw at the airport."

But Rachel and Adam were not listening.

"We need to find him," Rachel was saying. "We need to get Dad."

"Find him where?"

"Wherever they are."

"Go looking for them?" Adam sounded horrified.

"You heard what Gabriel said. Aren't you sick of running and hiding?"

Gabriel was on his feet now, throwing open drawers: looking for something.

"We're going to find Dad," Rachel said firmly to Adam. "And we're going to end this."

Adam sat on the edge of the bed. His features settled, hardened themselves into an expression of determination. He nodded at Rachel. "So where do we start?"

Rachel gathered up the letter and photograph from the bed in front of her. "She left us these for a reason," she said, waving them. She read part of the letter again. "Like she said; we need to go back to where it all began."

Gabriel had found what he was looking for. "Move over," he said, pushing between them and laying the huge map he had found in a drawer out on the bed.

He ran his finger slowly across it until he came to the place he was searching for. A small town in the middle of the desert that was home to an air force base in New Mexico. "There," he said.

Rachel nodded. "Alamogordo…"

Eighteen thousand kilometres away it was early morning in Australia, and at Perth Airport Brett Harkness was starting to sweat. Laura Sullivan's oldest friend, a man she had known since high school, was shaking his head and wondering aloud why he always did whatever she asked him to do; how he always let himself get badgered into doing such crazy things. An hour before it had sounded like a reasonable enough idea, like it would be a good laugh, but now…

"Relax," Laura said, seeing the worry on his face. "If we get caught, just tell them we talked you into it."

"You *did* talk me into it."

"Well, you shouldn't be such a pushover."

Kate laughed, but she was every bit as terrified as Brett was. Only Laura seemed truly calm, sizing up the cops and airport staff that seemed to outnumber the passengers lining up to go through the security checks by about three to one.

"We're just a couple of girls off to Europe on holiday." She touched Kate's arm. "OK?"

"OK," Kate said. She caught the eye of a cop near the metal detector and looked away quickly. Had he recognized her? She knew that by now her details would have been circulated to every force in the country and perhaps beyond. She was a wanted murderer and the first thing the police did when they were on the lookout for a killer on the run was to watch the ports.

She was doing just what they expected her to do.

Laura handed Kate her passport. She could see how worried her friend was. "Firstly they're looking for 'Debbie Crocker' and you're travelling on Kate Newman's passport. And even if they have got a picture, your new look's bound to fool them. So don't worry."

Kate nodded and ran her fingers through the hair that Laura had cut and dyed blonde the night before. She knew the risk she was running – the risk that Brett and Laura were running on her behalf – but if there was the smallest chance of getting Rachel and Adam back, it was worth it.

"You ready, mate?" Laura said, turning to Brett.

"As I'll ever be." Brett took a deep breath. "You owe me one, Sullivan."

"Let's go," Laura said.

The line of passengers moved forward, and they walked casually towards the metal detector. Ahead of them a family began loading their hand luggage on to the conveyor belt, moaning all the while about taking off their shoes and belts and arguing about whether the wife had any liquids in her handbag.

Laura leaned close to Brett and whispered, "Time to check if *you've* got anything dangerous in your bag."

Brett nodded and carefully lowered his small backpack to the floor. He checked to see that no one was looking and then reached inside and slowly drew something out. Pretending to tie his shoelace, he laid the object down at the feet of the woman behind him. She was too busy brushing her hair to notice – when she *did* notice, the scream made Brett jump, even though he knew it was coming.

"Snake!" she screeched, pointing and trying to push her way out of the line.

Brett stepped back theatrically and made sure his voice carried: "Bloody hell; that's a taipan!"

The name of the most venomous snake in Australia was enough to get everybody's attention, and the panic spread quickly. Passengers scattered and screamed, and half a dozen cops came running towards Brett, who had begun trying to pick the snake up.

The cops began to shout. "Don't be stupid!" "Get away!" "That thing'll kill you…"

The fact that the reptile in question was Brett's own pet, a harmless grass snake called Kevin, was just about the only thing keeping Brett calm. He continued shouting, while all around him cops drew their weapons and told people not to panic. All this caused enough of a distraction for Kate and Laura to slip, unseen, through the security cordon and begin walking quickly towards the gate.

A woman fainted when Brett finally picked up the snake and held it aloft. "Hang on," he shouted. "My mistake! Crikey, the bugger *looks* like a taipan, though…"

The cops holstered their guns and turned away, muttering and shaking their heads. Passengers began to shuffle back into line around him, and through the sea of faces staring disapprovingly at him, he could just make out the figures of Laura and Kate disappearing around a corner towards their plane.

He saw Laura turn back and nod her thanks.

"Yeah, you owe me big time," he said.

19

A giant white statue of a man stretched his arms out as if to welcome them to Pennsylvania Station. It was a simple sculpture, primitive and bold, yet somehow it diminished the fussy classical façade of Penn Station behind.

It was a bright morning, and Rachel and Adam felt rested after spending the night in one of New York's plushest hotels. They were also very full, having eaten a breakfast that would have fed a family of four for a week. Gabriel had grudgingly enjoyed the surroundings at the Waldorf, but had been relatively uninterested in sleep or food.

He walked into the crowded ticket office at the station and up to the front of the queue without anyone noticing that he had jumped a line some twenty people long.

He came back with tickets for Rachel and Adam as far as Cincinnati, Ohio: the first leg of their journey out of New York.

Voices echoed across the vast atrium of the main

station, fighting with electronic announcements. Above the cacophony, one announcement was coming through clearly: "Ezekiel One! The time is now! Tick-Tock. Tick-Tock. Prepare yourselves for the day…"

Rachel, Adam and Gabriel pushed through the crowds to find a group of people similar to the ones they had seen at the airport. They were gathered around a stand with the banner of the Triple Wheel over their heads.

"It's those Triple Wheel guys again," Adam said. "They give me the creeps."

Rachel was approached by a woman with a leaflet.

"Tick-Tock. Tick-Tock," she said, wagging a finger from side to side like a pendulum. "Are you prepared for the Gathering, young lady?"

"I'm not sure," Rachel said.

Gabriel stood next to her protectively, and a man from the group of Triple Wheelers, seeing the potential for a couple of converts, came and joined them. Gabriel took the leaflet the man was holding and read it.

"Do we have some converts to the Triple Wheel, Sister Sarah?" the man asked.

"I hope so, Brother John," the woman said, smiling blandly.

"Tell me about the Triple Wheel," Gabriel said.

"Glad you asked, young man," Brother John said, with a greasy smile. "The Triple Wheel is what the prophet Ezekiel saw come to earth. Pastor Crane likes to think of it as three hoops of energy that spin across one another like a gyroscope, creating a greater energy than can be found anywhere on earth. And it was in the Triple Wheel – what some call Ezekiel's Wheel – that the first Travellers came to earth. Isn't that right, Sister Sarah?"

"Amen, Brother John," Sarah said.

"And who do you think these Travellers were?" Gabriel asked.

"Pastor Crane says they are the ancestors who came to help humankind," John said, "and make us greater than the apes. The pastor is a direct descendant of those ancestors."

"But Pastor Crane says that we are a disappointment to them," Sarah added; "that we have messed with the world they helped us create, and so they are coming back… Coming back for the Gathering."

"And what will they do when they get here?" Rachel asked.

"Pastor Crane says we will be saved. They will know him as their leader on earth, and the bad will be destroyed." Sarah clasped the Triple Wheel brooch on her cardigan. "Amen."

Adam was starting to get impatient. He tugged at Rachel's sleeve. "C'mon; we don't have time for this… We've got a train to catch."

The man called John saw an opening. "You're right. We don't have time. Where will you be at the Gathering, young sir? Tick-Tock. Tick-Tock. The time is now."

Adam pulled Rachel away, and Gabriel followed.

"What a load of bunk," Adam said.

Gabriel shrugged and smiled. "I don't know. I think they may be on to something."

"Tick-Tock. Tick-Tock."

Pastor Crane wagged his finger at the make-up girl.

"The pastor likes to do his own make-up," Brother Jedediah said. "And only *I* am allowed to touch his hair." He wrung his hands and gave her a humourless smile.

Crane waved away the girl who was trying to dust him with powder. Her displeasure was clear. She went off to speak to the director of the TV show, to complain about their guest who was compromising her professional status.

Brother Jedediah closed the dressing-room door behind her and locked it. "Hair's looking good, Pastor," he said.

He teased a few candyfloss strands across the scar tissue at the side of Crane's ear and primped up the front to give it more volume. In another life Jedediah had been a hairdresser, and Ezekiel Crane's wig was his greatest achievement.

Crane poured a good slug from a bottle of vodka into his Dr Pepper and took a swig while Brother Jedediah snapped the top off a vial and filled a syringe with a clear liquid. Crane took the syringe from him and stabbed it into his own neck, just above the collar of his silk shirt. He made a grunt and then let out a long breath.

"Let's get this show on the road, Jed," he said.

*   *   *

The TV presenter gave Ezekiel Crane the kind of patronizing introduction he was becoming used to.

"We're live here today on Channel Six, and we'd like to welcome Pastor Ezekiel Crane, who thinks that the world as we know it is about to end in just a few days..." The presenter turned to the camera and gave a barely perceptible wink and a cynical smile to the TV audience – just enough to let them know that he thought Crane was a crank. He turned back to Ezekiel Crane.

"So, Pastor Crane, what should we be looking out for? A big explosion? An invasion of little green men?"

Crane swivelled in his chair. He crossed his legs and made a temple of his fingers, pressing them to his lips. He said nothing, and the dead air on TV was torture to the presenter for whom a nanosecond of silence was too long.

"Perhaps we're going to see flying saucers in Central Park?" the presenter continued.

Silence.

"Or is this more of a religious cult? The second coming?"

Silence.

The presenter was losing his composure. Live broadcasts were always risky, but you could usually rely on guests to *speak*. He was perspiring under the hot studio lights and his deep tan make-up was beginning to run, leaving marks on his white collar. Crane's unwavering stare made him wriggle in his seat. He tried another tack.

"Well, maybe Pastor Crane is trying to communicate with

us using his thoughts. I read in your book, *The Triple Wheel,* that in the future we will all be able to communicate without speaking. Is that right?"

Silence.

The presenter thumbed through the book, looking for something else to say, but in his panic he could find nothing. He looked stumped.

And then Crane spoke.

"Thank you for your kind introduction, and now you have got your prejudices out of the way, perhaps you will listen to what I have to say."

There was a whoop from the studio audience and one or two "Amens" from the Triple Wheelers among the crowd. Crane had them all in the palm of his hand. He got up from his seat and, walking over to the camera, put his face close to the lens so it would fill the screen of the viewer at home. He wagged his finger from side to side.

"Tick-Tock. Tick-Tock. The time approaches," he said. "For those of you with a brain, listen to what I have to say. Believe and follow, for that way salvation lies. Touch the screen of your TV and repeat after me... Tick-Tock. Tick-Tock..."

The studio audience repeated the mantra while, across the country, people in their thousands found themselves touching their screens and repeating Crane's words.

"The hive hears my voice and I know each one of them. They follow me. This will be your last chance not to be left behind and be a martyr of the tribulation," Crane continued. "When the trumpet sounds and the swarming happens the Gathering will have begun, and those that follow me will be saved."

There were more shouts and whoops from the audience. The director was telling the presenter through his earpiece to let Crane continue. And all across the country people were switching to Channel Six, as if guided by some collective hysteria.

Crane grabbed the edges of the camera and spoke close, sweat beading on his upper lip. His voice began to tremble a little with fervour. "I am calling the faithful remnant out of the lying corrupted cities and false TV ministries. Only the hive will escape when the swarming begins. Where will you be for the Gathering? Your time is running out. Ezekiel One. Amen."

Crane was pouring with sweat. There were screams of "Amen" and "Hallelujah" as he dropped to his knees, and a woman collapsed, her body racked with spasms, foam drooling from her mouth.

Crane grabbed the camera and pulled it to him. "Tick…" he said in a trembling voice. "Tock."

The director of the Hope Project shook his head at the mass hysteria developing in the TV studio. He watched as Crane was led away by his faithful sidekick and the presenter tried hopelessly to bring the studio back to order.

He switched the screen off. This Crane guy certainly had some good tricks. The director had become quite mesmerized himself from the comfort of his own office. He recognized some of the basic hypnosis tricks – but the way Crane put himself across and hijacked TV shows to his own ends was masterful.

And there was another thing; something that gnawed away at the back of his mind. A familiarity about Crane that he couldn't put his finger on. Nothing specific, but something in the man's gestures and his walk and his tone of voice... However, there were more pressing concerns at the forefront of the director's mind. Strange data was flooding in from the Astronomical Research centre in Alamogordo...

Meredith came in from the next office, interrupting his thoughts. Her smile told him she had good news. "The kids are here," she said.

"What – here in New York?" the director snapped sarcastically. "Here in the building?"

Meredith reddened. "Er ... not right here, right now, but they've *been* in New York. They've just taken a train to Cincinnati, Ohio, sir. We're on it."

"Excellent," the director said. "Make sure there's a welcoming committee for them."

20

Their train pulled into Cincinnati, Ohio, just after three in the afternoon. It was a typical spring day in Midwest America, bright and crisp, and although Gabriel showed no sign of feeling the cold, Rachel and Adam pulled on the hooded fleeces and leather jackets they had bought in New York. They shivered in unison as they walked from the train along the platform and out into the vast brightly lit concourse.

They had spent the long train journey planning out their route: a more or less straight line that ran through Pennsylvania, Ohio and Indiana, on through the central states of Missouri and Oklahoma and finally into New Mexico itself. They had decided that they needed to break the journey up and, more importantly, to vary the methods by which they moved from state to state. They would use rail and road and travel alternately by day and night in an effort to stay one step ahead of the forces they felt sure would be on their tails every step of the way.

"Keep them guessing," Gabriel had said. "Plus it's more fun and I've always wanted to see America."

Thinking about her father and what he might already be going through, Rachel had been in no mood to be light-hearted. "We're not on vacation..." she'd said.

Cincinnati station was busy.

For some the rush hour seemed to have begun early with commuters moving purposefully towards platforms – in a hurry to catch trains home to the suburbs. Meanwhile, those who had enjoyed a long lunch in one of the station's many restaurants hurried the other way, out on to the street. Students hung around near the exit, and a gaggle of tour-ists gathered in the centre of the main concourse, looking around and taking pictures, while their guide struggled to be heard above the noise of announcements and a busker sing-ing operatic arias over a backing tape.

Gabriel pushed his way through the crowd, then stopped suddenly.

"Danger," he said.

Rachel and Adam had already stopped a metre or so behind him. They could feel it too. In the short time since Gabriel had come back into their lives and "re-awakened" them, it had become obvious that in the two years since they had last seen him, their powers had strengthened; their intuition had become more finely tuned.

It had never been clearer than at this moment.

The danger was like a current buzzing across the shiny

floor, crackling through the walls. People very close meant them harm.

Rachel felt the blood rushing through her; her pulse slowing as she looked from person to person. She took in everyone around her, noting each detail of every face in no more than a few seconds. Gabriel and Adam were also studying the crowd, looking for the danger as closely as she was. It was as though time had slowed and they were the only three people still operating as normal.

A metre or so away Rachel saw a man whispering into a mobile phone. Two men in suits were watching her from the ticket office; a third lowered his paper, raising it again quickly when he saw her looking at him; a fourth, casually dressed and wearing headphones, was smoking a cigarette and adjusting the volume on his iPod.

A kid wheeled his bike in front of her.

A young woman loaded down with luggage tried to hurry along a reluctant toddler.

An old woman shuffled slowly past on a walking frame.

Rachel tried to speak to Gabriel and Adam with her mind, but it was as if the frequency were scrambled. She turned and spoke out loud. "Who?" she said. "It could be any one of a dozen people. There could be any number of them."

"Walk slowly towards the exit," Gabriel said.

They began to move.

"There're too many people," Adam said. "They wouldn't try anything in a crowd, would they?"

"Just keep moving," Gabriel said.

They drifted through the throng of people, who still appeared to be moving in slow motion, their eyes fixed on their destinations. They parted as Gabriel, Rachel and Adam walked towards the exit.

"Almost there," Adam said. "Maybe we were wrong."

"No."

And as Gabriel spoke, Rachel froze, seeing it too late. The hands of the old woman on the metal handle of the walking frame were smooth and unlined; her eyes were cold and dark. Before Rachel could speak, the walking frame was tossed aside and it became clear that the woman was actually young and strong. She reached for the toddler a few metres away, yanking the crying child towards her while at the same moment producing a gun.

"You know what I want, Rachel," she said. "Just hand over the amulets and there'll be no need to hurt anyone."

The child's mother began to scream. Others who saw the gun did the same, moving quickly away, until only six figures were left alone in the centre of the concourse.

Rachel, Adam and Gabriel.

The terrified mother and her child.

The young woman who was pressing the gun to the child's head.

"Please," Rachel said.

"It's very simple." The woman's voice was as calm and cold as her eyes. "Give me the amulets."

"Don't!" Gabriel said to Rachel.

The toddler's mother was hysterical, screaming at Gabriel, then at Rachel: urging them to do what the woman wanted.

Gabriel sighed and let his breath settle. He closed his eyes and focused, and a kilometre outside the station a signal on the line switched from red to green.

"You should listen to her," the woman said to Rachel. "Do you really want this child's life on your conscience?"

"Do you want it on *yours*?" Rachel said.

"I don't have one."

Rachel was finding it hard to focus. It was hard to think, to talk, above the high-pitched whine that was filling her head. She looked at Gabriel. "We've got no choice." She reached up and unfastened the leather thong round her neck from which one of the Triskellions hung. She gestured to Adam – who was carrying the second Triskellion – to do the same.

"That's good," the woman said. "Just hand them over nice and slowly…"

People were still screaming, and in the corner of the station a group of armed police had appeared. Their weapons were levelled – but with the child so close to the gun, nobody would give the order to open fire.

A pair of pigeons swooped low over the heads of the horrified onlookers and the automatic Tannoy system announced the arrival of a train from Washington DC.

"Take a step towards me," the woman said to the twins. She pressed the gun tighter against the child's head.

The child's mother dropped to her knees, saying, "Oh God, oh God, oh God..."

Adam handed his Triskellion to Rachel, and she held the two of them at arm's length in front of her and moved towards the woman holding the child.

"Nice and slowly," the woman said again.

"How do we know you won't shoot us?" Rachel asked.

The woman smiled. "You'll just have to read my mind." She put out her hand, beckoning; desperate to get hold of the amulets. Rachel leaned forward to pass them over.

The woman's eyes, which had been locked on the Triskellions, suddenly flicked away, widening in horror as the roar of an engine became almost deafening.

A second later a huge locomotive smashed through the station wall. Debris exploded across the hall, forcing people to run from cascading rubble and flying rock. Rachel seized her chance to run at the woman with the gun, but she was already tearing away in the opposite direction.

Rachel grabbed the toddler, passing him quickly back to his mother, before starting to run herself.

A few metres away, the engine careered across the floor. Sparks cascading in its wake, it crashed down on to its side before finally stopping, the first of its carriages embedded in the station wall; its wheels were buckled, its sides flayed and twisted like flaps of metal skin.

Rachel looked around, her heart thumping. Adam and Gabriel were right behind her.

"Here!" Adam said.

"We need to get out of here," Gabriel said. "Now."

Rachel followed his gaze and felt a stab of panic. Diesel was spilling from the felled engine, pooling out, thick and blue-black, across the marble floor. Near by, the man with the earphones was backing away and, without thinking, he tossed his cigarette on to the floor.

The twins and Gabriel sprinted towards the exit along with everyone else. A second later they heard a *whoosh* as the fire caught and felt the searing heat from the tide of flame that rolled across the station towards them. The screams of those trapped inside were lost beneath the blast and before Rachel knew what was happening she was picking herself up from the pavement. She was oblivious to the blood pouring from the cut to her head and the smell of burning as the three of them staggered out into the tangle of emergency vehicles waiting outside the main entrance.

"We need your car."

The man behind the wheel of the taxi-cab had been staring at the smoke billowing from the station; watching people spilling out on to the street – some with their clothes on fire with passers-by beating out the flames. Now he turned and stared into the eyes of the boy looking in through the cab's window.

"Get out of the car," Gabriel said.

Without knowing why, the driver did as he was told and stood by watching as Gabriel, Adam and Rachel clambered into the cab. Gabriel got behind the wheel, and a second later the car veered away from the kerb. Pedestrians jumped aside as it tore out into traffic and accelerated away, swerving to avoid the fire engines and ambulances that were speeding in the opposite direction to join those already massed around the station.

The screen went blank as the CCTV feed from the station in Cincinnati was burned out by the fire. The director cursed quietly and flicked through other available sources until he was watching the pictures from a Cincinnati news station.

The "welcome" he had arranged for the twins had got a little warmer than he had planned.

He saw fire crews dragging equipment into the station and paramedics tending to those who had been injured. He saw local newscasters interviewing those who had been caught up in the disaster – a young woman jabbered about the girl who had saved her child's life – and he watched as a cab lurched away from the chaos and was almost hit by an ambulance before disappearing into the distance.

The director turned from his wall of screens and looked down at the picture on his desk. A photograph of Rachel and Adam Newman. They were smiling. Happy.

He picked up the picture and stared at it. "Clever children," he said.

21

It was the morning of their fourth day back in America.

The day before, Gabriel and the twins had driven the commandeered taxi all the way from Cincinnati in Ohio to Indianpolis – the state capital of Indiana – one hundred and eighty kilometres to the west. They had checked into a small motel on the outskirts of the city, where each had tried to take in what had happened; what the terrifying incident at the railway station had meant; and what they would do next.

"Run," Gabriel had said. "Same as always. We just need to keep running."

Rachel had been unable to sleep. She had lain awake, finding it impossible to shake the terrible images that ran on a seemingly endless loop inside her head: a young woman with flat black eyes, a screaming child, a sheet of flame, screams, flailing limbs…

As cicadas sang in the darkness outside her room Rachel had picked up her grandmother's letter, reading it again and again until the insects had fallen silent and it had finally begun to grow light outside. As she had been transported back nearly half a century, she could sense that Adam was taking the journey with her; that the words and pictures taking shape in her head as she read were also coming to life in his.

The scorched earth and barbed wire of the air force base. The woman Celia Root had not been expecting to see. The terrible pain of it.

Now, on a Greyhound bus heading for St Louis, Missouri, those events were still with Rachel and Adam as they tried to catch up on the sleep they had missed.

God, it must have been horrible for her, Rachel said, eyes closed, mouth unmoving. *When that woman opened the door. His* wife.

Never mind the wife, Adam answered. *What about those kids? The eldest one sounds weird, and Hilary Wing was obviously a creep even back then.*

Rachel shuddered, as though mention of the name had conjured an icy blast that cut through to her bones.

Hilary Wing…

The half-uncle they had thought dead until he had reappeared – more creature than man – to hunt them down, determined to possess the Triskellions for his own dark and twisted reasons.

Adam could sense his sister's discomfort. *He got what was coming to him,* he said with his mind. *Back in Morocco.*

Gabriel sorted him out once and for all.

Rachel nodded. She did not know exactly what had happened between Gabriel and Hilary Wing two years earlier when they had fought in the Cave of the Berbers, but she could still recall the look on Gabriel's face – something hard had glittered in his eyes as he'd fastened the two Triskellions round her neck in the dark deep of the cave. "That creature you saw by your bed," he had said. "He won't be bothering you again…"

Gabriel was sitting on the seat in front of her. He had obviously been following her mental conversation with Adam. He turned and smiled. "Adam's right," he said. "No need to worry about him. And don't worry about your grandmother, either. She's drawing you to Alamogordo. This is what she wants."

"She's dead," Rachel snapped. "How can she want anything?"

"You want something badly enough, nothing can get in the way of it. Certainly not something as … *trivial* as dying."

"Trivial?" The bad temper Rachel had woken up in came to the boil. "What about those people caught up in what happened at the station yesterday? What about their relatives?"

"Nobody died," Gabriel said.

"You sure about that?"

"Some people were … hurt – no more than that. It couldn't be helped."

"Sometimes I think that you like hurting people; that you enjoy paying them back."

"I wasn't the one with the gun," Gabriel said.

Adam sat up in the seat across from Rachel. "I meant to ask you about that," he said to Gabriel. "Why didn't you just get rid of that woman's gun? Make it burn or vanish or jump out of her hand or whatever. You can do that kind of thing standing on your head."

"So can you," Gabriel said. "I'm not the only one with … party tricks."

Adam nodded slowly. "I know, but yesterday…"

"It didn't work," Rachel said. She knew because she had tried to deal with the gun herself – and failed. "And there was this noise in my head…"

Adam nodded. "I thought it was just because I was scared. I couldn't see where the danger was coming from, and then when I did, there was nothing I could do. I focused on the gun, tried to get rid of it, but it was as if all my strength was gone. I just hoped you'd be able to do it."

"I tried." Something passed across Gabriel's face and the worry was evident in the way his eyes drifted down to the floor. "That woman *had* something," he said. "Something that blocked my mind, and I just couldn't get to her. Using the train was the only thing I could do in the end."

"What do you mean, 'blocked'?" Adam asked.

"They've developed something," Gabriel said. "Moved on from their earphones and dark glasses – and whatever it is, it means that, until we can find some way to shut it off, we're in trouble."

"Great," Adam said.

"I'll figure it out," Gabriel said.

Rachel's mood was still black and bubbling. "Well, try not to hurt too many people in the meantime," she said. "Even if it can't be *helped*."

Gabriel turned away and slid down low in his seat.

"It wasn't his fault," Adam whispered.

Rachel said nothing. She turned her face to the window and closed her eyes against the fierce morning sun as the bus rumbled west along I-70.

"We've got an appointment with Detective Scoppetone," Kate said.

The officer at the desk stared at her.

"We're old friends," Kate added. The officer yawned. "She's expecting us…"

Kate and Laura had landed in New York the previous evening. They had gone straight to Kate's old apartment, and although Kate had been as disconcerted as the twins to find that her old life had somehow been … erased, she had at least discovered from the present owners that the children had been there. She had tried contacting Ralph at the university – but had run into another brick wall.

Laura had tried her best to be reassuring. "I'm sure there's an explanation."

"I'm not sure I want to find out," Kate had said.

She and Laura had found themselves a cheap hotel and

eaten dinner in virtual silence. Having travelled halfway around the world in search of the children, they were now at a loss as to what to do next. Then Kate had remembered an old friend from university.

She had put in a call and asked for a huge favour…

Angie Scoppetone was skinny and hard-faced, with bleached-blonde hair cut very short and a manner that suggested she was scared of very little.

"You don't look any different," Kate said. "What's it been, twenty years?"

"Twenty-one," Scoppetone said. "You look a little older."

Kate tried to laugh. "I've had a hard life," she said. She introduced Laura and then the detective led them upstairs to a small room at the far end of an open-plan office, a dozen weary-looking faces turning to stare as they walked past.

"You any idea how big this town is?" Scoppetone asked when she'd dropped into the chair behind her desk. "Any idea how many hotels there are?"

"I didn't know where else to go," Kate said. "You were the only person I could think of. I really need to find them."

Scoppetone stared at Kate and Laura like they were suspects and she was deciding how best to interrogate them.

"So, did you have any luck?" Laura asked.

Scoppetone waited a few seconds. "Maybe," she said. She began rifling through some papers on her desk. "Doing this job, you get to know the house detectives at most of the big hotels, and as it happens the guy at the Waldorf is a buddy of mine. According to him, two kids – a boy and a girl, both about sixteen, both dark-haired – spent the night before last in the presidential suite."

"That's them," Kate said. "That's Rachel and Adam."

"I thought you were looking for *three* kids," Scoppetone said. "My friend only saw two."

Laura understood, but decided not to try to explain. She knew that people only saw Gabriel when he wanted them to. "I'm sure that's them," she said.

Scoppetone shook her head. "God only knows how they managed to check in. That's one piece of detective work I don't have time for."

"Look, we really appreciate this," Laura said.

Kate leaned forward, impatient. "Are they still there?"

"Checked out," Scoppetone said, reading her scribbled notes. "My guy says they caught a cab to Penn Station. That's it."

Kate's face fell. She slumped back in her chair and looked helplessly at Laura.

"Or it *would* be," Scoppetone said, "if I wasn't such a damn good detective." She slid a large black and white photograph across the desk.

Kate leaned forward again and picked up the picture. It was grainy and blurred, but she recognized Rachel and Adam easily enough. She nodded. "It's them."

"They bought tickets to Cincinnati, Ohio." Scoppetone

looked serious. "I hope they weren't caught up in what happened there yesterday."

"What?" Kate tried to keep the alarm out of her voice.

"There was a disaster at the station. A signal failed and a diesel train crashed right through the buffers." The detective saw the look of horror on Kate's face and held up her hands. "Nobody was killed, thank God, but a few people were pretty badly hurt. I checked the local hospitals over there, though, and they didn't admit any kids matching their descriptions. So looks like you're OK…"

Laura reached over and laid a hand on Kate's arm. Then she turned back to Scoppetone. "Listen, thanks for this. Kate really appreciates it. We'll get out of your way—"

"One more thing," Scoppetone said. She pointed at the picture. "I only found this thing because somebody else had already punched it up. You understand?"

Kate and Laura waited.

"Somebody else is looking for these kids." Scoppetone shrugged and sat back in her chair. "You haven't exactly told me a lot, so I figure I'd better not ask, but just so as you know."

"Thanks," Kate said.

They made polite chit-chat for another minute or so, but Kate was eager to leave so that she and Laura could plan their next move. Scoppetone was equally keen to get on with her day, but the women's behaviour had sparked her curiosity: exciting those instincts that made her so good at her job. As soon as they were out of sight she picked up her phone and made a call.

"I need to run a name, OK, Tony? It's 'Kate Newman'. Yeah, I'll wait…"

She doodled while she waited. It never hurt to check these things. Somebody she had known twenty years ago getting in touch out of the blue was enough to make anyone suspicious. That, coupled with the fact that another party had called up the same photograph, had been enough to ring alarm bells.

Two minutes later the dispatcher came back on the line and gave her the information. She took down the details, saying "Oh my God" over and over again.

22

L aura held a bagel between her teeth and put her latte
next to the computer as she manoeuvred herself and
her bags into the seat. The internet cafe was quite
empty, but she still scanned the room and arranged her
things around her like a barricade: employing the caution
and fieldcraft that her years with Hope had taught her.

Her mouth dry, she logged on to the Hope Intelligence
Terminal. It asked for her password. She took a deep breath,
then typed it in:

● ● ● ● ●

She held the breath and waited a moment as the progress
bar crawled across the bottom of the window.

CONFIRM PASSWORD

Laura typed in the word again: ULURU.

A wheel spun on the screen. So far, so good. Laura waited. A chair scraped behind her and she jumped; turned around. A young guy with a beard, wearing a beanie, got up, slurping a smoothie on his way out of the cafe. A student from the nearby university, she guessed.

She turned back to the screen. The wheel was still spinning. She clicked the RETURN key impatiently. Perhaps the connection was slow – but it was more likely that the HIT database was checking and rechecking any incoming information.

The screen cleared and another window opened. The single word HOPE appeared in white across the top of the black page and a small box at the bottom of the screen asked:

> **AGENT NAME?**

Laura's hand trembled over the keyboard. She had not logged on to Hope for over two years. It was not unheard of; people who worked for the Project often disappeared into the field for years on end. Buried deep undercover, with new lives and new identities, agents could sometimes take that long to uncover important information. To gather intelligence from people who were themselves secretive – or had good reason to be hiding.

And the Hope Project was a very patient employer.

Laura typed in her agent identification: SHEILA.

It was the jokey name given to her by the American who
had recruited her from the University of Western Australia
ten years before. He had been an older man – in his mid-
forties when she was in her early twenties. He had been on
a sabbatical from an American university and was already
a professor – but he had been good to her. Laura, who had
not had a father to speak of, had responded to his friend-
ship, and his protection. He had been very confident and
knowledgeable, with expertise in Laura's field of archaeology, and had been happy to guide her research on
ancient sites. And then one day, before he left to go back to
America, he had asked Laura whether she would be interested in working for him…

A month later Laura had discovered that sums of money
from a company called the Flight Trust were being depos-
ited in her overdrawn bank account. All she had had to do
was share her research on Aboriginal Songlines and Bronze
Age burial sites across Europe. She had not felt as though
she were doing anything underhand or that she was being
exploited – this Flight Trust Company was effectively just
sponsoring her research, and more importantly, she would
have a job with them waiting for her when she graduated.

She hadn't realized just how undercover that job would
be until she had been asked to move to England and pass
on information about a certain burial mound in a village in
the West Country. A job had even been arranged for her as a
producer with a TV company; all the red tape had been cut,

taken care of at government level.

Her days in Triskellion seemed like a distant memory as she waited to log on to – or rather, to hack into – an organization she now knew to be more sinister and ruthless than she had ever bargained for.

"Sheila" was eventually recognized and the labyrinthine Hope Intelligence Terminal database opened up in front of Laura's eyes. The internet cafe computer was not as fast as she was used to. She would have to work as quickly as possible and search very carefully so as not to alert the watching eyes she knew would be monitoring activity on the site 24/7.

There was one thing she would have to risk typing. If the agents who had approached Angie Scoppetone and the NYPD were from Hope as she suspected, then these names would be at the forefront of activity on the database in the past day.

Laura typed RACHEL AND ADAM NEWMAN.

A new window opened rapidly. A box containing the word CLASSIFIED flashed in the middle of the page. Laura clicked on it. Another page opened; this time the box asked for another password.

Laura typed it in: TRISKELLION.

She waited for a spinning wheel, but this time the reaction was quicker...

ACCESS DENIED

Laura thumped the desk. She had been stupid to think that the code word would not have changed in her absence. She tried another route: CINCINNATI STATION, OHIO.

The screen became a flurry of data and email exchanges. Hundreds of reports had been filed on this topic in the past two days. Good; her enquiries would be hidden among the long list of agent names. Apparently, Hope had deployed thirty agents at the station. Serious questions were now being asked. How had they failed so miserably? Why had their agent let the targets slip through her fingers? Why hadn't the other agents closed in? How had the incoming train been so effectively sabotaged?

Who was responsible for such an operational disaster?

Laura shook her head. There would be trouble. Heads would be rolling, and once you had been excluded from Hope, the future was far from rosy. New name, new identity, exiled to the back of beyond and, rumour had it, worse. Former agents had died from drug overdoses, car crashes, unfortunate falls and food poisoning. Laura shuddered. She continued typing and then studied the results.

The targets had escaped by car: a taxi.

She opened a new window: one that accessed Hope's LPR – licence plate recognition – technology.

She typed again. LPR+TAXI+CINCINNATI+OHIO+TRACKING.

Half a dozen results came up. Hope was tracking cars heading in all directions out of Cincinnati. She narrowed the search: LPR+TAXI+CINCINNATI+OHIO+TRACKING+STOLEN.

The results filtered down to one. A stolen taxi heading along I-74 towards Indianapolis.

Laura clicked on the licence plate of the listed taxi, and another report appeared:

> **SUSPECTED CINCINNATI STATION TARGETS. TRACKING. DO NOT APPROACH. ORDERS FROM NYC. ALL OTHER INFORMATION STRICTLY RESTRICTED. NAMED AGENTS ONLY. CLASSIFIED LEVEL 5 BETA.**

Laura knew what Level 5 BETA meant. It meant Top Secret. It meant the case was being dealt with by Hope's most secretive department:

BETA – The Bureau of Extra-Terrestrial Activity.

BETA was based in New Mexico.

Laura quickly punched in GOOGLE EARTH, and then she entered: NEW YORK TO CINCINNATI.

A blue line, going west, developed across the landscape, linking the towns together. She changed the co-ordinates, tapping feverishly: NEW YORK TO NEW MEXICO. The map pulled out wider and the blue line extended across the country – from New York to Cincinnati, Cincinnati to Indianapolis, then on to St Louis, Missouri, and Tulsa, Oklahoma. Laura felt nauseous as she plotted the last leg of the straight line that ran across America and ended in New Mexico.

It appeared that Rachel and Adam were headed for the last place they should be going.

To Hope's headquarters in Alamogordo.

Kate was waiting outside, sitting in a hired Ford parked on a meter and sipping coffee.

Laura got in.

"Like the car?" Kate asked. "I got the police scanner from a store on Canal Street. It was made in China but it should be OK." It had been Laura's idea and was a way to monitor any police transmissions about wanted Australian fugitives.

"Did you get some supplies?" Laura asked.

Kate gestured to a supermarket bag in the back of the car.

"Good," Laura said grimly. "We've got a long drive ahead."

Meredith knocked and walked into the director's office, smiling.

"The HIT monitor has just reported a lot of activity, sir. They wanted to flag this up to you. The system's being hacked right now."

The director waved a hand dismissively, his eyes glued to the screen in front of him. "Thank you, Meredith, but I'm already on it."

Thanks to the information called up by the mystery hacker, the director now knew where the car they were after was headed. He watched the map open on his computer screen. A blue line had been plotted that joined New York to Cincinnati to Indianapolis. He watched it stretch across the country, following the three co-ordinates. It traced a diagonal line across the states into New Mexico.

The director allowed himself a smile. The children were driving themselves to exactly where he wanted them to be, saving him the trouble of taking them there. He logged back into the intelligence terminal, deciding to refresh and update his last message:

> **SUSPECTED CINCINNATI STATION TARGETS. TRACKING. DO NOT APPROACH. ORDERS FROM NYC. ALL OTHER INFORMATION STRICTLY RESTRICTED. NAMED AGENTS ONLY. CLASSIFIED LEVEL 5 BETA.**

He added another line:

DO NOT INTERCEPT. DO NOT ARREST.

He was pleased with his day's work. Things were beginning to swing in his favour. He started to compose an email to Crow in Alamogordo. The man might have an opportunity to redeem himself, the director thought.

As he was typing, Meredith handed him a piece of paper. She smiled, knowing that she had done something that would please her boss. "They traced the hacker to an internet cafe here in New York," she said.

The director studied the data on the printout.

A code name was highlighted in red.

SHEILA.

"Well, well," he said. "Laura Sullivan. Welcome back."

23

Rachel, Adam and Gabriel sat in a small hotel room. The curtains were drawn and the room was lit only by the flickering light from a small TV set in the corner. The atmosphere between the children had been tense and the conversation all but non-existent since the exchange on the Greyhound.

Adam was doing his best to lighten the mood. He thrust his hand deep into a large bowl of nachos and ate noisily, talking as cheerfully as he could between mouthfuls. "It's like being in a rock band or something," he said. "Another town, another hotel room, you know? Like being on tour and not knowing which city you're in."

"St Louis," Rachel said.

"Yeah, I *know*." Adam brushed crumbs from the front of his shirt. "I'm just saying that's what it's like."

"I guess." Rachel was lying down with her eyes closed. She was not particularly angry with Gabriel any more; she was too frightened for that. She sensed that as they drew ever closer to this mysterious place in the desert that they seemed destined to visit, the danger would only increase, especially if what Gabriel had said about their powers being "blocked" were true.

Now they would not even be able to recognize their enemy.

In those brief periods when the fear for herself and Adam faded a little, it was quickly replaced by an even greater fear for their father. If she had harboured any doubts about what the Hope Project and those who worked for it were capable of, they had evaporated at the railway station in Ohio. If they could threaten a child in the way that woman had, then there would be no limit to what they would do to Ralph Newman.

Rachel's only hope was that they would quickly realize that her father was of no use to them – but even that was of little comfort. She knew how ruthless Hope could be when it came to those who had become expendable.

Perhaps she and Adam were already too late…

"Maybe we *should* start a rock band," Adam said. "I mean, if we can speak any language we like, then I could probably play the guitar like Jimi Hendrix." He shoved in another mouthful of nachos, flicking through the TV channels at the same time. "And you can probably sing like Madonna. No, way *better* than Madonna. What do you think? Rachel…?"

Rachel was not listening.

"I'm going out," Gabriel said.

Rachel opened her eyes and sat up. "Where?"

Gabriel shrugged. "I just need some air."

"I'll come with you," she said. Gabriel was being evasive and she wanted to know why. But it was more than that – unwilling as she was to admit it to herself, she also craved time alone with him.

"No, it's fine," he said. "I think we're starting to get on one another's nerves anyway. I won't be long. Will you two be OK?"

Rachel stared at him, but Gabriel wouldn't meet her eyes.

"Yeah, no problem," Adam said, still munching on nachos. "Bring back a few beers, will you?" He glanced up to see Gabriel heading for the door with no intention of answering him. "Worth a try," he muttered.

At the door Gabriel turned. "Don't do anything stupid."

Adam raised his hands as if the idea were completely ridiculous. "Such as?"

"Anything."

Rachel waited less than a minute after the door had closed behind Gabriel, before saying, "Let's call Laura."

"What?" Adam got to his feet. "You heard what he said."

"He's not being honest with us." Rachel reached for her jacket. "And it's not the first time. Come on; don't you want to know if she's heard from Mom?"

"Course I do, but—"

"We'll go down to the lobby and use the payphone. Even if they *are* monitoring Laura's cell, we won't stay on long enough for them to trace it. Adam?"

"I guess it would be all right."

They walked down to the lobby, nodding politely at the seedy looking man who had checked them in, believing them to be old age pensioners from Alaska.

A man was talking on the public phone. Rachel caught his eye, and without a word he hung up and walked away.

Rachel dialled the number.

"Mel Campbell…"

"It's me."

"Thank God." The relief was plain in Laura's voice. "Are you OK?"

"We're fine," Rachel lied. "Do you know where Mom is?"

"She's right here," Laura said. "Hang on."

Rachel was relaying the conversation back to Adam when she heard her mother's voice on the line. "Mom? You OK?"

"Where are you?"

"Please don't ask me that," Rachel said. Tears sprang to her eyes. "I really don't want to tell you."

"Is Adam all right?"

"He's fine. He's right here."

"I'm fine!" Adam shouted.

"What are you doing?" Kate asked.

"We think we know where Dad is," Rachel said. "We're going to find him." She could hear that her mother and Laura were driving and she suddenly had the overwhelming sense that they were getting closer. "Are you in *America*?"

"We're coming to get you," Kate said.

"No!" Rachel shouted. "You need to go back. Turn round now and go back to Australia!"

"I can't go back."

"Why not? What's happened?"

"Nothing. Look, I'm just so worried about you both."

Adam was pointing at his watch. "That's nearly a minute," he said. "Time to hang up."

"I've got to go, Mom," Rachel said. "Love you."

Adam snatched the phone from her and shouted, "I love you too…"

He hung up before his mother had had a chance to answer. The twins began walking back across the lobby. "She sound OK to you?" Adam asked.

Rachel knew there was little point in lying when her brother could read her mind so easily. "There's something she's not telling us."

Adam was worried too but did his best to smile. "It's starting to run in the family," he said.

24

Neon lights that spelled the word FOX shone in the night sky and cast a red glow over the several thousand Triple Wheelers filing in through the main doors of the building. Across the front of it, a huge semicircular billboard, painted to look like a clock, had been raised.

A banner read: TICK-TOCK. TICK-TOCK – THE GATHERING DRAWS NEAR!

The "Fabulous" Fox Theatre on Grand Boulevard had been built in 1929 on the site of what was once home to the Grand Avenue Presbyterian Church. The theatre was rightly known as the Pride of St Louis, and just as every major motion picture had been shown in its magnificent five thousand-seater auditorium, almost every great entertainer of the twentieth century had, at one time or another, entertained the people of the city from its vast stage.

Frank Sinatra, Glenn Miller, Elvis Presley...

Now Ezekiel Crane was slowly stalking its opulent

corridors. He sucked in the air that was infused with a rich and magical history. He studied the photographs and play-bills that lined the walls before stopping in front of a framed poster for a Fox production from over fifty years before. The line-up of artists that had appeared in 1955 had certainly been impressive.

But Crane was drawn to this poster for reasons of his own.

1955 had been a significant year.

It had been the year when visitors from a little further afield had come to the United States…

In the polished glass, Crane watched his smile disappear. He felt a tingle at the ends of his fingers. He felt it spread across skin that had been harvested from the dead years before and grafted on to his own flesh.

He had known this moment was coming, of course. It was necessary. It was part of the scheme of things. The presence of these two … no *three* … children, while a threat, was certainly a necessity – for without them the show Crane had planned for a few days' time could not take place. It was to be the best and biggest show of all. And they were a vital part of the bill.

Ezekiel Crane's smile reappeared, spectacular as ever. He lifted up his dark glasses and winked at himself in the glass, before going to join his closest disciples backstage. Crane did this before every meeting. It was not so much a prayer meeting, but a pep talk to get his team ready to go out and work the audience up to fever pitch before he appeared on stage.

"May you use this energy – my gift to you – and pass it on to the people so that they may feel it too," Crane intoned in a dramatic voice. "Let them sing it from their hearts and believe it in their souls. I want to see eyes burning with zeal and mouths speaking in tongues. Reach out to every man, woman and child in the hive and let them know that they are the chosen few, the faithful remnant; they are my workers and my drones and their work has not been in vain. Let them know that I will deliver them. Amen."

In unison, the circle of Crane's closest followers mumbled "Amen."

Crane waved a vague blessing at his devotees and they hurried away to prepare for the show while he returned to his dressing room with Brother Jedediah to put the finishing touches to his wig.

"Biggest crowd I ever seen out there, Pastor," Jedediah said. He grinned obsequiously and rubbed his sweaty palms together.

Crane grunted. He knew the theatre would be full to capacity; tonight was going to be very special. He sat down in the padded make-up chair and rolled up his sleeve. He double-looped a rubber band round his arm, just above the elbow, and tapped his skin with two fingers, trying to raise a vein.

Jedediah was already going about his work; with hairspray

and the pointed end of a styling comb, he was teasing the back of Crane's hair into a blond roll over his high collar. "Got a new supply of venom coming in tomorrow," he said. "Top quality stuff from Mexico."

"Glad to hear it, Brother Jed." Crane flashed his teeth. "I'm going to need all the strength I can get in the next few weeks." He found a blood vessel and stuck the needle in, letting out a long sigh as he pushed down the plunger and the bee venom raced into his veins...

In the auditorium the band was playing a song. Drummers beat out the rhythm of a ticking clock, punctuated by stabs of brass and organ. The audience clapped as one and sang along:

"Tick-Tock, the day has come,
Tick-Tock, we are as one,
Tick-Tock, we're rising up,
To drink from Ezekiel's Cup.

"The Gathering, we will ascend,
The Gathering, our souls will mend..."

As the song ended, the jewelled curtain rose and the band struck up again with organ chords and a great blare of brass. Flash-pots exploded and pyrotechnics lit up the stage with bright-white light and smoke. A spotlight revealed the figure of Ezekiel Crane at the top of a flight of steps, his pale blue cape blowing in the breeze from a wind machine.

Shrieks and whistles tore the air. Men shouted and women screamed – some of them fainting or frothing at the mouth. Arms waved wildly and people jumped up and down on the spot. Others broke rank and ran around in the aisles, punching the air, their tongues lolling from their mouths as they chatted gibberish.

Savouring the moment, Crane slowly descended the staircase to more applause, eventually coming to a stop at a lectern at the front of the stage. He allowed the adulation to continue for a few seconds longer then raised his arms. The crowd fell silent.

"Brothers and Sisters, the day is nearly come," he said. "But first we must bury our dead…"

The main lights dimmed, and as a small choir was revealed by a spotlight at the back of the stage, a lidless white coffin was carried on from the wings. The pall-bearers walked slowly in step across the stage and laid the coffin down on a raised platform that was draped in the Triple Wheel flag. The choir lowered their voices and Crane began to speak.

"You are the lucky ones," he said. "You will be there when the day of the Gathering dawns. But others, such as our brother here, will not be so fortunate." He walked across the stage and stared down at the body in the casket, shaking his head and wiping away what might have been a tear. "He has been taken just a few days too soon. Just a few days before the world will change for ever. We mourn the loss of one of our own, and we wish him well on his journey – we *know* he will be watching when the great day comes." There were gasps and muffled sobs from the crowd and Crane walked back to the lectern. "Now, let us bow our heads," he said. "Let us remember a valued member of our hive…"

As one, the congregation did as Crane asked. He bowed his own head and closed his eyes – but not before he had glanced into the wings and smiled at the thumbs-up Brother Jedediah had given him.

"Thank you," Crane said to the crowd, opening his eyes. He held out his arms and raised his voice. "Now, which of you is burning to share? Which of you is hurting? Which of you is sick?"

There followed an hour or so of testimony and healing. One by one, members of the audience stood up, waiting, while one of the Triple Wheel support staff hurried across the theatre with a microphone. Each "witness" talked about how the Triple Wheel had changed his or her life or else gave details of the particular ailment that was blighting it.

Ezekiel Crane invited them all up on to the stage and laid his hands on them while the band played and the voices of the choir echoed around the auditorium. He eased the pain of bad backs and migraines, and caused those with walking frames to move unaided. A woman with failing eyesight claimed that the moment Crane touched her, she could see "clear to the back of the room". Another fell to her knees and announced that all her pain had "melted away" beneath the pastor's fingers. One old man joyfully threw away a pair of walking-sticks and all but ran back to his seat, dancing for joy and singing the virtues of Pastor Crane and the Triple Wheel.

The audience watched, spellbound and thrilled.

It was as great a performance as the Fox Theatre had ever witnessed.

"The three wheels are spinning mighty fast and powerful in here tonight," Crane said, chuckling. He was once more alone on stage, save for the body of the dead man in the coffin behind him. "I know that when my workers move among you with the collection buckets, you will feel that *power*. I know that you will dig deep into your pocketbooks and your purses. I know that... *I know that...*"

Crane stopped, his gaze fixed on a small boy three rows from the front: on the pale skinny arm that the boy had raised in the air.

The room fell silent; all eyes were on the boy.

"We've done with the healing for tonight, son," Crane said. His voice was weak suddenly; a tremble in it he could neither control nor explain. He could only watch as the boy pushed to the end of the row and began walking towards the stage.

"Maybe next time," Crane said. He tried and failed to summon up a nice big smile. "Give your name to Brother Jedediah..."

But the boy kept coming, burly Triple Wheel devotees stepping aside as he got closer, marching up the steps and walking across the dimly lit stage until he stood a few metres away from Ezekiel Crane.

Crane's mouth was dry and he could feel beads of sweat running down his face and trickling beneath the collar of his shirt. He wondered if he was coming down with something. Food poisoning, maybe…

He stared at the boy. He saw a mop of blond hair that hung down, almost obscuring the boy's bright blue eyes. He saw an open, easy smile. He saw a face which looked innocent – angelic even – but which made Crane feel as if he were on the edge of an abyss, or standing too close to an open fire.

It was exactly the face that Gabriel wanted him to see.

25

Nearly seven thousand kilometres away a dog named Merlin began to howl in the grand lobby of Waverley Hall, a stately home on the outskirts of the small English village of Triskellion. Upstairs, the master of the house – and its sole occupant for many years – woke and looked at the clock. It was 2.15 a.m. Muttering curses, he climbed out of bed and pulled on his dressing gown, and then, in between the cries of his Irish wolfhound, heard the ringing of the telephone.

Commodore Gerald Wing came down the stairs faster than a man with a false leg and nearly eighty years behind him was entitled to. He switched on the lights in the lobby and walked over to where the old Bakelite phone sat ringing on the polished oak table opposite the front door.

Merlin was waiting for him, sitting proudly next to the table, his job done.

"Good boy." The old man rubbed the dog's ears, then picked up the phone. "Wing," he said. There was a crackle and a pause before a woman said something he could not understand. "What?"

"My name's Angela Scoppetone," the woman repeated.

"Do you have any bloody idea what time it is?"

"I'm terribly sorry if I woke you, sir, but I'm ringing from the New York City Police Department. It's pretty important."

The police? Commodore Wing felt as though he had been punched in the stomach. He cleared his throat and stood up straighter, preparing himself for the news. "It's Hilary, isn't it?"

"Excuse me? Hilary who?"

"My son," Wing said. "He's … missing."

The commodore's only son had been involved in a terrible motorcycle accident a little more than two years ago, and in truth, the old man could no longer be sure if he was alive or dead. Wing's heart started to beat a little faster as he remembered the events leading up to the crash. It had been the summer the children were in the village: the one when the lives of a great many people, his own included, had been turned upside down. Exactly what had happened after the accident was a mystery. Hilary had vanished, and though the two of them had been far from close, the commodore was still deeply troubled by the fact that he had not heard a word from his son since that day.

It had been the day his own life had as good as ended – the day Celia Root had passed away; the day Gerald Wing had lost everything.

"I'm not calling about that," the woman said.

Wing tried to clear his mind, to focus on the conversation. "Sorry, what did you say?"

"This is not about your son."

"Is it the children, then?"

"Which children are we talking about here?"

"Rachel and Adam." The commodore felt a wave of regret, of shame, wash over him as he spoke the names of the grandchildren he had never acknowledged as his own flesh and blood. It had been because he was frightened; he had known what their presence in the village would mean. The uncovering of secrets so long buried had been painful, and costly.

"I'm calling about a woman called Kate Newman," Scoppetone said. "I know she was born there and I know that her mother was named Celia Root."

"That's correct," Wing said. His voice was weak and hoarse.

"The rest of it's a bit of a mystery. It says FATHER UNKNOWN on Ms Newman's birth certificate, so…"

"Go on."

"Well, I don't know much about how these villages work over there. I mean it's not New York, I know that much." Scoppetone chuckled. "So I used my initiative and called the local pub…"

"The Star."

"Right. Got the landlord out of bed too. He said you were the right person to speak to." Scoppetone paused, taking a drink of something. "He gave me your number."

"He was correct," Wing said. "I am the right person." He pulled a chair away from the table and sat down. He took a deep breath. His voice echoed in the gloomy old hall as he said something he should have done a long time ago: "Kate Newman is my daughter" – it felt good to say it – "so how can I be of help?"

"I'm sorry to tell you this, but your daughter is wanted for murder." Scoppetone paused again, this time for effect. "She killed a man. Shot him dead."

Wing struggled to find the right words. "There has to be some mistake. I mean, surely…"

"No mistake, sir."

"Where did this happen?" It had been more than two years since that terrible day when Celia had died and Kate and the children had left the village. He hadn't seen them since the funeral, and their whereabouts had been as unknown to him as Hilary's.

"In Australia," Scoppetone said. "But she was here in New York this morning. Now she's on the run."

"And what do you think *I* can do about it?"

"You can contact me immediately if Kate turns up over there. Or if she gets in touch. Tell her it's me, OK? We're old friends, and things'll go a damn sight better for her if I'm the one who brings her in. Make sure she understands that, sir."

"She won't get in touch with me," Wing said, sadly. "No reason she should."

"Well, if she does, you know what to do."

Wing muttered a vague yes, but he was barely listening any more. His mind was racing as he scribbled down the contact details the detective gave him.

"Thanks for your help," Scoppetone said. "I hope I didn't disturb you too much."

Wing was struggling to see how he could feel any more disturbed. "It's fine," he said.

"I'll let you get back to sleep."

Commodore Wing dropped the phone back into its cradle and pulled the dog close to him. He knew that sleep would now be impossible. It was cold, and he felt more alone, more helpless, than at any other time in his life.

26

The crowd of Triple Wheelers was becoming unsettled. They had never heard Pastor Crane remain silent for so long. He looked smaller, diminished somehow by the golden-haired boy who faced him on stage.

Crane croaked a "Welcome", knowing instinctively that he had to do something to salvage the situation. He swallowed hard and opened his arms wide.

Brother Jedediah began to applaud from the wings, grateful that the dreadful silence had been broken. A flutter of applause went through the band and began to spread across the stage to the choir. The clapping continued into the front rows and then crashed like a wave across the rest of the assembly. Triple Wheelers began to echo Crane's words. "Welcome, welcome, welcome."

Gabriel walked to the front of the stage and raised his hands. A spotlight was trained on him, making him appear to shine. He lowered his arms and the crowd fell silent.

"Thank you for your kindness to me tonight," he said.

"I come here to testify. I come here to tell you more about the day that you know is coming, and I come here to tell you the *truth*…"

Crane did not like what the boy was saying. He edged forward and clicked his fingers at the lighting gallery, instructing them to put a spotlight on him. It quickly appeared, but the boy's light burned twice as brightly.

"The truth…" Gabriel repeated.

"Amen to that," Crane said, putting an arm round the boy's shoulder. "We all know the truth… That's why we're here today, Brothers and Sisters, and I'd like to thank this young man for coming up here today and testifying. Amen."

"Amen!" the Triple Wheelers shouted.

Crane seized his chance to try and usher the boy from the stage, but Gabriel was not finished. He threw Crane's arm off his shoulder.

"Leave me alone," he said.

Crane nodded to his bodyguards in the wings. The men came forward and began to crowd around Gabriel, trying to edge him off the stage.

"Leave me alone," Gabriel said again, and threw his arms back.

The men screamed and fell to the floor as if they had been electrified. Gabriel's eyes burned with a new zeal and he strode back to the front of the stage. "I'll tell you the *truth*," he said. "What you have seen today are not miracles. What you have seen are party tricks, performed by a charlatan."

He pointed at Ezekiel Crane. "By a fake."

The audience began to shout, "No! No!" and Crane nodded in desperate agreement with them.

"This man will lead you to disaster!" Gabriel said. "He does not know what he is dealing with."

Crane strode across the front of the stage, and the Triple Wheelers began jeering at this boy who dared to say these things about their leader. They stamped the floor and yelled until the theatre was full of a noise like thunder.

Suddenly, Gabriel's voice boomed out, high above the noise. "If you want a miracle, I'll *show* you a miracle."

He clenched his fists and the spotlight on him glowed brighter still. High in the upper balconies of the theatre, bulbs began to pop and fizz, showering sparks into the air. They went out one by one until the only light came from the spotlight over Gabriel.

Gabriel walked over to where the open coffin stood. He closed his eyes and clenched his teeth together, summoning up all the strength he had. A light went on over the coffin, giving it an eerie glow.

The audience fell completely silent.

Then there was a sound.

A noise came from the coffin. A low groan like a wounded animal. Then a movement: a white hand raising itself, trembling, into the air.

Triple Wheelers threw their hands over their faces while gasping and crying out.

Ezekiel Crane drew back in horror as the dead man's body hauled itself up from the silk-lined casket.

The body was dressed in a black tuxedo; the head poking out above it was bald and white. Stray wisps of hair caught the spotlight, and the eyelids opened to reveal empty sockets where the eyes inside had shrivelled and gone. Pink embalming fluid ran from the man's nostrils and down over his jacket.

People in the audience screamed as the corpse twisted itself up and out of the coffin. Its legs hung over the edge briefly and then its whole body flopped to the floor. Gabriel stood near by, waving his hands over the body, like a puppeteer. The corpse staggered to its feet and raised its head. A stream of viscous liquid poured from its mouth and across the stage. It let out a horrifying cry of pain then fell, its legs and arms racked with twitches and spasms before it became completely still.

"*That* is a miracle," Gabriel said.

With a movement of his hand, he trained a spotlight on to Ezekiel Crane, who stood cowering with shock near the wings.

"What is my name?" Gabriel said.

Crane said nothing.

"*What is my name?*"

Crane blinked slowly. The silence was broken by a tremendous clap of thunder which sounded as if it would split the theatre in two. Doors flew open in the auditorium and wind howled through, blowing pamphlets and books into the air. There was another thunderclap and the lights flashed and fizzed as rain and sparks started pouring down from the roof.

Gabriel stood his ground in the spotlight and stared at Ezekiel Crane. "What is my name?"

Crane wiped the rain from his eyes and looked across at the golden-haired boy. "Is it Baal?" he asked nervously. "Is it Asteroth?"

"Is that what you think?" Gabriel said, recognizing the names of fallen angels. "Is that what you think I am?"

"I think you are worse than a fallen angel," Crane said. "I think you—"

Suddenly the remaining lights exploded above their heads, showering the audience and themselves with shards of splintered glass, and the theatre went black.

Rachel was suddenly aware that Gabriel was standing over her bed. She opened an eye. He was soaking wet and covered in blood and broken glass. Adam sat bolt upright in the other bed, a terrified expression on his face.

"What happened?" he bleated. "I had a terrible dream."

"So did I," Rachel said. "The dead body…"

"Yeah," Adam said. "And that preacher."

Rachel jumped out of bed and sat Gabriel down. She brushed away the splinters of glass from his chest and shoulders and then grabbed a towel and began to dry his hair.

"I'm afraid it wasn't a dream," Gabriel said.

Rachel dabbed at the spots of blood on his face with the corner of the towel. "Who is he?" she asked.

"He's that freaky preacher we saw on TV," Adam said.

"That's not what I mean." Rachel stared at Gabriel, waiting for an answer. "You know him, don't you?"

"He's an old enemy," Gabriel said. "Someone we need to stay well away from. For a while, at least."

"Why do I get the impression you're not being completely honest with us?" Rachel asked. She leaned her face close to his. "Why do I *always* have that impression?"

Gabriel almost smiled. "It's good to be suspicious. You just have to make sure you're suspecting the right people."

"So what do we do now?" Adam asked. He was thinking about the carnage they had left in their wake in Cincinnati and now in St Louis. "I thought we weren't supposed to be drawing attention to ourselves."

"Pack your stuff," Gabriel said. "We need to get back on the road."

27

The night they had spent in Indianapolis had left Laura and Kate feeling tired, tense and irritable.

Having made contact with the twins, neither had slept well. Their minds had been racing with thoughts and possibilities. They both needed to rest, but equally, both wanted to be up and on the road early, excited by the knowledge that Rachel and Adam were somewhere ahead of them.

Two hours out of Indianapolis Laura felt her eyes begin to droop. She swerved and narrowly missed an oncoming truck, the jolt of adrenalin suddenly bringing her attention back to the road in front of her. She looked over at Kate, who was sound asleep, her head resting against the car window. Laura saw a diner up ahead and knew that she would have to stop.

She pulled into the forecourt of the Moonshine Diner, where two cars and a camper van were already parked. Laura killed the engine. Kate stirred and opened a bleary eye.

"Where are we?"

"About two hours out of Indianapolis," Laura said. "I need coffee."

They got out of the car, taking their backpacks with them, along with the police scanner Kate had bought in New York. Laura felt it was a good idea to stay vigilant, but Kate seemed almost oblivious to the fact that she was wanted for murder on another continent. Her desire to catch up with her children was clearly of more concern to her than her own freedom.

The diner was bright and cheerful. They sat in a booth with shiny red plastic seats, its table laden with bottles of ketchup and sachets of every other condiment known to man. Laura smiled at the family in the next booth: a mother, father and two lively kids – a boy and a girl. They looked relaxed and happy, and their casual clothes suggested that they were on holiday.

"They look like they're having a great time," Kate said, sitting down.

"Lucky them," Laura said.

"It's a dim and distant memory." Kate smiled sadly, thinking back to a time when her family had looked like that.

A pretty, middle-aged waitress came to the table with her pad open and ready. A badge on her white overalls announced that her name was Estelle. "How you guys doing?"

Kate and Laura nodded, said that they were good, even though they weren't.

"What can I get you?"

Laura ordered coffee and scrambled eggs. Kate asked for a blueberry muffin.

They didn't talk much while they waited for their order. Kate flicked through the pages of a local paper and Laura plugged an earpiece into the scanner, which was crackling quietly in her pocket, and adjusted it to the local frequency.

Their food arrived, but just as Laura was about to eat her eggs, she saw a Harley-Davidson roar on to the forecourt. A large policeman dismounted and headed for the diner. He pushed open the door, took off his helmet and sunglasses and unzipped his leather jacket to reveal a big belly that stretched at the buttons of his shirt. Then he stomped over to the counter and sat at the same stool he obviously used most days of the week.

"How you doin', Scotty?" the waitress asked.

The policeman took a toothpick from the counter and stuck it in the corner of his mouth. "All the better for seeing you, Estelle."

Estelle smiled and asked him if he wanted the usual – which he did.

Laura watched Kate pick at her muffin, keeping one eye on the cop at the bar and one ear on the police messages that were coming through every few minutes on the scanner. She was about to say something when information she recognized cut through the interference and crackle:

"…Interstate 70, blue Ford rental, licence plate…"

Laura looked out of the window and across at their car; she listened again as the number of their licence plate was reeled off by the police controller on the scanner.

They were in trouble.

"Any agents in the vicinity? … Scotty, you out there?"

At the counter, Scotty sighed and reluctantly answered the call on his radio. "Yep, check you. I'm here." He filled his mouth with hash browns and a swig of coffee.

"Repeat: blue Ford rental, licence plate…"

Scotty swallowed the mouthful. "Nope, not seen nothing." He winked at Estelle, who poured him more coffee. "I'll keep my eyes open."

Laura stuffed the earpiece into her pocket and leaned over to Kate. "We need to go," she said.

"What's the matter?"

"We need to go *now*."

Hearing the urgency in Laura's voice, Kate grabbed her bag and got up from her seat. Laura threw a twenty on the table, and the two of them hurried out of the door.

Estelle came round the counter and walked towards their table, one eye on the fleeing couple, the other on the bill Laura had left behind.

"Everything OK over there?" the cop asked, seeing her puzzled expression.

The waitress shrugged. "They seemed in a bit of a hurry, is all."

The boy at the next table watched through the window as the two women hurried across the car park and climbed into his family's camper van.

"Dad…"

The family looked on, horrified, as their vehicle reversed and then drove off the forecourt, before speeding away west along I-70.

"Hey, that's our van!" the father shouted, rushing towards the door.

Officer Scott McAndrew levered himself from his stool just in time to see the cloud of dust raised by the stolen camper van and to register the licence plate of the blue Ford that was still parked in front of the diner.

Laura drove as fast as she could without drawing attention to herself, then slowed and turned off into a side road in an effort to shake off anyone who might be following. The camper van cruised along a tree-lined residential street, past rows of almost identical houses in a variety of colours. Freshly washed family sedans were parked in most of the neatly kept front drives.

"The suburbs," Laura said.

Kate looked out of the window. She barely noticed the smartly dressed young couple standing on the doorstep of a pastel-pink house set back from the road…

28

"Who could that be?" Barbra Anderson asked when the doorbell chimed. She rose from the breakfast table, brushing the crumbs from her blouse and adjusting her hair in the hall mirror before opening the front door.

She smiled warmly at the couple standing on her doorstep. They smiled back. The boy who lived next door cycled past, waving, and a squirrel scampered across the top of the white picket fence that edged the front garden of the pink house.

"Good morning, ma'am," the young man said. "We're from the Church of the Triple Wheel. Could you spare us a few moments?"

The smile of young woman next to him got even wider. "You'll be *so* glad you did," she said.

"Well, we're having breakfast," Barbra said. She looked at the man's smart grey suit before admiring the lovely blue twinset that his companion was wearing. She glanced up at the clear blue sky and remembered what her mother had always said about seeing the good in people; about how strangers were only friends you hadn't met yet. "But you're welcome to join us," she added.

"That's very kind of you," the man said. "Maybe just some coffee."

Barbra stood back and allowed the couple in. She led them into the kitchen and introduced her family. "This is my husband, Bob."

"Bob Anderson," he said. "I'm in computing."

Barbra laid a hand on the shoulder of each of her children. "And this is Eden ... and Tammy."

Eden, who was nine, and his older sister, who was thirteen, both said hello politely and grinned at the newcomers.

"My name's Brother Thomas," the young man said. "And this is Sister Marianne."

"You have a beautiful family," Sister Marianne said.

Barbra blushed and beamed and poured out coffee for her guests.

"There's oatmeal too," Eden said. "And Mom's pancakes are just the best."

"We don't want to take up too much of your time." Brother Thomas pulled out a chair. "It will only take us a few minutes to change your lives."

"I think I've seen you people on the TV," Bob said.

"Right," Eden agreed. "There's ads on the radio, too."

Sister Marianne nodded. "It's an important message," she

said. "We try and deliver it any way we can…"

Continuing to eat, the Andersons listened politely as their guests told them about Pastor Ezekiel Crane – about the wonderful vision of the man who had founded the Triple Wheel movement. A man who had new and amazing ideas about what it meant to be human.

"I've never heard anything like it," Barbra said. "What about you, Bob?"

"Sounds … unbelievable," her husband said.

"It *is*," Sister Marianne said. She leaned across the table and placed a hand over his. "It *is* unbelievable, but just listen to Pastor Crane and you'll know it's true."

"And you'll want to join us," Brother Thomas said. "Of your own free will." He grinned at the children. "Now then, you kids like presents?"

"Sure," Tammy said. "Who doesn't?"

Brother Thomas dug into his black backpack and produced several parcels. "These are gifts from the Triple Wheel," he said. He passed four watches across the table; each had the words TICK-TOCK and the symbol of the Triple Wheel emblazoned on its face. "They keep pretty good time too."

"Wow, thanks!" Eden said, already fastening the plastic strap round his thin wrist.

"That's very kind," Barbra said.

Brother Thomas smiled and took a slurp of coffee. "We've barely started." He handed over a book and a couple of CDs to each member of the family. "The words in that book will lift your hearts and excite your minds," he said. "They will help you prepare for the Gathering."

"What's that?" Eden asked.

Brother Thomas ruffled the boy's hair. "It's all explained in the book," he said. "All you have to do is read it. Better than Harry Potter, I promise."

The boy laughed and began flicking through the book.

"Is this music?" Tammy asked. She was studying one of the CDs and finding it hard to tear her eyes away from the picture of Ezekiel Crane on the cover.

Sister Marianne smiled. "Well, there's *some* music on it, but it's mostly just Pastor Crane talking. His voice is better than any music you've ever heard."

"Listen to these every night before you go to sleep," Brother Thomas said. "I guarantee they will give you the best night's sleep you'll ever have."

"That sounds good," Barbra said. She nodded at her husband and stage whispered, "Bob *snores*…"

Sister Marianne looked deep into Barbra's eyes. "Better than good," she said. She reached into her own backpack and produced four plastic containers, each one the size of a small lunch box and a different colour. "You each get one of these too. So who wants the red one?"

The children argued half-heartedly over the colours, but eventually each one of the Anderson family had a box to go along with their book, CDs and wristwatch.

"What's in these?" Eden asked. He held the box up to his ear and shook it, as if trying to work out what was inside a Christmas present.

"Those are not to be opened just yet," Brother Thomas said.

"These are your survival packs." Sister Marianne gently tapped the lid of Eden's box. "They are to be saved until the great day dawns, and then Pastor Crane will tell us all what to do with them."

"Sounds mysterious," Barbra said, laughing.

"It certainly is," Brother Thomas said. "It's the greatest mystery of all time, and you can be part of it. You're lucky we came to your neighbourhood today."

"Thank you," Barbra said. She smiled and reached out to take her husband's hand. "Now, are you sure we can't offer you anything to eat?"

Brother Thomas glanced over at his companion.

"We've got a lot of households to visit, Thomas," she said.

"I know, but I don't think any of them will be as warm and as willing to listen as this one." Brother Thomas looked around the table at the Andersons' four smiling faces. "And those pancakes *do* look pretty good..."

29

When Rachel was thirteen she had made a list of all the places in America that she wanted to visit. She had filled three pages of a notebook with the names. The major natural attractions were there, obviously – the Grand Canyon, Yosemite National Park, the Everglades – but Rachel had learned all about those places at school and it was the cities she had wanted to see, above all.

Nashville. San Francisco. Honolulu. New Orleans…

Even the names sounded exotic somehow, and she had lain awake at night in the apartment in New York City, trying to imagine what the scenery would be like, wondering how the people would talk. Back then, she had promised herself that she would get to all those places one day – she would travel as much as she could, ticking these amazing cities off her list one by one.

Now, driving through yet another city as they gradually made their way west towards Alamogordo, Rachel's spirits sank even lower than where they'd been when they had driven out of St Louis six hours before. The car cruised past the same chain stores in the same strip malls that they had seen in every other place they had stopped at, and she wondered why she had ever wanted to see these places, how she could have been so stupidly enthusiastic. Every coffee shop and pharmacy – each one a facsimile of a thousand others – only reminded her of how far away from home she was.

Only reminded her that she no longer *had* a home.

Adam read her mind. "It's hard to get excited about anywhere when you're running," he said. He put his hand on her arm. "When this is over, you can go see *all* those places you dreamed about, and I promise you they'll be every bit as exciting as you thought they'd be."

"Sure," Rachel said. "Thanks." She smiled at her brother – but he didn't understand. It was not excitement that she craved now; it was the opposite: gloriously dull and uneventful ordinariness.

Normality.

"Hey, what about that place?" Adam asked, pointing out of the car window. It was just after midday and they had been looking for somewhere to eat ever since they had first hit the outskirts of Tulsa, Oklahoma.

Their driver, a nice man called Elliott, who had told them he was an insurance salesman, pulled over and smiled at his three passengers as they climbed out of the car. Watching them walk away towards the roadhouse, he struggled to remember what on earth had made him stop and pick them up in the first place. Why, when he had only popped out to get milk from the grocery store, had he agreed to drive them all the way from St Louis to Tulsa? He waved a cheery goodbye and turned the car around to begin the six-hour drive home, wondering what he would say to his wife when he got there.

"Wow, look at these things," Adam said. He walked along a line of shiny motorbikes parked in front of the roadhouse.

Rachel was already peering in through the dirty window and shaking her head. "Oh, good choice," she said sarcastically. "It's a biker place."

"Sounds like fun," Gabriel said.

Adam shrugged. Stepping past Rachel, he pushed open the door. "Who cares as long as the burgers are good."

Inside, the roadhouse seemed to be lit solely by the neon signs that hung above the bar. The floor was sticky with a thousand spilled beers, and the smell of fried onions was just about winning its competition with the stench of sweat and motor oil.

"Nice," Rachel said.

They walked over to the counter and hitched themselves up on to stools. A young woman whose arms were covered with tattoos slapped menus down in front of them and went back to her conversation with a man at the end of the bar. The man was probably in his late forties and was dressed in a fringed leather jacket and torn jeans, with a battered cowboy hat on his head from beneath which multicoloured dreadlocks hung down to his waist. Rachel smiled at him when he glanced her way and got an oddly blank look in return. She turned on her stool and looked over to the far corner, where a group of bikers was gathered around a pool table, drinking beer. One of them – a stick-thin figure with a long grey beard – grinned at her, showing teeth that were all either gold or black, but the smile was neither warm nor welcoming.

Rachel turned back and looked at her menu. "Well, if *they* don't kill us, the food probably will…"

They ordered burgers and Cokes. Adam, knowing very well that ID would not be a problem, thought about asking for beer again, but he could see that neither Rachel nor Gabriel thought it was a good idea. He could see their point. It was probably sensible to keep his wits about him.

"What do you think we're going to find when we get there?" he asked. "In Alamogordo, I mean."

"God knows," Rachel said. "Dad, maybe." She knew it was a long shot, but there had to be some reason why they were being guided there; why their grandmother had sent a letter for them. "Answers, if we're lucky." She looked at Gabriel, hoping he might offer an answer of his own.

He did not look up from his plate. He finished a mouthful and wiped his fingers before saying, "Something that belongs somewhere else."

"The third Triskellion, you mean?" Adam asked.

"Maybe…"

Rachel did not need to see Gabriel's face. She could hear the darkness in his voice and sense the anger that was fizzing inside him. He had his own reasons for making the journey but, as always, Rachel knew that she and Adam were vital to whatever he was planning to do when they got there.

"Hey, darlin'!"

Rachel turned to see one of the bikers from the pool table staring at her. He was bald with a thick moustache and a smile that was even more disconcerting than the one Rachel had received from his skinny friend. He held up a bottle of beer and beckoned her to join him.

Rachel turned round again and found herself staring at the girl behind the bar. The girl ran her fingers through her long black hair and stared back at Rachel with dead eyes. "Must be your lucky day," she said. "Looks like Chopper's taken a fancy to you. You and your pretty dress…"

Rachel looked down at the dress she had "bought" at the vintage store in New York. She had never felt less pretty in her life. Wolf-whistles rang out from behind her and she was aware that Adam was now turning round to look at the bikers.

"Let's just go," she said.

"Come over here, sweet thing," the bald biker called Chopper shouted.

Adam got to his feet. "Hey, shut up!"

"Leave it, Adam," Rachel said.

"I'll deal with this," Gabriel said.

It was the skinny one who came at him first, waving a pool cue above his head like a Samurai sword and roaring like a wounded animal. Gabriel turned and his hand was round the biker's throat before the man could lower the cue. Gabriel lifted him clean off his feet, walked him back across the room and threw him crashing down on to the pool table.

Then all hell broke loose.

As the others rushed forward, Adam did likewise to help Gabriel, stepping in front of Chopper as the big biker came at them with a beer bottle, unaware that several of the gang had already produced knives.

"Adam!" Rachel screamed.

Her cry was lost among others as Gabriel calmly snapped the wrists of two bikers. Their weapons clattered to the floor, and Adam wrapped his hands round Chopper's bald head, driving it against the side of the bar, before turning to take on another of his friends…

Those bikers who could still walk were slowly hobbling out of the roadhouse. Others were being carried out and several still lay, unconscious or groaning, amid the shattered glass and broken furniture.

The man who had been sitting at the end of the bar raised his glass to Gabriel and Adam. "You guys are good," he said. "You guys are out of this world."

"We're stronger than we look," Adam said.

The barmaid was screaming at the injured bikers. She turned to scream at Rachel and the two boys, telling them to get out and never come back.

"You OK, Adam?" Rachel asked, ignoring her.

"Sure," Adam said. But his face was pale and he was leaning a little awkwardly against the bar.

"My name's Honeycutt," the man at the bar said. "You can call me BB."

"Nice to meet you." Gabriel casually picked up a French fry from his plate and turned to Rachel and Adam. "We should go," he said.

"Adam?" Rachel stepped next to her brother, and at that moment he fell forward into her arms. She laid him gently on the floor and then bent down to lift up his T-shirt. The meal she had just eaten rose back up at the sight of the blood, and she shouted for Gabriel.

"I'm fine," Adam said, weakly.

Honeycutt knelt beside him and looked at the wound. "We need to get him to a hospital," he said.

"No hospitals," Gabriel said. He looked hard at Rachel and spoke with his mind. *There'll be records. They'd be able to find us.*

He knelt next to Honeycutt and placed his hand on Adam's stomach. Blood flowed from the wound between his fingers. He closed his eyes. "It's missed all the major organs," he said. "He's going to be all right."

Honeycutt looked at their faces and saw that there was

little point arguing. "Well, at least let me help get him cleaned up. I know what I'm doing, OK?"

"Where can we go?" Rachel asked, instinctively feeling she could trust him.

Honeycutt smiled. "I'll take you to Nirvana."

30

Honeycutt's smallholding was twenty kilometres or so west of Tulsa. His pick-up truck bumped over the potholes, and Adam winced in pain every time they hit a rock.

Rachel sat in the front with Honeycutt and looked worryingly back at her brother lying across the bench seat, his face slick with perspiration. The blood had spread and now formed a dark wet patch from his chest to his groin. Gabriel sat by him and held his right hand over the wound.

"Trust me; he's going to be OK," Gabriel said.

Rachel was glad Gabriel was so certain, but part of her still felt furious with him. Once again, he had got them into unnecessary trouble. "Maybe if you hadn't attacked those butt-holes, this wouldn't have happened." But even as she rebuked him, she knew that she was not being completely honest with herself. Back there in the biker bar she had felt a surge of affection when Gabriel had stepped forward to protect her.

"Perhaps," Gabriel said. "But you can't always let these situations take control of you. You have to stand up and be counted. If you don't resist harmful forces, they will destroy you."

Rachel turned and stared forward. She did not want to see the smug look on Gabriel's face for fear she might lose her temper and punch him.

"I think it was a lucky escape," Honeycutt said. "Those punks are notorious around here. Personally, I'd have run."

They came to a fence at the end of a rutted track and Honeycutt got out of the car and unlatched the gate; a sign painted on its slats read NIRVANA. It opened on to small fenced field, with a horse, a few goats, chickens and bee-hives.

"You keep bees?" Rachel asked.

"Name like mine, it would be rude not to," Honeycutt said, with a smile. "Make my living selling honey."

They pulled up outside the house and Honeycutt helped carry Adam in. He held him under the armpits while Gabriel lifted his feet, and they carried him across the wooden veranda and into the main room. They lay Adam down on the sofa. He grunted with pain as they adjusted his position.

"You OK?" Rachel asked. She had had a burning in her lower gut that she took to be a sympathy pain ever since Adam had been hurt. She was feeling a little of what Adam was feeling.

"Been better," Adam whispered.

Honeycutt brought in hot water and dressings, and tore away Adam's shirt. He cleaned the blood from around a hole that was about the size of two fingers, the flesh puckering at its edges. Rachel felt a warm surge of love spread through her, and Adam smiled weakly. Ever since they had been tiny Adam had always been in the wars. If something bad was going to happen to someone, it would happen to Adam.

"Let me take away the pain," she said.

Rachel put her hand over the wound and concentrated. She felt her palm grow hot as she drew the pain from her brother and into herself; she felt the gnawing in her gut grow stronger and sharper. Shutting her eyes, she visualized the pain as a black ball that in her mind's eye she pushed out of her body like a tumour and sent flying out into space. Then it was gone. Rachel felt nothing more and Adam's face relaxed. She wiped the sweat from his brow.

"You guys are full of surprises," Honeycutt said. He gave them some cotton bandages and Band-aids, and Rachel began to dry the cut and dress it.

"You should put some of this on it," Honeycutt said. He passed Rachel a brown glass pot and a small vial containing yellowish liquid.

"Royal jelly?" Gabriel asked.

"Yep, from the queen bee. Best medicine there is." Honeycutt grinned and Gabriel nodded his approval. "And there's propolis in the other one – bees make it themselves from tree resin and gum. It's a powerful antibiotic…"

Rachel smeared the edges of Adam's stab wound with the royal jelly and rubbed a little of the waxy propolis over it, before dressing the area with a cotton swab.

"The beehive's a totally sterile environment, did you know that?" Honeycutt began to arrange logs, paper and kindling in the stone grate of the fireplace. "It's nature's pharmacy."

Within minutes Adam was asleep in front of the fire, and Honeycutt put bread and honey on the table, along with plates of cheese and glasses of beer. As they ate, Honeycutt began to tell them about the problems he was having; making honey for a living was hard enough, he said, but when more than half your bee colony had disappeared in a single year, it was almost impossible.

Rachel had heard a lot about Colony Collapse Disorder from, among others, Salvador Abeja, the beekeeper who had befriended them in Seville, but she had yet to hear two theories that matched. "So what do *you* think is happening to the bees?" she said.

"Most people in this part of America think it's due to crop-spraying. You know, all the new sorts of chemicals being put into the ecosystem." Honeycutt dipped his finger in the honey and put it in his mouth. "Others say that importing bees spreads disease that certain species don't have the resistance to fight off. You know, in the same way that introducing the common cold to an Amazonian tribe would kill them all."

"But what do *you* think?" Gabriel asked.

Honeycutt looked from one to the other as if he was about to say something stupid. "You won't believe me if I tell you," he said, stifling a laugh.

"Try us," Gabriel challenged.

"Bee Rapture," Honeycutt said.

Rachel had not heard the phrase before. "Bee *what*?"

"Rapture," Honeycutt repeated. "I don't think they're actually dying off; I think they're going back to where they come from."

"Where?" Rachel asked, incredulous.

Honeycutt pointed skywards. "I seen them, in the evening. I've been out in the yard, feeding the chickens and the goats." He began to paint pictures with his words in a voice that was very deep and appropriately honeyed. "Just as the sun is going down, you know when that golden light hits everything and makes it look warm and magical, you can hear a buzzing in the sky, and you look up, and there's a black column flying above. At first you think it's birds way, way up, but then you see they're closer – and the buzzing gets louder. Then they stop. They hover over the farm like a dark cloud and I see other bees ... *my* bees, join them, spinning up into the sky in a spiral and the whole thing spins like a black tornado. Faster and faster, louder and louder, and then" – Honeycutt clicked his fingers – "they're gone. Vanished."

"Where?" Rachel asked again.

"To the land of milk and honey, I guess." Honeycutt smiled. "And who can blame them? It's like they were here to do mankind good and we do nothing but damage them and mess them around. So, they are withdrawing the privilege."

"You may be right," Gabriel said.

The sun was lowering in the sky by the time they had finished talking and the golden light that Honeycutt had spoken of flooded across the fields. He insisted they stay the night. Adam still slept soundly by the fire and the colour had returned to his cheeks. Gabriel took a walk outside and across the prairie, studying the big Oklahoma sky, while Rachel offered to help Honeycutt feed his goats and chickens.

She had taken an immediate liking to this warm and relaxed man. She envied his life. She could see herself ending up somewhere remote like this – feeding livestock in the pale evening light. It was unlikely to happen for some time, though, she thought.

Given her current situation.

"So I guess you and your brother are from New York or somewhere like that?" Honeycutt said.

"That's right; we're New Yorkers," Rachel said.

"Have to say you're nice and polite for New Yorkers," Honeycutt said. "They're usually up their own butts, pardon my Spanish."

Rachel chuckled. "Maybe. We've spent time in England and quite a few other places, though."

"I can see that. You look like you've … seen things."

Suddenly, Rachel wanted to tell this man everything;

to confess it all would have been a huge relief – but she knew she couldn't, even though she sensed that he would understand.

"Where's the other guy from, though?" Honeycutt narrowed his eyes. "Gabriel?"

"I don't know for sure. We met him in England."

"Hmm. He's smart. I can see that. He's got something else about him, though – but I can't put my finger on it."

"Yeah, he's like that," Rachel said. "A bit of a mystery."

Honeycutt hesitated a moment and looked out to where Gabriel stood in the cornfield. "And you like him, right?"

Rachel was about to contradict him, but felt herself redden and knew there was little point.

"That's nice," Honeycutt said. "Just don't let him get you into any more trouble."

Rachel was silent. Trouble of any sort was the last thing she wanted, but with Gabriel around they seemed to draw it to them like a magnet. "Thanks, BB," she said quietly.

31

hey had driven down to the lake in the blue Packard.
Eleanor had gone to spend a couple of days with
friends in Albuquerque and Gerald had leave to take
the boys off to swim and explore around the lagoon thirty kilometres away from the base.

They had eaten a picnic by the side of the lake and then
Gerald had instructed the boys to run along and play. Only
when they could see the boys splashing around in the middle of
the lake, silhouetted in the bright sunshine, had Gerald dared
to lean over and place his hand on Celia's bare leg and kiss her
lightly on the lips. "Don't worry; they can't see us," he said.

Celia and Gerald had been lovers for nearly a year now.
Their relationship, even back in Triskellion, had had the
feeling of something forbidden about it. Now that feeling
was even stronger, and Celia lived with the guilt of it every
moment.

No one had done more than Eleanor Wing to make her feel
at home in Alamogordo. She had enjoyed the confidence and

the kindness of this woman and had then betrayed her by stealing her husband.

"Please, darling," Celia said, pushing Wing's hand away. "I really don't feel comfortable here. Let's just talk."

Wing fell back on his lounger and shielded his eyes from the sun with the back of his hand. The lunchtime wine had made him feel unusually talkative. "I need to tell you something really important," he said. "You are the only one who will know what it means. It will enable you to understand why I was never allowed to write; why I had to keep this secret."

Celia looked over at him. She could see that beneath his hand a tear was trickling down his cheek. She wiped it away. "Tell me, darling."

"It was ten years ago," Wing said. He spoke quickly. It was as though he were afraid his nerve might fail him; as though he were desperate to reveal a secret he had kept for far too long. He kept his hand over his eyes. "Nineteen fifty-five. I had just come back from Korea and the Yanks had recruited me into the test pilot scheme here. I was only twenty-four, so breaking the sound barrier on a daily basis during peacetime was very appealing." He paused, took a breath. "It was a perfect June morning and I had taken a new Super Sabre up to do some altitude tests over the desert. I remember it so vividly because it was a perfect flying day; the sky was clear as far as the eye could see. Once I got above the clouds everything was so bright and blue I felt I could have been in heaven. I was still in radio contact and they told me to climb higher still to really test the *kite. I must have been doing seven hundred miles an hour or so – just subsonic…" He paused for a moment in his story, his voice cracking a little.*

"Go on," Celia said. "I'm listening."

Wing was almost in tears. "Well, then I saw something, you see. People at the time were always talking about seeing cigar and saucer shapes in the sky. We were all terribly paranoid about spying in those days, as you know. But this was different. It was more like a vision. As I climbed to a higher altitude I saw a golden shape coming straight for me. It was travelling very slowly and, although I was going at high speed, it did not seem to get closer quickly at all – so I was able to get a good look at it. It was a light … well, more like three lights, spinning and intersecting like wheels of energy. It drew close and I began to see it was more solid, like a gyroscope.

"My radar was registering nothing, so I spoke to them on the ground. I told them that a flying object, gold and bright, was heading almost straight for me. They asked me to confirm the sighting because nothing was showing on their radar either, and then told me to try and make radio contact with it. But when I tried, using different frequencies on my radio, all I got was a high-pitched whine, like singing voices: metallic and strange.

"There was a delay on the ground as if they were deciding what to do, and then a voice told me to open fire. To open fire on the instructions of the president himself! At that moment the thing came closer. I took evasive action and it passed me.

*As it went by I swear I saw a figure standing in the middle
of the spinning wheels looking straight at me. I told them on
the ground that there was no need to shoot; that it had gone
past. They told me to pursue, but I didn't need to. The thing
had taken a wide circle and was coming round in front of me
again. I swear, Celia, as it circled me in that bright blue sky,
way above the clouds, I felt an immense feeling of peace. And
do you know, I did a really foolish thing: I waved at it…"* Wing
stopped, gathering his thoughts.

"And then…?" Celia pressed.

"It circled me again and I told them on the ground that it
just seemed to be observing me."

"And what did they do?"

Wing's voice caught in his throat. "They told me to fire, or be
shot down myself. And when this spinning wheel approached
me again I was sure that whatever was inside it was smiling
at me."

"So what did you do, Gerry?"

"I blew him to bits," Wing sobbed. "I let off both rockets and
got a direct hit when he came in for the fourth time. The thing
exploded into a million balls of light that burst like bubbles as
they hit my plane… I felt as if I had made a friend and then
shot him down. It felt so wrong."

"Oh my God! What happened after that?" Celia asked,
astonished.

"I remember nothing until I was on the ground. As I was
being dragged from the cockpit, I could see the remains of a …

body on the tarmac. It was naked and had been torn apart; its broken back and ribs were spread out like wings."

"Oh my God," Celia gasped. "Were you injured?"

"That's the thing," Wing said. "There wasn't a scratch on me. After I was pulled from the plane, I just sat there on the tarmac with this ... thing in my hand."

"What thing?"

Wing was wiping away his tears with a big white handkerchief. "That's what really frightened me, Celia – I was holding a ... a Triskellion."

"Like the one in our village?"

Wing nodded.

Celia leaned across and kissed the tears from his face. Suddenly there was a noise behind them and they turned to see a boy standing there.

"Hilary," Gerald said, attempting to compose himself. "What is it, old boy? Has Rudi been bullying you again?"

But Hilary Wing kept looking at his father and Celia, his face collapsing and his mouth opening in a howl as he turned and ran crying towards the lake.

32

There was plenty more of BB Honeycutt's honey at breakfast, slathered over toasted rolls, mixed into cereal and poured over natural yoghurt. Adam's enormous appetite was a clear sign that he had fully recovered. He told Honeycutt he was feeling much better and thanked him for all his help, but he kept the bandage on, not wanting Honeycutt to see that the wound had completely disappeared.

Once breakfast was cleared away, Rachel told Honeycutt that they needed to move on.

"You never said where you was headed," he said.

"West," Rachel said. "The desert."

The beekeeper stared at her, waiting for her to say more – but when he saw that she had told him all she wanted to, he simply nodded and wished her a safe journey. "And remember what I told you last night," he said; "you and your brother got to watch out for yourselves…" He turned to find Gabriel standing behind him.

"I'll watch out for them," he said.

"You'd better. I don't care what I saw you do to those bikers yesterday; these two come to any harm, I'm going to come looking for you."

Gabriel nodded. "We need to get a bus towards New Mexico," he said. "You know where—?"

Honeycutt held up a hand. "Can you kids drive? I know you're not old enough, but…"

"We can drive," Adam said.

"You won't need the bus." He led them out into the yard and across to a weather-beaten wooden garage. Chickens scattered and rats scurried into the shadows as he opened the door. Light filtered down through holes in the ceiling, casting thin beams on to the roof of a dusty old car.

"My daddy bought this thing forty years ago," he said. "Thing was in pieces when he got it, but he worked every weekend for two years until it was good as new. She's been sitting in here gathering dust since I was in my twenties." He wiped a sleeve across the wing. "You're welcome to take it if you want."

"Don't you need it?" Adam asked.

Honeycutt shook his head. "I use the pick-up to make my deliveries. Got no real use for this old thing." He carried on wiping at the wing, clearing away the grime to reveal the shiny blue metal beneath. "It's yours if you want it," he said. "She's a sixty-one Packard. They made these things to last."

Rachel stared at the car, remembering her dream from

the night before: another vision of her grandmother's old life. Celia Root and Gerald Wing – her grandparents – together by the side of a lake. This was the car that had taken them there: her grandfather's blue Packard.

"We'll take it," she said. "Thank you."

Honeycutt nodded, smiling, as though he had always known what Rachel's answer would be.

Ten minutes later they had said their goodbyes and Adam was driving the old car out through the gates of Honeycutt's farm. Rachel waved from the back window and watched the figure of the beekeeper receding as they accelerated away and out on to the main road.

"This is the same car, isn't it?" Adam said. "The one they drove to the lake in."

Rachel nodded. As always, Adam had been privy to the same dreams and visions as his sister. She knew that finding Honeycutt and being given this car had not been a coincidence. "It's the way we were meant to get there," she said.

Gabriel looked at Rachel, read her thoughts. "When you meet someone with the same name or when two neighbours find themselves on the same beach on the other side of the world, *that's* coincidence" – he smiled – "this is something else."

"We're going there because of the crash, aren't we," Rachel said. "Because of what my grandfather shot down."

"Partly," Gabriel said.

Adam sounded the car's ancient horn as a sedan swerved

in front of them. "They left him with a Triskellion."

"Yes. Another Triskellion stolen from a Traveller not exactly welcomed with open arms."

Rachel sat back. The car's cracked leather seats seemed perfectly moulded to her body and the smell of the interior was oddly familiar and comforting. "Things are starting to add up," she said.

"They've always added up," Gabriel said. "It's just taken you two this long to do the maths."

By the time Laura and Kate were awake and had freshened up in the public toilets, the wholefoods store they had looked at the night before was open.

The previous day Laura had taken back roads to avoid driving on the interstate as much as possible. The journey had taken twice as long, but they had hoped that by travelling through small towns and rural areas and staying off major routes they would avoid drawing attention to themselves.

The sun in the early evening sky had been golden, and Kate and Laura had admired the expanses of cornfield that had extended into infinity on either side of them. They could have passed for a pair of ordinary women, enjoying their independence by driving coast to coast across the US.

As it was, their situation was very different.

They had found a small village unmarked on the map, some forty kilometres outside Tulsa, Oklahoma. It had been empty as they'd driven through at eleven in the evening, and

Laura had thought the lack of activity made it the perfect place to stop. At the centre of the village they had noticed a store:

Fresh, Fruity and Totally Nuts
General and Wholefood Organic Store

Now, the owner, a plump middle-aged woman with long silver hair, welcomed them warmly and encouraged them to try the coffee before they so much as thought about buying anything.

The coffee was every bit as good as the woman had promised, as were the Danish pastries that Laura and Kate bought to go with it. Once they were finished, they loaded up a basket each with supplies – fresh fruit and bottled water, cookies, bread and cheese – and carried them to the checkout.

"Long journey ahead?" the woman asked as she rang up their purchases.

"Not really sure," Laura said. "Hopefully not that long."

"I'll give you a flask of coffee to take with you," the shopkeeper said. "On the house."

Kate could not have explained why this simple act of kindness affected her so much. But, eaten up with worry for her children and herself, fearing for the lives of everyone she loved, lost and far from anywhere she might remotely call home, she suddenly found herself bursting into tears.

"Your friend all right?" The woman handed Laura a handkerchief for Kate.

"Just tired," Laura said. "She'll be OK."

The woman behind the till turned as the bell on the door rang and a man walked in. She smiled and said, "Hey, BB! How's tricks? Want some coffee?"

"Let me unload your delivery first, Martha, then I'll be right with you…"

He stepped out again and returned a few minutes later with a crate of jars, which he began to unload on to the counter. Each was labelled HONEYCUTT'S PREMIUM HONEY. BEE-LICIOUS!

"Can we buy a jar of that?" Laura asked.

"You certainly can," the man said, passing her one.

Laura added the honey to her basket and Martha rang it up.

"Where are you ladies from?" the man asked. "That's not an accent I'm familiar with."

"I'm Australian," Laura said. She turned to Kate, who was still dabbing the tears away from her face. "But my friend's from New York."

"Now that's an accent I *do* know. Matter of fact, I just had breakfast with some kids from New York. Two very nice kids, who…" He stopped, seeing the look on the women's faces. "Did I say something wrong?"

Kate shook her head and, using every ounce of strength

she could, summoned a smile. "What were their names?" she asked.

"Rachel and Adam," the man said.

Kate had to lean on the counter for support.

"Where are they now?" Laura asked.

"Well, they just—"

They all turned as the bell rang again and a woman entered the store. Seeing who it was, Kate felt all the hope and joy that had begun to flood through her evaporate in an instant.

"Hello, Kate," the woman said.

Kate nodded, her eyes searching frantically for a way out.

Scoppetone stood with her back to the door and said nothing for a few seconds. Sensing the atmosphere, the store owner demanded to know what was going on. Scoppetone took out her ID and flashed it at her without taking her eyes off Kate Newman.

"This is where it ends, Kate," she said. "And if you're smart, it ends nice and peacefully. We just walk out of here."

Kate shook her head. "I can't do it, Angie. I have to find my kids."

"Is there some kind of problem?" Honeycutt asked.

Scoppetone flashed him a look. "Not your problem, sir. Please stay back and keep quiet. Kate?"

She shook her head again. "I'm sorry." She began to edge towards the back door she had noticed on her way in.

"What are you doing?" Laura asked.

Scoppetone took a step forward. "Listen to your friend, Kate."

"They're here," Kate said. There were tears in her eyes again as she looked at Laura. "You heard what he said. The kids are *here.*"

"I've got half a dozen men out there," Scoppetone said. "And bearing in mind what you did, you don't need me to tell you that they're serious guys."

"I can't…"

"You understand me?"

"She's upset," Laura said. "Can't you see that?"

Scoppetone sighed. "I don't want to take you out of here at gunpoint." The detective reached into her jacket and produced a pistol. "But you made the call."

As the gun was raised, Honeycutt jumped forward and grabbed Scoppetone's arm. He shouted at Kate, "Run…!"

The crack of a gun sounded and Kate fell on to her face. The storekeeper dived behind the counter, and a second later the lifeless body of BB Honeycutt crumpled to the floor.

"Stay down, Kate!" Scoppetone shouted.

Kate Newman curled into a ball and began to scream as the store was peppered with bullets while a few metres away, with jars and bottles exploding all around her, Laura Sullivan ran for her life, crashing through the back door and into the street.

33

"**D**o let me get you a real drink, Celia." It was the second time Eleanor Wing had asked.

"No, really," Celia said; "I'm fine with lemonade."

Eleanor wandered away to minister to her other guests; to continue playing the perfect party hostess. The cocktail party was in full swing.

Celia was agitated; she needed to talk to Gerry urgently. She needed to tell him it was time to come clean with Eleanor; to tell her the truth about their affair – they no longer had any choice.

Then Eleanor Wing would understand why Celia was not drinking alcohol…

As soon as she saw her chance Celia marched outside and pulled Gerry round to the back of the house, on the pretence of talking about work.

"Hang on. Celia, what's—?"

"I'm pregnant, Gerry."

The blood drained from Wing's face. "Oh God. You know

what this means. We were never supposed to…"

"Well, it's happened," Celia said. "So now we have to deal with it."

There was silence for a minute or two, and then they began to talk. To make the necessary plans. "I must tell Eleanor about the baby, of course," Wing said. "Perhaps this is the perfect opportunity for you and me to make a clean break. To get away…"

"What about the children?" Celia asked. "Eleanor's children?"

"We'll need to talk about Hilary, obviously. He's my flesh and blood." He was pacing back and forth, chewing at a loose fingernail. "I've tried my hardest with Rudi, but we've never been able to get close. I think he's always resented me, and to be honest, I've never really warmed to him… Well, you know the boy, there's something … disconcerting about him."

They talked a little more about Eleanor Wing's oldest son, who was now thirteen years old, unaware that he was sitting no more than a few metres away from them, curled up beneath the porch. Almost afraid to breathe in case he was discovered, he was hanging on every terrible word of the conversation going on above him and his was body shaking with fury.

A few hours later those few guests who had not left the party already were encouraged to do so by the raised voices coming from Gerald and Eleanor Wing's bedroom; they were driven away by the cursing and the sound of glasses smashing against walls…

It was not long before the only other people left in the house were Celia and the children. Hilary and Rudi sat in different corners of the living room, glaring alternately at each other and at her. Both had odd expressions that Celia could not quite fathom: knowing yet fearful.

The bedroom door suddenly burst open and Wing marched out, his face drawn and pale, his wife's screeched curses still ringing in the air behind him. He took Celia's arm and led her out on to the porch and down the steps.

"Get into the car and wait for me," he said. "I need to try and explain to Hilary."

Celia hurried over to the blue Packard and climbed into the passenger seat. She turned to watch Gerry go back into the house. He walked past Rudi, who was standing on the porch, a strange half-smile on his face, which he turned on Celia before following his stepfather back inside.

Ten minutes later Wing came out again and climbed into the car beside her without a word. He fired up the Packard's engine, then hesitated when he heard his wife's voice. He glanced in the mirror to see Eleanor come running from the house towards the car.

"Wait, you son of a bitch…" she shouted.

Celia was suddenly frightened, and thought for a second that Eleanor might physically attack her. Instead, she just yanked open the driver's door and told Gerry to get into the passenger's seat. "You're too drunk to drive." She looked over at Celia.

"I can't say I'd be devastated to see her *dead, but you're not leaving my kids without a father."*

Wing did as he was told, moving over into the passenger seat, while Celia clambered into the back and Eleanor got behind the wheel. The car lurched away, throwing up a cloud of dust that prevented anyone inside from seeing Rudi.

The boy had come tearing from the house, panic-stricken. He began chasing after the car, desperately shouting at his mother, pleading with her to stop as she accelerated away.

The dust had not yet settled again when the peaceful night air was torn apart by the noise of squealing brakes, shearing metal and shattering glass...

The Packard had not needed gas and had seemed to drive itself smoothly along the highway and then off into the scrubland of the New Mexico desert. Gabriel was behind the wheel now, and sitting in the back seat, Rachel and Adam had drifted into the most disturbing glimpse yet of their grandmother's past.

The party, the angry confrontations, and the dreadful ... *fatal* consequences.

As the vision had unfolded in their minds, the same car that had fulfilled Celia Root's terrible destiny forty years before now carried them towards their own – and inexplicably, a thousand-kilometre journey which should have taken the best part of twelve hours had taken less than half that time.

It was only the weather that had made the drive remotely

difficult. The day had never become bright. The sky was purple and blotchy, and a howling wind had blown up, throwing tumbleweed and scraps of rubbish into their path and across the windscreen.

Hailstones battered the bonnet of the Packard and drummed menacingly on its roof. Rachel curled up on the springy back seat, where her grandmother had sat decades before, glad that the steel of the car's body was thick and protective.

"Looks like a tornado," Adam said. He pointed across the desert to where the clouds seemed to be pressing down on the land. A plume of dark vapour spiralled out of the cloud and twisted down to the ground. As they drove towards it, the tornado threw up grit, sticks and plants as if the desert was protesting at their presence – or at least was trying to prevent them from continuing.

It was only mid afternoon when signs for ALAMOGORDO AIR FORCE BASE started to appear but it was already dark. Adam was driving again. He steered the Packard over the last few kilometres and they saw lights in the distance. As they approached, they could tell that the base was the size of a small town. A perimeter fence sparkled with bright white lamps, and spotlights raked the sky and surrounding desert from conning-towers on each corner.

"Looks welcoming," Gabriel said. He smiled at Rachel. "You ready for this?"

Rachel did not feel in the least bit ready, but if there

was any chance at all that her father was being held here then she had no choice but to go in. Her anxiety was only heightened by the reactions of the Triskellion round her neck: it had been vibrating and getting warmer for the last twenty kilometres.

"Can you feel it, Adam?" she asked.

Adam fished into his shirt and held up his Triskellion. It spun on its leather thong and glowed bright in the dim light inside the car. "You bet," he said.

They pulled up at the checkpoint by the main gates and spotlights immediately focused on the old car.

"This'll be a test," Adam said. He wound down the window and waited for someone to come from the sentry box. It was empty.

They waited a few seconds, wondering what to do, until the electronic barrier in front of the car lifted, opening the way for them. Adam looked to Gabriel for guidance.

"Go on," he said.

Adam accelerated and drove the car under the barrier. A pair of armoured gates swung open, and they found themselves inside Alamogordo Air Force Base. It appeared to be completely deserted. The gates swung shut behind them.

"Nice work," Adam said to Gabriel. "You made the gates do that, didn't you?"

"No," Gabriel said. "Pull over."

Adam stopped the car behind an army truck.

"Can't you hear that?" Gabriel said.

Adam and Rachel concentrated for a second.

"I thought it was just me," Rachel said. She could hear a faint high-pitched ringing in her ears.

"I've got it too." Adam rattled his little finger in his ear.

"They're blocking us," Gabriel said. "Like they did at the station in Ohio. Try talking to each other; use your minds."

Rachel tried and failed to communicate with her brother. It was as if the frequency in their heads were scrambling their words.

"So if you didn't open the gates," Adam said, "why did they let us in?"

"I don't know," Gabriel said. "And that's what worries me."

34

High above New York City, in the glass observatory at the very top of the Flight Building, the director cranked up the powerful refractor telescope.

BETA-coded reports had been landing on his desk all day. The office had been on high alert after operatives had begun reporting freak conditions in the sky from New Mexico all the way up to Alaska. Reports of similar meteorological events were also coming in from Canada, the UK and North Africa.

Whatever was happening up there was *big*.

The Hope astronomers had identified a rare constellation that, according to them, could only happen once every ten thousand years – an alignment of the planets that appeared to be causing hurricanes, freak tides, storms and today, a partial eclipse. The base in Alamogordo was also reporting more than usual activity in the desert sky.

There was always activity of one kind or another in the skies above Alamogordo, which was why the base had been built there in the first place. Then, of course, there had been the incident in the 1950s and the evidence that had finally convinced the government to take the reports seriously – so seriously that they had created a fake incident some kilometres away to take the attention away from Alamogordo itself.

The incident...

The director crossed to the solid steel door behind his desk. It was built into the only wall that was not floor-to-ceiling glass. He reached out a hand, laid his palm flat against the metal.

He could *feel* it, he was certain – could feel the *power* of it, sitting there locked away, waiting for its two companions.

Whenever he took the Triskellion out to study it, he was excited by the way it made him feel. Just looking at it was enough to make him hyperventilate; enough to make his heart dance in his chest and send the blood coursing a little faster through his veins.

He could barely imagine what would happen when the three of them were finally reunited. His throat tightened and his mouth went dry just thinking about it. He smiled. Wasn't that how people sometimes described being in love?

The director walked back to the telescope, leaned down to the eyepiece and focused on the star they had been watching for days. It appeared to be getting closer. It pulsed with light, and through the powerful lens, the director could see auras of colour radiating around it, flickering and flashing like a signal.

A signal that none of them could decode.

The director's BlackBerry buzzed in his pocket. He looked at it. A text message from Alamogordo: THEY'VE ARRIVED.

Commodore Wing was watching the sky.

Merlin had been howling all day at the terrible storm that had driven rain through the leaky windows of Waverley Hall and ripped tiles from its roof. Wing had spent the afternoon with his ground staff, chainsawing trees that had blown over and were blocking the main drive to the hall.

It had been the same all over the village. Hundred-year-old trees had been torn from their roots, crushing cars and demolishing houses. It would take months to clear up the debris the storm had left in its wake.

The sky had cleared during the evening and now Commodore Wing swung an old brass telescope around before fixing it on a bright star. He took a reading with a sextant and jotted down co-ordinates on a pad by his side. An ancient yellow document covered with diagrams and calculations was unfolded on his desk. It had been drawn up centuries before and held in the family's library ever since.

There were Triskellions etched in three corners of the parchment, and at its centre was what appeared to be a flower shape – as if three Triskellions had been laid one on top of the other.

Commodore Wing compared his co-ordinates with the figures on the piece of paper, and for the hundredth time that evening, read the words written at the bottom of it:

Wind, Fire and Water
Will come to pass,
When Three Become One
In the City of Glass.

Disease, pox and famine,
The world will be done,
If the heir of my house
Is Ezekiel One.

Commodore Wing knew very well what Ezekiel chapter one was about. It had been one of the favourite Old Testament readings in the village church since he could remember.

But the meaning of the rest of the verse escaped him.

He took a sip of whisky, and then another, and began to doodle in the corner of the telephone pad on his desk. Flipping over the page, he saw the note he had written down a few nights before: DETECTIVE ANGELA SCOPPETONE, NYPD.

And suddenly he knew exactly where the City of Glass was.

35

Ezekiel Crane was more nervous than he could ever remember having been before – but it was understandable. He was only human, after all. It had only been two days since the bizarre and troubling events at the theatre in St Louis and he was a matter of hours away from the biggest show of his career.

A matter of days away from the Gathering...

The Franklin Field stadium in Philadelphia held fifty thousand people, and tonight Ezekiel Crane would draw each one of them to his cause. He would swell the ranks and the coffers of the Triple Wheel, ready for the moment of Truth and Change and Transformation – when the waiting would be over and the journey would begin.

From every corner of the United States, his followers would be drawn to a city a hundred and fifty kilometres east of where he was at that very moment.

"Gonna be a big crowd out there, Pastor Crane." Brother Jedediah brushed lint from Crane's gold and white striped suit, which was hanging on the back of the dressing-room door. "Yessir, you gonna make history tonight."

Crane flashed a sickly smile at Jedediah in the mirror. "It's only a rehearsal, Jed. Just you wait."

Jedediah nodded and chuckled. "Just a rehearsal. Amen…"

The man was hardly the sharpest tool in the box, but Crane tolerated him. He admired his loyalty, and besides, he was the only one Crane trusted to secure and handle the precious bee venom – an invaluable service now that Crane needed shots of venom three times a day.

"I was meaning to ask you," Jedediah said, his voice high-pitched and nervous. "About the other night…"

"What about it?"

"That boy. What he did with … with the body…"

"Mind control," Crane snapped. "Nothing more. Mass hypnosis of some sort, and amateur pyrotechnics." He was trying to stay calm, but the anger was bubbling to the surface; clear in his voice, it distorted his unnaturally smooth features into a dark furious mask.

"I was just asking," Jedediah said. "You seemed a bit shaken, is all. I've never seen you so upset."

Crane blinked, remembering those few hours of madness following the events at the Fox Theatre. The rage which had gripped him. The power he had felt surging through him as he had crashed around backstage, smashing equipment, clawing at the walls and screaming curses at anyone who had tried to calm him down. "There are forces such as those *we* represent," he said. "And then there are those whose motives are a little harder to fathom – those who hide in the shadows, who can only spread lies and doubt, and live purely to cast suspicion."

"So all that stuff he was saying…"

"What *stuff?*"

"About your miracles being party tricks and you being a … being a fake."

Crane turned round in his chair. "What do *you* think, Brother Jedediah?" Jedediah stood stock-still and open-mouthed, like a mannequin brandishing a clothes-brush. "Do *you* think I'm a fake?"

Jedediah shook his head vehemently.

"That's good," Crane said. "Because I'm not."

And he wasn't…

He knew many people who claimed to have been born again in a religious sense, but none could claim as he could, to have been born again *twice*. Crane could not explain why, but since the second of his … rebirths, he had found himself able to perform such "miracles" as those he demonstrated at the rallies and meetings. He could make pain disappear and restore feeling where there had been none.

He had acquired the power to heal.

Jedediah had given up preparing the costumes for the evening's show. Instead he had fallen to his knees in front of Crane and was muttering heartfelt thanks for Ezekiel Crane and for being allowed to help – albeit it in a small and insignificant way – in the wonderful work the Triple Wheel was doing.

But Ezekiel Crane could not enjoy the moment. He was still thinking about the boy at the theatre, remembering the look on his face as he had stared across the stage at him and the light in his eyes that had seemed to be blue one moment and green the next. *What is my name?*

No, Crane was not a fake.

But neither was the boy…

Crane felt a surge of anger move through him, and suddenly he was out of his chair, clamping his hands tight to the sides of Brother Jedediah's head. "Do you doubt me, Brother Jedediah?"

His assistant opened his mouth to speak, but only a whimper emerged as Crane's grip tightened still further.

"Do you doubt my *power*?"

The whimper became a low moan, and Jedediah's eyeballs rolled up until only the whites were showing, and he began to tremble.

"Good, because faith is important. Faith can change the world, and very soon that's exactly what is going to happen. I was given this power for a reason. Do you understand that?"

Jedediah just about managed a nod. The trembling had now taken hold of his entire body and he was beginning to bleed.

"*I* was given it!" Crane continued. "*I* was chosen! And I will do *whatever* is necessary to ensure that when the time comes that power is put to its proper use." He was shouting now, his hands clamped tight round Jedediah's head, the fingers whitening as he increased the pressure. "Now, you're either with me or against me, is that clear?"

The blood was running down Jedediah's shirt, dripping on to the floor of the dressing-room as it poured from his nose and ears.

"You need to choose a side, Jedediah." Crane stared down at the man on his knees in front of him. "You need to decide, and you need to do it fast. Tick-Tock, Brother Jedediah. Tick-Tock..." He leaned down until his face was only inches from the bloodied and agonized face of his assistant. "Because power like mine can work in all sorts of ways. I can take pain away..." He released his grip on the man's head, and with a groan, Jedediah dropped to the floor. Crane smiled before turning and walking calmly back to his chair. "Or I can make it happen..."

Adam drove the Packard past what looked like the base head-quarters − a two-storey building above which the United States air force flag was highlighted by a single spotlight − and parked it on a narrow street opposite a small row of shops: a grocery store, a hairdresser's, a post office.

Everywhere appeared to be deserted.

Not wanting to take any chances, they moved quickly into

an area of shadow and crept along a block of warehouses, which Rachel guessed housed military vehicles or other heavy equipment.

"It's getting stronger," Gabriel said. "This way..." He pointed.

Whatever else happened, they needed to do something about whatever was blocking their abilities to communicate with one another – or else they would be unable to use their powers of persuasion to deal with any immediate threat.

They were sitting ducks.

"There..." Gabriel said, and they ran across a parade square and over an area of lawn towards a low grey building. Its walls were metal and windowless. A low hum was coming from inside and there was a light issuing from a glazed roof, but there seemed no obvious way in.

They moved all the way round the building until they came back to where they had started. Gabriel pressed himself against the wall, slapping his hands against the metal in frustration. "It's in there," he said. "Whatever's doing this to us."

"That's the problem," Adam said. He was staring into the gloom of the base, keeping an eye out for trouble. "While it's blocking us, there's not very much we can do to *get* at it."

"We have to find some way to get in there," Gabriel said. "Some ... *ordinary* way."

"Where's Rachel?" Adam asked suddenly.

Gabriel turned round. There was no sign of her. Adam

was about to risk shouting his sister's name when he saw
her moving through a shaft of light at the far corner of the
building. He grabbed Gabriel's arm, and the two of them ran
to catch up with her.

"What are you doing?" he asked.

"We need to go this way," Rachel whispered. "It's the way
she went."

Adam started to protest, but Rachel was already moving
off again, walking towards another grey and utilitarian
building fifty metres away.

"Maybe she knows where they're keeping Dad," Adam
said.

They followed her.

The building had DANGER signs and symbols indicating
the presence of hazardous materials posted every six metres
around its perimeter. Rachel was walking calmly towards it,
moving in and out of shadow as the automated searchlights
from the conning-towers moved across the landscape.

Adam was a few metres behind her. "When you say 'she'
you mean our grandmother, right?"

"It's the same feeling I got in the back of the Packard," she
said. "That we're walking in her footsteps, you know."

"So what are we looking for?" Adam asked.

"I'm not sure. But I think we'll know when we find it."
She stopped dead suddenly, her hand flying to her neck – to
the amulet that hung from a thong round it. "Can you feel
that?"

Adam nodded. The Triskellion was vibrating again. It felt hot against his skin.

Although this building was also windowless, there was at least a visible way in: a single door was outlined against the dark metal by the skein of light round its edge. Rachel took a step towards it and wrapped her fingers round the handle.

She looked over her shoulder at Gabriel. "My grandmother stood here," she said. "Over forty years ago. Right here on this spot." She closed her eyes and pushed. The door was unlocked. She felt a wave of energy – white-hot and danger-ous – wash across her from inside, and when she opened her mouth to speak, the back of her throat felt burned and raw; it tasted of the perfume her grandmother had worn when she was alive. "And she was *terrified*…"

36

"Is that a British accent?" the man asked.

"New Zealand," Laura said, bending the truth a little.

"That's in Canada, right?"

"That's right," Laura said. It suited her that geography was clearly not the man's strong point.

He had picked her up just outside Oklahoma City. She had already hitched a ride on a truck out of Tulsa, eager to get away as fast as possible from the terrible scene in the store. She had borrowed a cap from the truck driver and had tucked her hair into it. She knew Scoppetone would have put a search out for her and her red hair and Australian accent would make her conspicuous. She would have to keep moving, and keep moving fast. As an attractive woman, she had had less trouble getting lifts than she might have otherwise had and her current driver was by no means immune to her charms.

"Larry Douglas," he said. "I'm from Kalamazoo." He held out a smooth pudgy hand for Laura to shake and she realized he was waiting to hear her name.

"Mel Campbell," she said.

"Lovely name for a lovely lady," Larry said. He raised one eyebrow and smiled what he clearly considered to be his very best lady-killer smile.

Laura groaned inwardly. The last thing she needed right now was to be hit upon by a Midwest salesman who smelled strongly of aftershave. She had more important things to worry about. While Larry droned on about sales figures and the new car he was going to buy, Laura's eyes darted around nervously, watching for police cars, her mind racing. What on earth was happening to Kate?

The man Kate had killed back in Australia had been an American. She was an American citizen, so she would be tried in the US. Scoppetone had arrested Kate in the state of Oklahoma with local backup, so she would have to stay in the state until a judge decided to send her back to New York – or not. Scoppetone would want her in New York, but the local small-town force might try to keep her in Tulsa. They would see it as a feather in their caps to have such a high-profile international case on their patch.

A sickening thought began to dawn on Laura. Oklahoma still had the death penalty. If Kate was tried here, she might face…

"Penny for your thoughts," Larry said.

"Sorry, I was daydreaming. I'm real tired."

"I can stop at a motel, if you like," Larry said, putting his hand on Laura's knee.

Thirty seconds later Laura was walking along the road-side, waiting anxiously for her next ride. She was pleased to see a bus approach over the horizon and even more delighted when she saw that one of its destinations was Amarillo.

She was heading in the right direction.

The winds had died down a little, but the rain was still torrential and Commodore Wing could barely see the road ahead of him as he carefully steered the Land Rover away from Waverley Hall and around the village green towards The Star.

The pub was as full as the commodore could remember seeing it, with villagers gathered in clusters round tables or standing several deep at the bar. They were talking in hushed tones about the terrible storm: comparing notes and telling horror stories about the dreadful havoc it had wreaked. Many were temporarily homeless and were getting ready to spend a second night in sleeping bags at the church or the village hall.

"Commodore..."

"Sir..."

"Good to see you, Commodore..."

Wing acknowledged the greetings with a nod and limped across to the bar, Merlin loping along at his side, faithful as always. He signalled to Tom Hatcham, the landlord, who immediately began pouring a large whisky, then he turned to see a familiar face, smiling at him from the end of the bar.

Creased, cracked and all but toothless, Jacob Honeyman looked as though he'd struggled for miles through the horrendous weather to get there. He looked bedraggled and confused. It was exactly the way he usually looked.

"Good evening, Jacob," the commodore said.

The beekeeper grunted a hello and nodded towards the door. "It's all going on."

"The storm, you mean?"

"All of it," Honeyman said. He grinned, showing off the few brown teeth he had left. "Reckon it's time to start building an ark."

"How are the hives holding up?" Wing asked.

Honeyman downed what was left of his beer. "Empty," he said. "Haven't got a single bee left." He leaned in close as if imparting a secret. "They've all gone home…"

Tom Hatcham walked over with Wing's whisky. The commodore downed it in one. "Get everyone a drink, will you, Tom?"

"What, the whole place?" Hatcham said.

Wing nodded.

Hatcham banged an empty glass on the bar to get everyone's attention and announced that the commodore was buying a round for the whole pub. There were predictable cheers and backslapping and a raucous rendition of "For He's a Jolly Good Fellow". The commodore smiled politely, waving and nodding to his fellow customers – some of whom he had known his entire life. Those who knew him well would

have recognized the fear visible in the lines around his eyes
and the corners of his mouth.

Hatcham was one of those few. "Are you all right, sir?" he
asked. "It's not about that phone call the other night, is it?
Sorry for giving that woman your number, but I didn't know
what else—"

Wing waved the landlord's concerns away and leaned forward. "I need to ask you a favour, Tom."

Hatcham nodded. "Name it."

"Will you look after Merlin for a while?" He gestured at
the dog lying at his feet. "I have to take a trip and there isn't
anyone else I can think of to ask."

Hatcham said that he would be happy to take the dog and
asked the commodore where he was going. When he didn't
get an answer, he tried to lighten the mood by telling the commodore that he had certainly picked the right time to take a
holiday – what with the atrocious weather and everything...

Wing nodded slowly, then stood up and walked towards
the door. The dog scrambled to its feet, but Wing raised a
hand, and the animal stayed where it was.

"How long will you be away?" Hatcham called.

Wing kept walking. His stick rattled against the wooden
floor, and those gathered at the bar stood by silently and
watched him leave. Behind him the dog began to whimper.

"Stay, Merlin," Wing said. He shut his eyes tightly against
the tears and took a deep breath before yanking the door
open and stepping out into the storm.

37

The first room was a laboratory.

Rachel felt the sting of industrial disinfectants drive away the memory of her grandmother's perfume.

Adam switched on the lights. They flickered on, revealing workbenches and rows of sinks. There were microscopes and centrifuges on every surface, and the shelves were stacked with files and boxes. Adam took down a file. It was marked BETA CLASSIFIED. He opened it and saw diagrams of DNA structures. Thousands of samples were listed alongside graphs and figures.

He showed Rachel the file and she shrugged. "Doesn't mean anything to me," she said.

"DNA," Adam said. "Looks like they study genetics here. I thought this place was going to be all about rocket science and stuff."

Rachel looked at Gabriel. He was pale and shivering. "You OK?" she said. She reached out and laid a hand on his arm.

"No," Gabriel whispered. "This is all wrong. Someone has *let* us in here. Someone wants us to see all this and I don't know why."

Rachel suddenly felt sorry for him. He looked lost and lonely; she put her arm round him.

He began to cry. "My mind won't work. I can't stand this noise, and I just feel we're close to something very bad."

Rachel didn't know what to say, so she just pulled him tighter to her. She hated it when Gabriel showed any weakness. If *he* didn't know what to do, who did?

Adam was looking at a computer at the end of the lab. A Triskellion screensaver was moving slowly across its screen.

"Click on it," Rachel said.

Adam hit the RETURN key and the screen came to life. On the desktop was an MPEG: a clip of film.

Adam double-clicked on it.

A grainy silent black and white film loaded, revealing a desert landscape. Mechanical debris was scattered around, and as the camera zoomed in, it became clear that they were seeing the aftermath of a plane crash. Military policemen and airmen were hurrying around the area in jerky fast-forward. The camera cut to a man on a stretcher. They recognized his face and then a subtitle confirmed it:

GROUP CAPT. WING.

His eyes were open and he looked around wildly. His face was dirty and scorched.

The camera cut to something on the ground. The film was

blotchy, but they could see the outline of a body. The image tightened, but they could make out little more than a head.

The film changed to an interior. A lab. The light was brighter and men in white coats stood around an operating table. The camera pushed between the men and they moved aside to allow the camera to see what they were working on.

"No," Rachel said. She thought she was going to be sick.

Adam kept watching, horribly fascinated, but Gabriel stepped forward and stabbed at the PAUSE button. "No!"

The horrifying image remained, frozen on the screen – the opened belly, the guts laid out on one side…

Before Gabriel had paused the film, they had seen that the arms and legs, although strapped to the table, were moving. The eyes were open and the head was rolling from side to side. Despite being smashed and torn apart, the body these men were operating on was still alive, and conscious.

"Keep moving," Gabriel said. His face was white and he was shaking as he pushed them away from the screen.

They opened a heavy door into another room. It was much cooler than the first and lit by pale industrial lights. There were jars and bottles on the shelves, and one whole wall was covered with what looked like a vast stainless steel filing cabinet. Rachel looked closely at the jars. They appeared to be filled with human body parts: internal organs, slices of brain, eyes…

"It's the morgue," Adam said.

Seeing him close his eyes, Rachel understood that he was

seeing the same thing that she was; they were once more seeing through their grandmother's eyes. She could taste that perfume again, feel her grandmother's fear. This was what Celia Root had been so terrified by...

Celia had made a decision. She needed to know everything! What Gerry had told her by the lake wasn't enough – she wanted to see it for herself.

Her heart was thumping against her ribs as she knocked on the door of Gerry's office in the senior airmen's block. After waiting a moment she reached for the handle and was amazed to find the door unlocked. She stepped inside, calling out Gerry's name, though it was clear there was nobody there.

She wandered behind the desk and dropped into the seat, and began absently flicking through the papers piled up on the leather desktop. There were reports marked URGENT *and* STRICTLY CONFIDENTIAL *and many files were marked* BETA: TOP SECRET...

"What on earth do you think you're doing, Celia?"

She looked up to see Gerry in the doorway. "I was just waiting for you. We need to talk. We—"

"These things are secret."

Celia grabbed the pile of files and folders from the desk and threw them across the room at him. "I'm sick of secrets," she said. "I want to know! What you told me by the lake—"

He strode over to her, took hold of her shoulders and shook her. "You want to see?"

She nodded.

"Right…"

He all but frogmarched her out of the office, across the compound and into a newly built building she had passed plenty of times but had never been inside. The armed guard acknowledged Wing and then glanced at Celia. Wing nodded. "She has Grade One BETA clearance," he said.

They pushed through several sets of doors until Celia became aware of the quiet, and the cold.

She was suddenly afraid.

"You want to see." The fury was still there in Wing's voice. "That's what you want, isn't it?"

"Please, Gerry…"

They had stopped at a set of metal doors in which a large round combination lock had been inset. Wing stepped close and began spinning the lock, first one way, then the other.

With every click, Celia's fear was ratcheted up a notch.

When Wing pushed open the door, the blast of cold air took her breath away.

He stepped aside. "After you, darling."

Celia's breath hung in plumes in front of her face and she stepped into the room. She saw a row of long wooden laboratory benches, each laid out with racks of test tubes, microscopes and Bunsen burners. There were blackboards with diagrams she could make neither head nor tail of and charts filled with columns of figures that made her head swim.

She walked further into the room and turned to a small alcove that was all but hidden from view by a translucent curtain. She stood frozen. Her hand was raised to move the curtain aside, but she was unable to go any further. In the alcove beyond she could hear something bubbling. A hiss and a hum.

Wing stepped quickly past her and pushed the curtain to one side. "Is this what you wanted to see?" he said.

Rachel and Adam opened their eyes at Gabriel's anguished cry. He was standing at the far end of the room, holding back a plastic curtain, his weeping eyes fixed on what lay behind it.

Rachel approached. Behind the curtain was a glass cylinder, some two metres tall, its surface coated with frost. The light above shed a ghostly glow into the liquid filling the tube.

Floating in the cylinder was the body of a naked figure.

Despite the ragged scars that criss-crossed the body, Rachel thought it looked remarkably peaceful: rotating slowly in its liquid grave. As the body turned and the face came into view, she saw that the hairless skull was fine and domed with high cheekbones and the now empty eye-sockets were almond shaped.

She realized it looked like Gabriel.

Gabriel was transfixed by the figure; his hands were pressed to the cold glass of the cylinder and tears coursed down his cheeks.

"Why do they want us to see this?" Adam asked.

"To leave you in no doubt about what we do here."

The voice – gruff and American – came from behind them. They turned to see a tough-looking man with a broken nose. "Thought you'd rather find out for yourselves than take the guided tour."

Rachel was waiting for Gabriel to do something, but he stood still, looking at the floor as if he knew the game was up. She reached out to him with her mind, but the ringing noise was louder than ever.

"This is where we find out what makes them tick," the man said. He flicked a finger towards Gabriel. "What makes you *all* tick. Hope you're going to be helpful…"

Suddenly, Adam rushed at the man, ready to kill, but two black-clad military personnel materialized behind him, Taser guns raised. The last thing Adam, Rachel and Gabriel felt was the agony of the powerful voltage coursing through their bodies as they fell to the floor.

part three:
the swarming

LD

ITICS

INESS

RTS

S

Freak Weather Linked to Stars

Global warming is once again being seen by many as the culprit for the extraordinary weather systems currently sweeping the US and many other parts of the world.

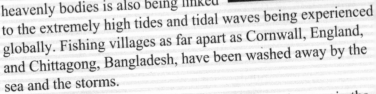

However, government astronomers in New Mexico are blaming the storms on a constellation that occurs only once every ten thousand years.

This near-unique alignment of heavenly bodies is also being linked to the extremely high tides and tidal waves being experienced globally. Fishing villages as far apart as Cornwall, England, and Chittagong, Bangladesh, have been washed away by the sea and the storms.

In New Mexico activity from long-dormant volcanoes in the Zuni-Bandera region has triggered earth tremors that have been felt along a previously unknown faultline that reaches from Arizona all the way to the east coast.

Tribes across Africa and Australasia are gathering at sacred sites – some convinced that the world is about to end, others that they are about to see a new beginning.

What is in no doubt, and a subject on which astronomers, scientists, astrologers and New Agers agree, is that something very unusual is happening in the sky…

Search

Other stories

Insurers Refuse Fox Theatre Payout

The mysterious electrical fire that almost destroyed the Fox Theatre in St Louis, Missouri, was caused by an "act of God", according to insurers who are refusing a payout. The Church of the Triple Wheel, whose followers were holding a rally in the theatre at the time of the fire, is expected to foot the bill.

⊙ Home news

Australian Murder Suspect Goes on Trial

Kate Newman, the woman arrested in Tulsa, Oklahoma, for the suspected murder of a man in Australia, appears in court today. The forty-year-old mother of two, who has dual British and US nationality, is appealing to be transferred to New York, where she will face a prison sentence rather than the death penalty. Her companion at the time of her arrest, an unnamed Australian woman in her thirties, remains at large.

⊙ Full story

Rebuilding Starts on Cincinnati Station, Ohio

Investigators draw a blank on causes of the crash.

⊙ Full story

New York Janitor Dies Rescuing Cat

Harry Hoffman, a sixty-five-year-old East Village janitor, died yesterday after falling from a fire escape. Residents say he slipped after rescuing a cat that had become trapped on the roof in East 11 Street. "Harry just loved Bilk said eighty-six-year-old Irma Winkleman, a distressed neighbour. "This is a tragedy

⊙ Full story

Colony Collapse on Rise

The New York Federation of Apiarists has reported a ninety per cent decline in bee colonies in the state. Experts are still divided over the cause of the collapse.

⊙ Environment

38

"It is time," Ezekiel Crane said.

He put down his copy of the *Pennsylvania Globe* on the map table of the motor yacht. The *Ezekiel One* – a sleek forty-foot Predator – had been purchased with generous donations from his loyal followers.

They had left Philadelphia in triumph. After Crane's barnstorming rally, another fifty thousand pilgrims would be coming to the Gathering; another fifty thousand who had pledged dollars in tens, twenties, fifties, hundreds to the Church of the Triple Wheel – as followers had from all across America.

Crane, Jedediah and a dozen or so trusted disciples from the Triple Wheel's inner circle had picked up the boat at Tom's River, a small harbour town on the Atlantic coast. Crane had always said that when the time came they would arrive in New York from the sea. He knew very well that when the great day came, all the major road and rail routes would be completely gridlocked.

"Hallelujah and amen," Brother Jedediah croaked. He put down the pastor's drink with a hand that now had a permanent tremor and watched with his remaining good eye as his master took out a bottle of pollen and tapped a small mound out on to the back of his hand, before sniffing the yellow powder up each nostril like a drug. Crane snorted the pollen back into his sinuses and let out a long sigh of pleasure. He added a splash of Dr Pepper to the vodka in front of him and drank it down.

"Anything else, Pastor?" Jedediah asked timidly. He had looked queasy since they'd got on the water, but he barely spoke now anyway for fear of offending Crane again – the shaking hand and the patch over his blinded eye permanent reminders of what could happen if he did.

"Hold this down for me," Crane said. He spread a rolled-up chart out across the map table. It was a facsimile of something very old and was covered in numbers and calculations, with a large symbol in the middle and smaller ones in three of the corners. At the bottom was a verse.

Brother Jedediah held down its corners with trembling hands. "Looks very old, Pastor," he hazarded.

"Older than anything in this God-forsaken country," Crane said. "It's English. I kind of grew up with it."

Jedediah looked at him, realizing that Crane had suddenly spoken in an English accent. Crane seemed to realize at the same moment and tried to cover it by continuing, braying mockingly like a comedy English toff, "Another time, another place, another life, old boy. It's a prophecy, don't you know?"

Jedediah smiled. "That's real funny, Pastor. You sound real different. Like someone in a movie."

Crane grunted and returned to his chart. He unfolded another map, a modern one this time, of Manhattan Island and New York City. Putting the two side by side, he began marking co-ordinates taken from the numbers on the old chart on the map of New York.

"Look, Pastor," Jedediah said. The excitement had raised his voice to a fevered squeak.

Crane already knew what he would see. It was not the first time he had done this – he had checked and rechecked the map references and locations numerous times. Each time he did so the same pattern emerged: the co-ordinates plotted three intersecting circles over the centre of New York City.

Triple wheels. And where the three wheels intersected they formed a symbol.

A Triskellion.

And the centre of the Triskellion bounded an area of downtown New York, with one building at its heart. Crane knew the history of that building, and its significance. He knew that this was where the prophecy would be fulfilled. This would be where Ezekiel One would happen again, and where he would gather his followers to him for whatever fate awaited them.

They were now motoring away from the New Jersey coast and across the harbour towards Brighton Beach. In the distance Crane could see the glittering spires of downtown Manhattan twinkling in the sun, and he felt he was about to fulfil his destiny, to do something for which he would be remembered for ever.

When the visitors came, he would present himself to them as their rightful representative on earth. As a direct descendant of the English Traveller, he was surely the natural ambassador. He would deliver up his loyal followers to the visitors – to do with as they saw fit. To breed the next super-generation with Crane himself as their leader. He was in absolutely no doubt about the role he was to play. He had not always felt this way – but he had finally come to recognize that his remarkable survival, his new-found powers, his re-birth, his *lineage* had all marked him out as the Chosen One.

Him. Not two snotty American kids from a bastard gene pool.

The water was becoming choppy and clouds gathered over the Manhattan skyline. A red sun hung heavily in the sky, casting a pink light on the glass towers. The boat powered up into the East River, past the buildings of the Lower East Side, until it found a berth alongside Roosevelt Island.

Crane gathered the crew on the teak deck.

"Look at the sunset, Brothers, and remember this day."

He took the hand of the two disciples on either side of him, who, following his lead, took the hand of those next to them and so on, until all on the deck were linked. The sun, huge now and blood-red, was sinking down behind the bristling spires and towers that yearned towards the pink-streaked sky.

Crane dropped his head in prayer. "Remember where you were on this day. Remember who you were with, and remember the sun going down on a world which from tomorrow will have been changed for ever. Amen."

"Amen!" Brother Jedediah's croak sounded above the low voices of the others.

Crane let go of their hands and smiled benignly at the group. "Tick-Tock," he said breezily. "The time has come." He looked down at the large Triple Wheel watch on his wrist, watching as the second hand swept round, waiting until it reached twelve.

And then he pushed the button…

In a pastel-pink house on a quiet tree-lined street in a suburban neighbourhood between Indianapolis and Tulsa, Barbra and Bob Anderson and their two children had just started to eat dinner. Meat loaf with gravy and mashed potatoes. Apple and raspberry cobbler to follow. It was Bob's favourite.

"Meat loaf's as great as always," he said.

Barbra smiled. "Thanks, honey."

The children rolled their eyes at each other and made

kissy-kissy noises. Their parents told them to be more respectful and then laughed, unable to keep straight faces.

Then the alarms sounded.

Four separate alarms on the four wristwatches the family had been given by Brother Thomas and Sister Marianne. Gifts from Pastor Ezekiel Crane and the Church of the Triple Wheel.

Bob Anderson gently laid down his knife and fork. Barbra, Eden and Tammy did the same, their eyes fixed ahead, the tinny *beep-beep* of the alarms continuing to sound as they pushed back their chairs and rose from the dining table.

Bob and Barbra joined hands and walked slowly into their bedroom to gather their things together. Coats, bags, car keys.

Eden and Tammy were already by the front door, ready and waiting to go, when their parents re-emerged; their four smiles were fixed and serene, their eyes wide and unblinking. Barbra opened the door, stepped out and took a deep breath. The air was crisp and scented with the honeysuckle that grew in huge pots at the edge of the driveway.

It was the perfect day for it.

The family climbed into Bob's station wagon, and as the car reversed out on to the road, Eden and Tammy waved at the family next door, who were pulling out of their drive at the same time.

Bob eased the big car out into the stream of slow-moving traffic. He nodded at Barbra and she nodded back. Their alarms and those of the children in the back began to syn-chronize: the tinny music of each one harmonizing with the others, until the car was filled with a sound like robotic bird-song.

They drifted towards the freeway, content to make the journey in silence. Bob and Barbra, Tammy and Eden. Each head was filled with the words they had read and heard every night.

The promises.

Each one was blissfully happy to be joining the others.

39

The noise changed from time to time, becoming either a high-pitched whine or a low buzz and shifting in pitch and intensity, but it was always there in Rachel's head. Constant and maddening. She knew it was the same for Gabriel and Adam – the terrible noise that only they could hear, the sound of the interference, of whatever was neutralizing their abilities – and she knew her face was twisted into the same tortured expression as theirs.

She could see it: hunched over and staring at herself in the polished metal of the cell wall. Blurred and indistinct as the reflection was, the pain and frustration were clear.

She felt hopeless.

Powerless…

The sounds within the cell itself were no less unpleasant, no more comforting. The rustle of the plastic suits was like the whisper of something terrible whenever she, Adam or Gabriel shifted position; whenever they turned over on the floor or stretched to fight off the cramp, fighting against the pain as the handcuffs cut off the blood to their wrists. Pressing themselves against one another for comfort or inching away in an effort to be alone for a while, they tried to deal with the noise, and worse with the sickening realization that the journey they had begun in a small English village a little over two years before would end here, like this.

Lost and helpless. A long way from home.

In those first few terrible hours after their capture, Rachel came to accept that the only possible escape was into herself. The interference hissed and hummed until the headache was barely noticeable any more, and there were moments when, if she focused hard enough, she found herself able to sink beneath it. To hide for a few minutes at a time in that part of her brain that they would never reach. In the tangle of synapses that still sparked; that still fired the strange and unsettling images she had lived with since she and Adam had first set foot in the village of Triskellion.

The part of her that dreamed; that saw the truth.

Now she felt the first flashes of a strange new vision. The lights in the cell never dimmed, but Rachel, studying the shift patterns of the guards, knew that it was night; that it was dark outside. She closed her eyes and surrendered her consciousness to the darkness within. She let herself drift down into it, towards bright explosions of light and sound, until her mind was like a screen and she could watch images move across it.

She lay her head down against the cold metal floor and dreamed the past...

The girl remembered the tree and the fields of maize that had surrounded it.

The stranger had taught her Wappinger tribe to cultivate this well-watered and fertile island they called Manna-Hata. As far as she knew, he had been there many years: longer than her father and her grandfather – the chief – could remember. They called him Achak-Aranck, which meant "Spirit from the Stars". He had seemed ageless and tireless, and had been regarded by the tribe as a medicine man and shaman.

The story told to the children was that he had brought the bees with him.

His gift to the tribe.

He had taught the tribesmen how to plant and cultivate maize, so they no longer had to live purely on meat. He had shown them how to burn off the crop to ensure greater fertility the next season, and the bees had pollinated many new species of plant around the island. He had taught them new techniques, so they could harvest shellfish from the bay and could manage the herds of buffalo that roamed freely across the plains.

He had helped the tribe to develop. He had turned them into a civilized and peaceful people.

The Wappinger had wanted for nothing once the stranger had arrived. They always had enough food to last through the winter, and the stranger's good deeds and kindness ensured that they all lived side by side in peace and prosperity. Manna-Hata had been an earthly paradise: a land of milk and honey.

Until the European came.

Her father and the other braves had rowed out in canoes to meet him when his ship had arrived in the harbour. They had greeted him with gifts of honey, corn and dried meat. They had never seen such a man, fair-skinned and bearded, and they met him with good fellowship in their hearts as they had the stranger many years before.

For the Wappinger, the arrival of travellers had always been a good omen.

But this man was different.

His voice was rough and angry, and so were his crew. Once they had come ashore they behaved like animals: eating like pigs and forcing themselves on the women of the tribe like wild beasts. Protests had been met with violence. The Wappinger braves were proud and had fought back, but they had been no match for the exploding powder that the Europeans used to blow them to bits.

They had killed her father.

Achak-Aranck had called for a truce. He had offered the Europeans corn, buffalo, fish, beads and carvings to leave, but they had wanted more. They had wanted the land. Achak-Aranck had become angry. He had paced in a circle all night, entering a trance and shouting at the stars. Then the storm had come; torrential rain had washed away the crops and tossed the European ship aground in the bay.

The Europeans had become nervous at the power of the tribe's medicine man, unnerved by the strange-looking shaman who seemed to be able to control the weather.

So they had killed him.

The Europeans had overpowered Achak-Aranck. They had run him through with a sword, spilling his guts on to the fertile land for the dogs to eat. Then, while he had still been alive, they had filled his mouth with their gunpowder and blown his head off.

A warning to the tribe.

And then the skies had really opened. The storms had battered the coastline, wrecking oyster beds and blowing away the tepees of the Wappinger. Swarms of bees had covered everything and everybody, stinging and dying as if to punish humanity for its folly. The European privateers had broken out in sores and died agonizing deaths in their beds, pus weeping from every wound.

As soon as his men had repaired the ship, the European captain had taken his remaining crew and limped away into the Atlantic Ocean, never to return.

They had gone, but the girl had known that nothing would be the same again. The braves had chopped down the tree where Achak-Aranck had died. They had carved it into a totem in memory of their shaman, the Spirit from the Stars, and had planted it where the tree had stood, in the same place that they buried their own dead.

She looked at it now: its stylized image of the stranger's face, placid-looking and almond-eyed; the halo of bees round his head;

the three-bladed amulet he had always worn round his neck carved underneath – the amulet from which he derived his power; the one torn from him by the European in his dying moments and taken away.

She looked at the wings that reached skyward from the top of the totem pole and saw a future: wood turning to brick, turning to steel on the same spot, growing and changing, thrusting ever higher, until a vast sparkling tower – glassy and jewel-like – stood on the spot where Achak-Aranck had perished. And at its top were two enormous silver wings poking up into the clouds.

And she was sure she could see two figures – spinning human fireballs – falling through the sky…

Rachel opened her eyes; dragged from the dream by the noise, metal against metal, she watched the guard slide the last of the three trays across the floor towards her and the others.

She blinked. She could still see the stranger's image on the tree; a face that refused to show pain…

"Eat up," the guard said.

The glass door slid shut, and only then did the guard holster his Taser.

Gabriel was awake. He looked down at the tray in front of him, then pushed it away with his foot.

"I'll eat yours," Adam said.

Gabriel shrugged and continued to stare through the glass at the guard.

Rachel watched him and wondered if he could possibly be feeling as wretched as she was. She knew he did not feel things in quite the same way as she and Adam did; she sensed that somewhere inside him was a strength she could never understand.

Yet despite all those things about Gabriel that were extraordinary, that defied belief and rational thought, he was still just a boy tied up in a prison cell. A boy to whom, she had come to accept, she would be inextricably tied for ever.

He turned to look at her. "Aren't you hungry?" he asked. He nodded towards Adam, who was tucking into what looked like porridge, then back at Rachel's untouched tray.

Rachel shook her head.

"Bad dreams?"

"Bad enough," she said. She inched across the floor and laid her head on Gabriel's shoulder. "But this is worse…"

40

Laura had spent the night in Amarillo: holed up in a cheap hotel and doing her best to stay awake. She had drifted off for an hour or two, but had spent most of the night watching the door and listening for footsteps outside the room or to the noise of cars drawing up in the car park. She had aided and abetted Kate's escape from Australia and fled the scene of the shoot-out in Oklahoma.

Now the police would be looking for her too.

She had caught the bus to Alamogordo first thing, sharing the journey with half a dozen airmen heading back to the base after a few days' R&R. Now, six hours later, she found herself approaching the base's sentry-box, trailing behind those returning airmen and watching as they casually flashed their identification cards before marching through the gates.

Her mouth was dry and her heart was thumping in her chest.

"Help you, ma'am?"

The sentry peered at her from behind mirrored sunglasses.

He was chewing gum and looked as though he could shoot her where she stood without giving it a second's thought.

Laura took out her old Hope ID: a card she had not used for over two years, but which she hoped might be enough to get her inside. She tried to smile, to look relaxed, as she passed it across.

The sentry chewed his gum. He looked at the card, then at Laura. She could feel the sweat popping out across her forehead and prayed the guard would not see it. Long seconds crawled past before he slid the card back towards her. "Welcome to Alamogordo Air Force Base, Doctor Sullivan…"

Laura could scarcely believe her luck. It had been her only hope but she had still been certain that her clearance would have long since been revoked. Perhaps they had simply forgotten. Perhaps they had never dreamed that she would have had the nerve to walk back into a Hope Project facility.

Whatever the reason, she was not about to question it and she hurried through the gates, her mind racing, wondering if the children were here and how on earth – now that she *was* inside – she was going to find them.

And what she would tell them when she did.

As she was walking past a block of single-storey buildings, a man in uniform rounded a corner and walked swiftly towards her.

"Doctor Sullivan?"

Laura nodded and tried to summon that relaxed smile again.

"I've been sent to escort you to the base commander's office," the airman said.

She fell into step with him. "And that would be…?"

"Major Todd Crow. He's kind of … new."

Laura nodded. Maybe that had been why she had found it so easy to get on to the base. Maybe this "new" commander was a little less security-minded than his predecessor.

Laura and her escort exchanged small talk as he led her into one of the low granite buildings on the base's main square. They walked quickly through to the rear of the building, past window after window; Laura glanced into each one in the hope of catching a glimpse of Rachel or Adam. They eventually stopped outside a simple brown door. The airman knocked twice, sharply, and when the order was given to enter, showed Laura into the commander's office.

The man behind the desk stood up. He was a little shorter than average but built like a soldier, with a broken nose and blond close-cropped hair. He stepped forward to shake her hand, and Laura found herself thinking it was unexpectedly soft in contrast to his tough militaristic appearance, with its pristine uniform and rod-straight back.

Crow sat down again and took a file from his desk. Laura saw her name and photograph at the top of the document.

It was her Hope file.

He tapped a finger against it. "Lots of good work," he said. "Interesting research. Up until two years ago, that is. Then there's just … nothing."

He looked up at her. She stared back at a face that she guessed could be extremely frightening if he chose it to be. But there was the ghost of a smile there, too, and she thought she could see something vulnerable lurking beneath the brass buttons and the bravado; something sensitive even. She was probably just imagining it. Not many people moved up the ranks of the Hope Project by *caring* a great deal about anything.

"I'm not going to pry into these two missing years," Crow said. "I know how these things work."

Laura nodded. She sensed that it would be best to say nothing, but she was beginning to understand why she was being given such an easy ride. She knew that according to Hope protocol, those engaged in "research" were often, in reality, agents operating under "deep cover". She was, and always had been, a scientist, pure and simple, and had since turned her back on everything Hope stood for – but those two missing years could easily be misinterpreted as time spent on a top secret assignment.

"You've been working on the Triskellion project," Crow said. "With the Newman children."

"It's a fascinating project," Laura said.

Crow nodded. "An important one too – one that's very close to the director's heart."

"Do you know the director well?" Laura asked.

Crow shrugged. "Well enough." He leaned back in his chair. "I'm not exactly flavour of the month with our beloved leader right now. That's why I'm here, if I'm honest." He gave a mock grimace. "In exile…"

Laura waited, unsure how to react.

Crow slapped his palms on the desktop. "I think I'll be back in the old man's good books pretty soon, though." He cleared his throat and inched forward. "You know we have the children?"

"The children?"

"I presume that's why you came…"

"Absolutely." Laura nodded, but the questions crashed around her head, panic and confusion rising up from her gut. What did he mean by "have the children"? How could they have been captured? And more importantly, how was she going to get them out?

Did Crow have the Triskellions? Worse, did the director already have them?

"Would you like to see them?" Crow asked. "The children? I could take you across there now, if you like…"

They walked back outside, and Crow showed her to a Jeep, explaining that it was a ten-minute walk to the cell block, which, considering the heat, was probably unwise.

He drove quickly around the perimeter of the base, the Jeep's wheels throwing up rust-coloured clouds behind them. He shouted above the growl of the engine, telling her that he was a New Yorker and still hadn't got used to the conditions out there in the New Mexican desert. She shouted back that she was right at home: it was like being in the Australian outback. He said he would like to visit Australia someday and she told him he would love it.

The chit-chat ceased immediately once they reached the cell block. Crow, having shown his ID to the armed guards on duty outside, was silent as they entered, signed in at a command point and then descended in a lift to the basement level.

His footsteps echoing, Crow led Laura along a corridor encased in solid steel. More armed guards were stationed every five metres or so and cameras mounted high up on the walls swivelled to track their progress as they passed.

When they arrived outside the cell where the children were being held Laura fought hard to stifle a gasp...

The doors were made entirely of a glass which Laura guessed to be several centimetres thick. She stepped up close to it and stared in at the children, who were huddled together against one metal wall in the corner of the three-metre cubed box. Their wrists were bound with plastic handcuffs and they were wearing white plastic bodysuits. Their faces looked pale and empty. Laura was wondering if it was one-way glass, when she saw Rachel glance up and notice her.

Her heart leapt in excitement and terror. She prayed that Rachel would not give the game away by looking pleased to see her. She could only hope that Rachel would read the warning in her face and not react.

Rachel just stared.

"Open it." Crow gestured to one of the guards, who entered a code into a keypad mounted on the wall.

Adam and Gabriel looked up as the glass doors slid open, but before Laura had a chance to worry further about how they might react, she was aware of Crow close behind her, his mouth pressed to her ear.

"In you go, Doctor Sullivan," he said. The change in his tone made it clear that this was an order, not a request. She turned to look at him, but his hand was already in the small of her back, guiding her across the threshold.

"We know exactly why you're here," he said. "And we've been waiting for you."

A guard stepped forward and wrapped plastic cuffs round her wrists before she had a chance to struggle. Crow turned away as she was bundled into the cell.

"Now you can go and join your friends," the guard said.

The glass doors slid shut and Laura had no choice but to walk over to join the children. She dropped to her knees when she reached them, well aware that Crow was still standing on the other side of the door, staring at them through the glass. Studying them as though they were lab-rats.

41

The Oklahoma State Penitentiary at McAlester was not designed to be pretty. Kate Newman knew that well enough, but she was still amazed at *how* breathtakingly ugly it was. It was as though every brick and barred window had somehow been infused with something rancid and poisonous; something that sucked the hope out of people and filled them with despair.

She avoided the hard stares of fellow prisoners as she was led to a table in the visitors' centre; as she was guided to a chair and shackled to the tabletop.

"You know how this thing works?" the guard asked.

Kate nodded. She had seen it in the movies. A solid sheet of Plexiglass divided one side of the table from the other and she would only be able to talk to her visitor through a phone that was built into the divide.

Once the guard had left, Kate sat and stared at the door, waiting for her visitor. She was thinking about Rachel and Adam – and trying to keep the tears away. She thought, too, about her ex-husband, Ralph, who for reasons she could not fathom had been coming into her mind a great deal in recent days.

Perhaps it was because she was back in the US. But whatever the reason, his presence in her thoughts this often was something she had not been used to for a few years. Not since the divorce.

When they had settled down to a new life in Australia, she had made the difficult decision to sever any contact with those from their previous life. They had always known that the Hope Project would do anything to find them and that included attacking those closest to them. So how ever cruel it had seemed to keep Rachel and Adam away from their father it had been the only way to ensure his safety.

The man she had once loved, who she presumed had loved her in return, had become as good as dead to her.

It was strange, but thinking about him now, she had difficulty picturing his face clearly. She knew that these things happened as time passed, even to those with whom you were most familiar – but this felt like something else. It was not that Ralph Newman's face had just become indistinct or blurred by failing memory – when she pictured him now, it was as if he were in shadow.

As though a darkness had fallen across his face.

And it frightened her…

The lawyer was twenty minutes late.

She watched Nick Georgiades bustle in through the door.

He was a stocky man with curly black hair and stubble that stood out against a ruddy complexion. He sat and picked up the phone.

"Sorry I'm late, Ms Newman." He was pulling papers from his briefcase and piling them up on the table in front of him. "You doing OK?"

Kate picked up her own phone – but she had nothing to say. It was not one of the lawyer's cleverest questions.

"Yeah, the traffic out there today's unbelievable," Georgiades said. He was still looking flustered, trying to get his documents in order. "This weird trek people are going on... You know about that?"

"I haven't really been keeping up with the news."

"People are coming from all over the country." The lawyer shook his head in disbelief. "Hundreds of thousands of them in cars, planes, boats, trains, whatever. Bicycles for Pete's sake, or walking if they have to. All started yesterday and now every freeway's pretty much at a standstill."

"Where are they going?" Kate asked.

"One-way traffic all the way to New York City," Georgiades said. "Some kind of rally for that weird cult. It's been all over the news."

"Like I said, I haven't really—"

"I know, I'm sorry." He held up a hand. "And now we really need to talk about your case. If we're going to appeal or push for extradition, we need to get your story straight. We need to go over all the facts..."

Georgiades kept on talking, but Kate was no longer listening. She knew as soon as he had begun to describe what was happening outside, the strange journey that so many people were making, that it had something to do with the children, and with Gabriel. She had no idea what was going to happen in New York, or why – but she knew that Rachel and Adam would almost certainly be heading there too, if they were not there already.

"I need to get out of here," she said.

The lawyer stopped speaking and stared at her for a few seconds. "Excuse me?"

"I have to get out and find my children."

"I don't think you quite understand, Ms Newman." He loosened his tie. "There is no possibility of getting out. In fact, there are much more … important things to worry about."

Kate shook her head, waving his concern away. "Look, once they find out what happened in Australia—"

"You shot a government agent."

"He wasn't from the *government*!" Kate shouted. "He was from the Hope Project, and he was after my children."

Georgiades stared down at his notes. "We cannot find any evidence that this 'Hope Project' you keep talking about even exists or that there was ever any threat to your children. The prosecution have made it very clear that they will be seeking the maximum penalty for these offences."

"No," Kate said; "they'll find out what happened."

"You shot a man; you've admitted that much already."

"They'll see that it was an accident and they'll drop the charges." Kate stared through the glass and saw the worry in the lawyer's face. Suddenly doubt flooded through her. "Won't they?"

Georgiades did his best to sound cheerful. "There's always hope."

Kate swallowed back a sob. She felt every one of those ugly poisonous bricks pressing in on her. Is there? she thought.

42

First came the tears, then the questions.

In the time since they had seen one another, so much had happened to all of them. Rachel and Adam fell into Laura's arms and, although hampered by the handcuffs, they hugged as best they could, until they could hardly breathe: all craving human contact and comfort. The comfort was missing one important element.

"Where's Mom?" Adam asked.

Laura wiped the tears from her cheeks and blinked at the twins through red eyes.

"Where is she? What's happened?" Panic rose in Rachel's voice. She knew it was bad news.

"She's in prison," Laura said.

Rachel and Adam's relief was palpable. "Thank God," Rachel cried.

"We thought you meant she was dead." Adam almost laughed with relief. "She's probably safer than we are."

The expression on Laura's face didn't change. She didn't

know how to tell them, but she had long since pledged to tell
the truth – how ever bad it might be.

"She's been arrested for murder," she said.

Rachel and Adam looked at each other in disbelief.

"Mom? Murder?" Rachel shook her head.

"Who did she kill?" Adam asked.

"A man," Laura said. "A Hope agent who was after you."

"Shit," Adam said.

"If she hadn't, you would never have got out of Australia.
Hope was on to you. You left just in time."

"I think you mean that I came for them just in time,"
Gabriel said. He had been silent since Laura had entered
the cell, curled up on a metal bench that ran the length of
one wall, his face between his knees. He looked lost and
confused, as if his brain were not functioning properly.

"Hi, Gabriel," Laura said. "Yes, you came just in time.
How are you? You look terrible."

It was true. Robbed of his powers, Gabriel looked wasted
and emaciated. Laura put her hand on his bony shoulder
and, unusually, he stood and embraced her.

"Where is Mom, exactly?" Rachel asked when they had
finished hugging.

"In Oklahoma," Laura said. "In the state penitentiary."

"What's going to happen to her?" Adam asked.

"She should have got a lawyer by now. And if he's any
good he'll be trying to get her extradited to Australia, where
it happened, or at the very least back to New York."

"Why does she need to be moved?" Adam asked. "What's the worst that can happen?"

Laura paused a moment. The truth, she remembered. "Oklahoma still has the death penalty," she said.

Adam sat down heavily on the bench next to Rachel; both their faces drained of colour. Visions of their mother strapped to a gurney awaiting a lethal injection flashed through their minds. They leaned against each other and cried. They had thought their situation couldn't get any worse, and it just had.

"We'll find a way," Gabriel said.

"Sorry if we don't seem very convinced," Rachel cried. "Mom's on death row and we *still* have no idea where our dad is. We thought he was going to be here, but…"

Laura laid a hand on Rachel's shoulder, but said nothing.

"I'm beginning to think he might be dead," Rachel said.

"He might just as well be," Adam added. "I'm not even sure I want to find him now, anyway. If he hadn't left Mom, none of this would have happened. We wouldn't have been sent away, we wouldn't have met *you*…" He stabbed a finger at Gabriel.

"Don't be so sure," Gabriel said.

Laura nodded. If there was one thing she was certain of, it was that Rachel and Adam would never have lived an ordinary life. She looked at Gabriel. "First, we need to get out of here," she said.

"Can't you hear that noise?" Gabriel asked, trying to point

out the shrieking frequency that hurt his brain. "It's torture. It stops any of us from being able to connect."

Laura listened, but heard nothing.

"We can't even think straight," Rachel said. "Let alone overpower anyone or hypnotize a guard. We're completely helpless."

"And they've taken the Triskellions," Adam said. "They disabled us with stun guns and took everything." He thumped the polished steel wall with a resounding boom. "They're Nazis."

The word chimed with Laura. She had thought exactly the same herself. She remembered a conversation she'd had with Clay Van der Zee a few years ago during which he had told her exactly what Hope had had in mind for the twins.

It was one horrifying truth she decided to keep to herself.

"The Triskellions are still in the safe," Crow said. "Under armed guard."

"Very good." The director sounded pleased.

Crow took a sip of the bourbon on his desk. It was just after 7 p.m., four hours since Laura Sullivan had arrived on the base, sixteen hours since the children had been captured.

Crow had needed a drink.

He had liked the Australian as soon as she had walked into his office. She was direct with a personal warmth, and was obviously good-looking. He had felt uncomfortable locking her up. He would have far preferred to have spent the evening having dinner with her or just talking. After New York, Crow was incredibly lonely in Alamogordo, and Laura Sullivan's company was exactly the kind he craved.

"I've put Doctor Sullivan in with the children as you instructed," he said.

"Are they wired?" the director asked.

"Of course, sir."

"Good. Let's see what she can get out of them."

"They've been talking plenty – about the mother and so on. The father, too."

The director said nothing for a few seconds. Then: "What about the *other* boy, Crow? Let's not forget what we're dealing with here."

"Under control, sir. The inhibitor frequency appears to have completely blocked his powers. He seems to be very weak."

"Good. Once we've broken him a bit more, I'd like you to isolate him, then run the tests."

"Very good, sir."

"But my immediate concern is the Triskellions. I want your personal guarantee that they will be on their way to New York on a military jet tomorrow."

"You have it, sir."

"Good work, Todd." His voice sounded almost warm.

It was the first time Crow could ever remember the director using his first name. It might be the first stage of my rehabilitation, he thought. "One more thing," he said; "what about the twins?"

"Get a team working on them in the BETA lab first thing in the morning. I want full genetic profiling, plus a CAT scan analysis of every inch of their bodies, with tissue samples to back up the scan: brain, gut, reproductive, everything. We need every scrap of information analysed and compared with samples from the other one – Gabriel, as you say they call him."

Crow suddenly felt cold. "Full tissue sample analysis, sir?" His mouth had dried and he took a sip from his glass. "But that means we have to—"

"I *know* what it means, Crow," the director said. Any glimmer of warmth was gone from his voice. "Now get me those Triskellions and get on with your work…"

A few minutes after the director had slammed the phone down on him, Crow left his office and walked along the corridor to the small room at the end. Nodding to the armed officer outside, Crow took the key from the chain attached to his belt and opened the door.

It was warm inside and the air smelled stale. Crow felt his heart start to beat that little bit faster. He crossed to the huge metal safe built into the far wall, rubbing his hands across his legs to wipe the sweat from his palms. He reached forward to key in the combination, then froze and span round, suddenly overcome by the sense that there was someone else in the room with him.

The room was every bit as empty as it had been when he'd entered it.

"What am I doing?" he muttered to himself.

When he had opened the safe, he took out the pair of small brown leather pouches which held the Triskellions. He had not once given in to the temptation to look at them since they had been taken from Rachel and Adam Newman, but suddenly, for reasons he could not fathom, he wanted more than anything to see them again for himself.

He tipped the pouches one at a time and the amulets dropped into his palm.

It felt as though he had been wired up to the mains… The surge died away as quickly as it had come, but it left a … buzz inside him. All at once, he felt stronger and unafraid – of the director and his stupid threats. Of anything…

Staring down at the objects in his hand, his vision blurred; he was transfixed by the warm glow that was spreading across his palm. It slid up his arms and into his chest…

"Beautiful," he heard himself say.

Would anyone know if he simply took them and ran? he wondered. Would they ever catch him…?

Taking a deep breath, he forced his eyes shut. It was far from easy. Keeping them closed, he shoved the Triskellions back into their pouches and back into the safe. Opening his eyes again, he stood there, staring at the gunmetal grey door of the safe, until he felt almost normal again.

Then he locked the room behind him and hurried back down the corridor to his office.

Back to his bourbon.

43

Major Todd Crow could not remember feeling worse.

He had drunk a lot more bourbon than he had intended to the night before – all but finishing the bottle once he was off duty – and his throbbing head and churning stomach were not helped by the fact that he had barely slept. Normally that much whisky would have put him out like a light, but he had lain awake, slick with sweat, thinking about the prison cell on the other side of the base. Thinking about Laura Sullivan and the three children with whom she was being held prisoner.

What little sleep he *had* been able to get had been punctuated with dreams that were full of blood and bright lights, and thinking about them now made the burning in his gut even worse; he wanted to run out into the desert and lie down until the images faded and the sand crept over him.

Crow had not known a great deal of contentment since his transfer to Alamogordo, but he could not imagine how things could be worse than this. For the last few days carrying out his orders had made him feel physically sick. He had looked away when the children had been brought down with Tasers and had felt something like a stone in his chest as he had ushered Laura Sullivan into the cell to join them.

He was a soldier, not a prison governor.

He drank the best part of a large bottle of water and stared down at his desktop. "I didn't sign up for this," he said.

"Excuse me, sir?"

Crow looked up and saw his assistant in the doorway. "Sorry, Parker, just talking to myself."

Parker stared back blankly, then nodded. "I have the director ringing through from New York, sir. It sounds urgent."

"It's always urgent," Crow muttered. He stared at the phone as Parker scuttled back into the adjoining office, fantasizing about telling the director he was quitting – he could find some other patsy to do his dirty work.

The phone rang. The fantasy evaporated and Crow snatched up the handset.

"Good morning, Todd." The director sounded as chipper and glad to be alive as Crow felt gloomy and thick-headed. "Thought a nice early reminder might be a good idea."

"Reminder, sir?'

"My Triskellions, Todd. I presume they are already on their way here."

"Sir, not as yet, sir…"

The director's mood blackened in a heartbeat. His voice

dropped, took on an edge. "How clear do I need to make this, Crow? There is nothing, *nothing*, as important as getting those two amulets to me as soon as possible. Do you understand? I don't care if we're invaded – I don't care if every country under the sun decides to launch missiles against us – you get the Triskellions to New York, and you do it now."

"Yessir." Crow could feel his stomach start to roll and burn, the jackhammer behind his skull picking up speed.

"You just need to follow orders, Crow. It's not difficult, is it?"

"No, sir, but there are still … issues we need to resolve."

"Issues?"

"The children, sir."

There was half a minute's silence. Crow could hear the director's breathing. "They are no longer your responsibility, Major. You've done your job … not as well as I would have liked, mind you … and now it's time to let the scientists get on with theirs."

"I still don't—"

"I'm authorizing the research process to begin at once. Have the lab prepped and get things started."

Crow's breathing felt laboured; the stone in his chest had doubled in size. "Which … one…?"

"We'll save the Gabriel character until last, I think. He should yield the most interesting results. You can start with the Newman children."

"Yessir."

"You sound a little worried, Crow."

"I'm fine," Crow lied.

"Good, because it's just science. Nothing to get hot and bothered about. We clear?"

"Clear, sir." Crow turned away from the bright light streaming through his office window. He had never felt less clear about anything in his entire life. "I'll get right on it."

"And my Triskellions?"

"On their way. I'll get an F-35 fuelled up and brief my best pilot."

"Bring them yourself," the director said. "There's no better pilot on the base, and I know I can trust you." He let his words hang for a second or two before adding, "I *can* trust you, can't I, Todd?"

Rachel had dreamed about the building again – and the greed and terror that had given birth to it. She had seen the glass tower rising from earth, stained with the blood of a man called Spirit from the Stars, the sweep of its metal wings across the clear blue above her...

It was a building Rachel knew well, one she and Adam had seen many times growing up in Manhattan.

The Flight Building.

But why were visions of it coming to her now? She thought about the dreams of a knight and a maiden that had troubled her so much when she had first arrived in the village of Triskellion. Later there had been dreams and visions of a Traveller and the ancient North African tribe whose lives he had transformed.

Marriage and twins. Treachery and murder.

Rachel shuddered at the images that were as real, as *vivid,* to her as her own memories: two hearts cut out and entombed in a church, a stranger's flesh consumed by flames, brains dashed out on a rock to be picked clean by sea birds.

The dreams always ended in death – those threatened or afraid always killed the outsider they did not understand – and they always meant there was something that Rachel and Adam had to do…

Rachel described what she had seen to Gabriel, Adam and Laura. In the past she and Adam had often shared the same dreams, but whatever was blocking their powers was clearly interfering with that ability too.

"Mine was a little more basic," Adam said after he'd heard about her dream. "I was in a band. There were lots of hot girls…"

Laura grinned, punched Adam on the arm.

"What is it we're supposed to do?" Rachel stared at Gabriel.

"It hardly matters," he said. He lifted up his wrists, still bound with the plastic cuffs. "Not if we're stuck in here."

"It's important, though, isn't it?"

"It's how all this finishes," Gabriel said. "How it was *meant* to finish."

"Basically we're screwed," Adam said. "Right?"

Gabriel shrugged, unable to argue.

"We can't do a thing," Adam said. "Trussed up in here like Christmas turkeys." He kicked the metal wall, kept on kicking it. "We can't help Mom; we can't *find* Dad…"

There was a click and a hiss and the glass doors began to slide back. Laura looked at Adam. "I think you're making them mad," she said.

Two guards had stepped into the cell, their Tasers pointed at the children. Adam stopped kicking. He sank down to the floor and turned away. "They're just bringing breakfast…"

Rachel's voice was quiet, a catch to it. "No," she said. "They're not."

Two other figures had come into the cell and were marching between the armed guards towards the children. They wore protective bodysuits and face masks.

"No…!" Laura screamed.

The men grabbed Rachel and Adam and hauled them to their feet. Gabriel stepped forward to protect Rachel, but he was pinned to the wall by one of the guards, and when Laura tried to fight off the man who was dragging Adam out of the cell, she was hit by a Taser and fell, convulsing, to the floor.

It was all over very quickly. By the time Laura was back on her feet, Rachel and Adam were gone. She and Gabriel could only watch as the glass doors slid shut and sealed them in.

Neither of them spoke at first. They both knew where the children were being taken, and why.

Laura rushed at the door and began pounding her fists against it. She was filled with rage and panic and roared out her demands, spittle running down the glass as she continued to smash and shout at it.

"I need to see Crow!" she screamed.

But the glass was thick and she knew the guard who stared back at her from the other side could barely make out what she was saying.

She looked up and noticed the tiny camera mounted high above the doors. She stared into the lens, her fists still clenched and the veins all but popping from her neck.

"Crow, I need to talk to you *right now*! I've got information..." she said.

44

Two military policemen frogmarched Laura into Crow's office and then stood behind her, holding her shackled arms.

"What can I do for you, Laura?" Crow said. He sat down behind his desk, formalizing the distance between them.

"Tell me where the children are."

"You need to talk to me first," he said.

"The stuff I need to tell you is classified to the highest level," she said. "I can't risk speaking with these monkeys here." She nodded backwards at her two guards, who showed no offence at her comment. "And it would be great if you could take the jewellery off." She shook her wrists.

Crow considered a moment, then instructed the guards to remove Laura's cuffs and leave. He locked the door behind them, and while his back was turned, Laura took the opportunity to straighten her clothes and tie her hair back. She knew she would only get one shot at this and she wanted to look presentable. Then she leaned forward quickly, saw a letter to Crow on his desk and checked his first name.

Crow sat down again. "Drink?" he asked, taking the bourbon from his desk drawer.

"A little early for me," Laura said. "But it's not been a great day so far, so why not?"

"Yeah, sorry about the Taser." Crow poured out two tumblers of whisky and sat back. "I'm listening," he said.

In a medical laboratory, somewhere deep beneath the Alamogordo base, Rachel and Adam were strapped to surgical gurneys. They had been wheeled through scanners that had X-rayed every millimetre of their bodies, providing a complete picture of them in cross-section. The doctors, faceless behind paper masks and safety goggles, analysed the brain scans briefly and then began to take swabs.

Rachel shuddered as an orderly pushed cotton buds into her nose, mouth and ears, carefully logging the samples and placing them in sealed plastic containers. He roughly clipped her fingernails and toenails as if she were a corpse.

She heard Adam scream as the first of many blood samples was drawn, and then, as a needle was inserted into the base of her spine, her screams joined those of her brother...

"I've been with Rachel and Adam Newman for over two years." Laura emphasized her words by banging her hand on the desk. "I've followed their every move. I know everything about them. I'm the world expert on these kids, and I'm telling you they need to be kept alive."

"What makes you think they *won't* be kept alive?"

Laura might have laughed had the situation not been so terrible. "What do you think your scientists are doing to them?"

"Research," Crow said. It did not sound convincing. "Just running tests, gathering data."

"I don't believe you're that naïve."

Crow looked away. He wasn't. He knew the Hope Project's agenda and as much as it sickened him, he had played his part in it. All he could do now was try and justify his actions.

"Orders from New York are to 'neutralize' them to get all the information we can," he said. "They're a real danger to society, Laura. Given a couple of years they might breed, and then all hell would break loose. Imagine it, Laura, interbreeding with … aliens."

"You don't understand." She thumped the table again. "They're not *aliens*. These people have always bred with us. We're all descended in some way from the Travellers. It's just that these kids are *direct* descendants. Their family hasn't moved from the same spot in England in three thousand years, and because of some family legend, the two branches of genes that were handed down from the first couple have never come together until *now*. These two kids are the most important human beings alive in the world today."

She sat back and drew breath. She didn't know how much more persuasive she could be, but she thought she caught a hint in Crow's eye that he might be wavering. "Listen, Todd," she continued, pressing her perceived advantage.

Crow looked surprised. "You know my name?"

"I know quite a lot about you," Laura said. "For instance, I know where your family comes from. Crow is the modern version of the Old English Crowe.

"My family's from Michigan."

"That's just this century. The Crowes were first recorded in England over a thousand years ago. They in turn would have been descended from Vikings who went over and raped and pillaged the Norfolk villages a few hundred years before that." She pointed. "*That's* where you got your blond hair from. The American Crowes came over with *The Mayflower*. But if we looked at your DNA, I would put money on you having some Viking genes, because it's just not that long ago in evolutionary terms."

"What's your point, Laura?"

"No one's blaming you for your ancestors being rapists and vandals, are they?"

Crow looked puzzled.

"In fact, it's probably seen as an evolutionary advantage that the Vikings mixed their blood with the Anglo-Saxons' to spread that blond hair everyone in the world seems to like so much. The same thing's true of the kids – they're the start of a better race. Something new and improved."

Crow finished his drink. "One big difference, Laura" – he looked serious suddenly – "something I heard once from the director…"

"What?" Laura asked.

"Rachel and Adam Newman didn't just evolve. They were *bred*. Bred for research by the Flight Trust."

"That's ridiculous."

"That's what he said. 'They *belong* to us…'"

45

Rachel could not believe the intensity of the pain, but with the frequency squealing in her head, there was nothing she could do with her mind to overcome it. No one else seemed interested in trying to alleviate her agony either. In fact, one of the orderlies actually seemed to be monitoring her pain levels with some kind of machine positioned by her head.

Her mouth had been clamped open wide and samples of dentine were being drilled from her teeth. As she tried desperately to block out the pain, the dreadful black and white images from the video she had seen in the lab on the night they had been captured raced through her mind...

"Look," Laura said, forcing Crow to look at the image she had called up on his laptop. The image of the live autopsy that had been conducted in the 1950s.

"I've seen it," Crow said. He looked away as the grainy figure thrashed around on the screen.

Todd Crow had seen many horrible things. As a soldier in the first Gulf War, he had seen the population of an entire village murdered by their own people for belonging to the wrong tribe. During a tour of duty in Africa, he had seen a church full of villagers killed by fourteen-year-old militia for the same reason.

He had seen enough horror and brutality to last several lifetimes. He had promised himself that he would see no more once he left the military. His secondment to Hope had seemed exactly that – full of hope. Looking to the stars and making contact with whatever was up there. He had not reckoned on the paranoia and cynicism of the whole organization, from the director – the man who had wrecked his life and exiled him to the desert – down.

Now, stuck in the wilderness, presiding over the near-vivisection of two American teenagers because of *their* genes, Crow finally realized how far he had strayed.

"And these," Laura said, calling up yet more images from the Hope BETA file. "This is what they did when we were in Morocco two years ago."

Crow looked at the film on the screen. It was in colour this time and the camera was panning across a row of bodies on a beach: twin boys, their faces and bodies battered; a pair of beautiful girls, bloated and drowned. The image tightened on two tiny corpses: a little boy and a girl, their eyes also closed peacefully in death. They were holding hands.

"They were called Morag and Duncan," Laura said. "They were eight years old."

Crow felt a hot tear run down his cheek and splash on to the desk. He felt Laura Sullivan's hand on his shoulder, felt it squeeze.

"You know I'm right," she said. "Do it my way."

Crow picked up a phone and rapidly stabbed in an extension.

"Crow," he barked. "Abort research immediately. Change of plan. Do what you can to make them comfortable. Whatever it takes." There was a hesitation from the lab assistant on the other end of the phone. "On *my* authority," Crow shouted. "Just do it."

"Thanks," Laura said, as Crow put down the phone.

"OK. Now that you've probably cost me my job, what next?" He felt a weight lift from him instantly, now that he would no longer be taking orders from Hope. He'd met some tough cookies in his time, but this Australian woman took some beating. She could convince him that black was white if she wanted, and probably just had.

"Here's the deal," Laura said. "You tell the director I have classified information for his ears only. You tell him that only *I* know how to put the three Triskellions together and only *I* know what will happen when they come together; that *I* need to be there when that happens."

"OK," Crow said.

"And one more thing…"

Crow rolled his eyes. "Go on."

"Tell him I'll show him everything I know about the Triskellions on one condition: I want Kate Newman sprung from the Oklahoma State Penitentiary."

She laid her hand on top of Crow's. "Please."

Gabriel looked up when the cell door slid open. Rachel and Adam stood there, wrapped in blankets, looking pale and shaken. They could barely speak, their lips puffy with recently administered anaesthetic. Laura and Crow were on either side of them.

Gabriel walked across to Rachel. He touched her face. "Are you OK?"

Rachel could feel the pain and numbness immediately begin to fade. "I am now," she said.

Gabriel nodded. "The noise is gone too."

"I switched the blocking frequency off," Crow said. "You've got your powers back."

Gabriel smiled and looked down at the plastic cuffs round his wrists. They began to smoulder and stretch until they fell away, blackened and useless.

"He's switched sides," Laura said, nodding at Crow. "And he's going to take us to New York."

Gabriel looked pleased. "We're getting out of here?"

"Sure," Laura said.

"How are we going to get there?" Rachel asked, feeling her numb lips with her finger.

"I'll take care of it," Crow said.

"Well, we'd better hurry," Gabriel said. "It's only hours until everything *really* kicks off."

It was Laura's turn to be surprised. "Hours? Why didn't you say?"

"Nobody asked."

Crane sat on the deck of *Ezekiel One,* enjoying a leisurely lunch. He knew there would not be much time for eating from this point on, so he had ordered Jedediah to provide something special. Oysters, champagne, soft-shelled crabs, steak. Followed by a large slab of waxy honeycomb.

Brother Jedediah had hovered nervously, trying desperately to please, fussing and pouring wine until Crane had become more than usually irritated by him; until he had dismissed him by throwing a heavy glass tumbler at his head.

The wheels for the Gathering were now in motion.

There would be no turning back now, and Crane needed a few moments in peace to reflect. The sky had been doing strange things all morning: a pink dawn had been followed by torrential rain and then a flurry of thick unseasonal snow. Now the sun was shining and Ezekiel Crane was enjoying the warmth of its rays on the taut skin of his face.

A face that did not really feel like his own – probably because it wasn't.

But it was a useful mask to hide behind. He thought back to the terrible accident; to the burns that had robbed him of his own features and melted them into something frightening, skull-like. He didn't look so bad now, he thought. He had seen pictures of a New York socialite whose plastic surgery had made her look like a monster-movie freak.

At least he looked human.

It never ceased to amaze him that this first near-death experience had triggered something almost supernatural in him; instead of breaking him and making him weaker, it had made him stronger.

And his second near-death experience had made him stronger still, releasing powers he never knew he had.

Now he felt invincible.

He lit a cigarette, inhaled deeply and looked up at the sky through his telescope. The clouds were boiling, twisting and racing by at unnatural speed, and Crane had never felt more certain about his destiny.

He swung the telescope around to look across at Manhattan and down towards Central Park. He could read the banners of the Triple Wheelers who were filling the streets. He had seen them on the TV: camping in the park, being interviewed by CNN journalists.

"Tick-Tock; the time has come," they had told the cameras, their faces open and innocent. "Ezekiel One! The time is now!"

The journalist had handed back to the studio with the wry look of a professional used to interviewing lunatics.

They would learn, Crane thought. Very soon…

He watched his followers converge on an already crowded Central Park and a verse of a children's song came back to him – something dredged up from his memory; from his childhood in England: *If you go down to the woods today, You're sure of a Big Surprise...*

Crane chuckled to himself and called to Jedediah, who came running from the other end of the boat, a cold compress held against the bruise on his head.

"Yes, Pastor?"

"Batten down the hatches, and prepare for the Gathering, Brother Jedediah." Crane pointed across the water towards the towers of Manhattan. "We're going ashore."

46

The director looked out across the East River from the sixtieth floor. He could see queues of cars gridlocked down below and people on foot crossing the bridge from the Brooklyn side. He saw more groups of people being disgorged from the ferries and marching up Roosevelt Drive, and even from his vantage point way above, he could read the banners that they were unfurling to proclaim their commitment to their organization.

THE CHURCH OF THE TRIPLE WHEEL.

The picture feed was the same on the screens that lined the wall of his office. Cars were blocked in the Holland Tunnel on the New Jersey side, and families in their Sunday best were arriving on foot from Hoboken and Union City. They were converging on Central Park, having travelled through the rain, through the snow, through the burning sun – through all the bizarre meteorological conditions that were sweeping the country – to get here. News channels were showing the airports at a standstill as disciples of the Triple Wheel continued to arrive from all over America.

But there was one image that puzzled the director more than the others.

He had recorded the biggest Triple Wheel rally to date, which had occurred in Philadelphia a couple of days before. Ezekiel Crane's face, rigid in freeze-frame, was flickering on the plasma. The director pressed PLAY and watched him stride backwards and forwards across the vast stage, holding fifty thousand people in his thrall. The director could not pinpoint exactly what it was about this charismatic man that captivated all these people, but as he watched he sensed that he was being mesmerized himself. But it was more than that: there was something in the walk, in the gestures, in the voice that chimed with him; something that awakened a long-dormant memory from somewhere deep in his mind.

He had done plenty of research on Ezekiel Crane. Since the preacher had first got his attention, the director had instructed Meredith to get him every press article and photograph on him. He had given others the job of digging into Crane's background. Extraordinarily, for an intelligence agency, they had drawn a virtual blank.

A copy of Crane's passport, gained from US immigration, had revealed that he had been born in the USA in 1957. But very little else.

It seemed Crane had arrived in society fully formed, little more than a year before. There was no record of him before that anywhere in the world. And in just over a year he had gained this phenomenal following. The director wanted to know how.

And even more importantly, why.

He understood the Ezekiel One legend: the belief that gods or aliens had come to earth in a burning chariot. He knew all about how ancient legends still guided people's lives. But what he wanted to know was how Crane knew that the time was *now*.

How could he have known that the unique alignment of heavenly bodies happening now had been imminent? It had taken Hope's astronomers twenty years to come up with the calculations. Everything the director had worked for throughout his life was about to come to fruition, and now this freakish charlatan seemed about to muddy the waters with superstition and guesswork.

He sat down and tried to think it through.

He remembered his childhood in the desert, watching the skies and looking for answers; waiting for something to happen. He remembered his time at the military school where they had broken him down and then built him up again. Made him fit and ready to do a life's service for the government.

He remembered his early training as a scientist at Alamogordo; his forensic work on the specimens there and the research he had done on their DNA; how it had tied up with the archaeological research they had been doing in the UK and elsewhere.

He remembered his initiation by the Hope Project: how they had cauterized any feelings he'd had, so that he could work without guilt or compassion for anyone. Not that he had had much guilt or compassion to begin with.

Most of the good feelings had stopped when his mother had died. When she had been killed.

He reflected on his loveless marriage: a union arranged by Hope for the convenience of his work and research. A marriage of genetics rather than personalities. He thought about the children it had produced, the ones he had never been able to love. Children who were now as fatherless as he had been. He was glad he would never see them again.

He picked up the phone. "Meredith. Get me Crow on the line."

He continued to watch Crane strutting on the screen, and seconds later the line buzzed. He picked up and heard Crow's voice, high and crackling, above the noise of jet engines. "Where are you, Todd?"

"We're in the air somewhere over Pennsylvania. Just past Pittsburgh. But we have a problem, sir."

It was not what the director wanted to hear. His silence forced Crow to continue.

"I've spoken to JFK and LaGuardia; they're completely shut down."

"You have Grade One clearance, Crow!" the director shouted.

"I know, sir, but they don't even *have* an airstrip they

can clear. It's mayhem down there. All the main roads are jammed up too. What's going on?"

"There are a lot of people visiting the city today." The director thought for a moment. "OK, here's what we're going to do. I'm going to scramble a Hope chopper. I want you to divert to Stewart International Airport up by West Point and we'll pick you up there. I'll get Meredith to make sure you have clearance. Now get to it. Time's running out."

He put down the phone and looked at the large clock on his wall: he still had time. He had waited the best part of his life for this to happen.

He guessed he could wait an hour longer.

47

A s soon as Crow had broken radio connection with the director, he switched on the intercom and spoke to Rachel, Adam and Gabriel, who were out of sight behind him in the main cabin.

"We can't get into JFK," he said. "We're being diverted to the military airport and we'll get a chopper into the city from there. Puts another thirty minutes on the trip, that's all. I'll let you know when we're coming in to land."

He turned and looked at Laura, who was seated next to him in the cockpit. "Did you hear the director's voice? It was weird."

Laura nodded. "He's excited. This is a special day for him." She looked to her right and saw the fields of Pennsylvania laid out below her like squares on a quilt. "Shame it's not going to turn out quite like he planned…"

With an F-35 jet capable of carrying no more than two people, Crow had fuelled up the Hope Project Gulfstream back in Alamogordo, and they had been in the air within fifteen minutes of his call to the director – the call during which he had outlined Laura Sullivan's demands.

"Doctor Sullivan seems to think she's holding all the aces," the director had said.

"I reckon she is." Crow had smiled at Laura, who was standing next to him.

"So the research on the children has been put on hold? I can live with that for now. But as for the rest of it, for her claims about the artefacts themselves … how do I know she isn't bluffing?"

It was then that Laura had snatched the phone and spoken to the director herself. "You *don't* know," she'd said; "but can you afford to take that chance?"

"If you try to play me for a fool, you *do* know there will be consequences, don't you?"

"I know," Laura had said.

"Just get my Triskellions to me. And then we'll see which of us is the *bigger* fool…"

The Gulfstream banked to the left, then straightened, and Laura watched the sun's reflection slide up from the fuselage until the cockpit was bathed in golden light.

"So … *do* you know how to put them together?" Crow asked. "The Triskellions. Do you know what's going to happen?"

Laura shrugged. "Not a clue, mate."

Crow smiled and nodded – but it wasn't long before the concern returned to his face. "We don't really have any aces at all, do we?"

Laura thought for a few moments, shielding her eyes from the glare and fighting off the exhaustion, then nodded back towards the main cabin where the children were. "We've got *them*," she said.

Rachel ran a finger across the Triskellion that was back hanging round her neck. She glanced across and saw that Adam was doing the same. It felt good to have them against their skin again; to be reunited with objects that were as much a part of them as bone and sinew.

Rachel felt re-energized: ready for the fight she knew was coming.

"I've always fancied a trip in a private jet," Adam said. "I'd kind of hoped it would be under different circumstances, though, you know. Cocktails, and hot girls as cabin crew, and the latest movie on a big screen…"

From the seat facing Rachel, Gabriel smiled and raised his eyebrows. "We'll see what we can do later on."

"Cool," Adam said, his eyes stupidly wide. "Can you maybe arrange it so I can ride up front with the captain too? I've always wanted to do that."

Rachel reached across the aisle and took her brother's hand. She knew exactly what he was doing; it had been the same ever since she could remember. Adam would play the fool whenever someone needed to. He would try to diffuse the tension or create a diversion when things were looking hopeless.

He could help them to stop being afraid.

Rachel remembered what Gabriel had said earlier about this being how it was meant to finish. "It's funny," she said. "That this is where it all finishes, I mean. We've been all over the world and we end up back in New York."

Gabriel smiled. "Like I said; it's how it was always meant to be. Sometimes you have to travel a long way from home to know where it is."

"I hope it still feels like home when we get there," Adam said.

Rachel took a few seconds to find the right words; to form the question she had been afraid to ask. "If you know what's *meant* to happen," she said, "does that mean you know what's *going* to happen?"

Gabriel didn't answer immediately. He turned to look out of the window and Rachel did the same. Far below they could just make out the line of the freeway and the thousands of vehicles that crawled eastwards along it: an artery clogged with dark fat. Gabriel pointed down towards it. "Unfortunately," he said, "there are others being drawn to the same place we are."

"Others?"

"Forces I have no control over."

They settled into silence for a while, and Rachel, tiredness creeping across her like a blanket, was just drifting off to sleep when Crow's voice came across the intercom.

"We're starting our descent," he said. "We'll be on the ground in ten minutes."

Rachel saw the same smile on Gabriel's face that she had first seen more than two years before. It felt like a *million* years before, and a million miles away at a village cricket match.

"I know how I *want* things to turn out, obviously," he said.

"I suppose a happy ending's a bit much to ask for," Adam said, looking from Rachel to Gabriel and back again. "You know, given how things have turned out so far."

The jet began to descend quickly and Rachel's stomach lurched. She closed her eyes. Happy ending or not, she thought, they would all know soon enough.

48

E zekiel Crane stared out of the gondola past the steel girders of the bridge. Below him, seventy metres above the East River, he could see cars, nose to tail across the bridge, and hundreds more vehicles were gridlocked along Roosevelt Drive. Above and beyond the various towers and spires that made up the river front, the silver wings of the Flight Building were spreading into the sky, shining in the sunlight.

The Roosevelt Island Tram was an aerial lift that carried commuters into Manhattan. When the old Queensboro Bridge had become too rickety to accommodate foot passengers, the tram had become hugely popular and it still offered what many considered to be the best view of the city.

Crane's followers had commandeered the tram, and now fifty or sixty of them surrounded him inside the gondola, eagerly anticipating their leader's triumphant arrival in Central Park. Crane took in the skyscape of glittering mirrored towers and remembered the verse that had fired his imagination all those years ago:

Wind, Fire and Water
Will come to pass,
When Three Become One
In the City of Glass.

He instantly recalled the smell of beeswax and dust in the library and the brooding atmosphere of the grand house in England where he had pored over the old books and documents on long afternoons.

Documents that had foretold of this day.

And he remembered a time years before that: the afternoon at the lake when he had overheard the story for the first time from the mouth of his own father. The revelation that had changed his life for ever.

He had once denied his fate – denied his connection to Rachel, Adam, Gabriel, and the ancient Travellers. But since then he had been reborn, not once but twice, and he had finally come to accept this link; to know what it was that made him special.

It was what marked him out for greatness and power.

"We're descending, Pastor," Brother Jedediah said. He wrung his hands, then pointed excitedly at the mass of Triple Wheelers assembled below them at the tram terminal.

"I can see that," Crane said. "Make sure none of them

touches me when we get out."

The red and white gondola clanked into the terminus and the crowd of Triple Wheelers below gave a collective gasp as many of them saw their leader in the flesh for the first time. Crane stepped out onto the platform high above them and waved. Some reached out for him; others screamed, wept or spoke in tongues while he walked down the steel stairs, protected by his phalanx of bodyguards. He climbed into the open-topped stretch limo that was to take him the final kilometre into Central Park.

The sea of people parted and the car began its slow progress down 59th Street. They watched in awe as he went by.

The man who had promised them the world.

Stewart International Airport lay ninety-five kilometres north of Manhattan in the southern Hudson Valley. It had been developed in the 1930s as a military base, but had since grown into a major airport as well as being an emergency landing facility for the space shuttle.

It was also one of the many locations across the country where the Flight Trust housed its aircraft. As per the director's orders, a helicopter had been standing by when the Gulfstream touched down, ready to transport Todd Crow and his precious cargo directly to the Flight Building.

"I can't believe it's never struck me before," Rachel said. They were hurrying across the tarmac towards the chopper;

its blades were whirring noisily and its headlights blazed in spite of the bright sunshine.

"What?" Adam asked.

She pointed towards the helicopter. "How much they look like bees. The way they hover and dip." She blinked, remembering the attack helicopter that had almost killed them two years before. "The way they buzz and sting…"

"*Angry* bees," Adam said.

Crow led Laura towards the front of the helicopter and clambered up into the pilot's seat. He checked his instruments quickly, then turned to make sure that Rachel, Adam and Gabriel were safely on board.

Gabriel had stopped on the tarmac. Rachel and Adam ran back to him.

"I'm not coming with you," he said.

"What?" Adam stared at Rachel, his eyes wide in disbelief.

"I'll catch up with you. There's somewhere else I need to go first."

Rachel shook her head. "We can't go in there without you. I don't *want* to go in there without you."

"You're strong enough now, and you'll be even stronger when you need to be." He reached out towards the Triskellion that hung round Rachel's neck, nodded towards the one round Adam's. "Besides, you'll be safe enough if you give me one of those."

Rachel began to unfasten the leather thong.

"They're less likely to kill us until they've got all three."

Adam was doing his best to sound casual, but the worry was clear enough in his eyes and in the slight tremble round his mouth. "That's what you're saying, right?"

Gabriel took the Triskellion from Rachel and hung it round his own neck. "That's what I'm saying."

Crow stuck his head out of the small window in the helicopter's cockpit. "We should get going!" he shouted.

"Be careful," Rachel said. She leaned forward to check the fastening on the Triskellion; to brush her fingers across the back of Gabriel's neck.

He lunged forward suddenly and threw his arms round her. She wrapped her own round him in response, feeling his ribs through his thin shirt, his breath on her cheek. But before she could say anything, he had broken away and stepped across to embrace Adam.

Adam hugged him back and then stepped away and nodded a little awkwardly. Gabriel's green eyes flashed behind the thick strands of black hair being blown across his face by the draft from the rotor blades.

The twins turned and ran to the chopper. Within a few seconds of shutting the door they were watching the ground drop away from them as the aircraft rose quickly into the air.

Laura smiled grimly at them from the cockpit. Next to her, Crow was pulling back on the joystick, pointing the helicopter south towards New York City.

"Should be fifteen minutes or so," he said.

Rachel pressed her hand to the window and stared at the figure on the tarmac below them. The noise inside the helicopter was almost deafening, but Rachel heard Gabriel's voice as clearly as if he were sitting next to her with his mouth pressed close to her ear.

You be careful too, he said. *It's a dangerous place.*

Gabriel was little more than a dark speck against the earth now.

Where? she asked.

The belly of the beast.

49

E zekiel Crane had never heard applause like it as he mounted the stage in Central Park. The clapping and the singing drowned out all other noises; it was so loud that even the clatter of the helicopter flying low over the park could not be heard.

Bands had been playing all day, filling the park with music, and the people who had gathered had danced and sung themselves into a frenzy. One of America's greatest performers, a country and western legend and recent convert to the Triple Wheel, finished his song and welcomed his leader. "Ladies and Gentlemen," he said; "Tick-Tock ... the time is now. I would just like to take this opportunity to thank the man who has come to save us all. Without his vision I would be lost and in the wilderness. He has shown me, he has shown you, he has shown *all of us* the way. Amen. Ladies and Gentlemen, please show your appreciation for the Archminister and Founder of the Church of the Triple Wheel ... Pastor ... Ezekiel ... Crane!"

Crane had saved a dazzling silver suit for the occasion, and the sunlight hit him, making him visible from far across the park. His hair and teeth were peroxide white and blown up to gigantic proportions on the screens on either side of the stage. He raised his arms and the cape that Jedediah had draped over his shoulders billowed behind him, making him look like he might be about to take off and fly.

"I love you," he shouted. The crowd roared. "I love you, and I have come to show you the way." He lowered his arms and continued in a sonorous voice, a whisper that rolled across Central Park like a gathering wind. "Hush, Brothers and Sisters; hush, and hear these words. Today we are gathered for the last time in this life. Tomorrow we will begin anew in the Promised Land. I will lead you to our new fathers; I will guide you to the Rapture. I am Ezekiel One, and I will show you the light! I will show you the light! *I will show you the light!*"

"Say it again!" people howled from the front of the stage.

"I will show you the light. Sing with me…" Crane picked up his guitar and began to play, and as one, the hundreds of thousands of people in the park began to sing words that they had all come to know by heart…

"Tick-Tock, the day has come,
Tick-Tock, we are as one,
Tick-Tock, we're rising up,
To drink from Ezekiel's Cup.

"The Gathering, we will ascend,
The Gathering, our souls will mend,
The Gathering, this is the end..."

Gabriel pushed through the crowd.

All were on their feet – singing, swaying, holding children on their shoulders – their eyes fixed on the stage. He needed to be closer in order to get control of the man he knew was his nemesis – the devil who had tried to undermine everything Gabriel had worked for as long as he had lived.

Gabriel stumbled over a twisted picnic blanket and accidentally kicked open a bright-red plastic lunch box. The feeling of foreboding that had been threatening to overpower him since he'd entered the park suddenly made sense. The lunch box contained bottles of pills and vials of liquid barbiturates. Enough drugs to kill an entire family. All were branded with the Triple Wheel.

He found another lunch box and another; their owners were far too obsessed with what was happening on stage to notice Gabriel going through their belongings. Each box was packed with the same cocktail of lethal drugs.

What was it that Crane intended to do?

The director imagined that this must be what it felt like to be a child on Christmas morning. Standing just inside the door that led out on to the building's restricted-access helicopter pad, he was watching the sky, listening for the sound of the rotor blades, and imagining that this was how it must feel to anticipate a wonderful gift.

A brilliant … *spectacular* … surprise.

If the director of the Hope Project had had a normal childhood, he would have *known* that feeling, but as it was he could only *guess* at what it must be like…

He had learned many other things, of course, during his troubled adolescence and the strange and interesting years that had followed. He had studied archaeology, astronomy and history, the twin disciplines of science and war.

He knew about the Travellers who had visited over many centuries and he knew what they had brought with them. He knew about the Triskellions and where they had been found, and it had been his life's work to see them united.

To see the Three Become One.

He had *engineered* it…

What nobody knew, what no amount of research could tell anyone, was exactly what the unification of the three amulets would bring about. The director could not possibly know *what* would happen, but he knew that the one who *made* it happen would be at the centre of the most powerful force that the planet had ever experienced. He knew that the one who brought the Triskellions together would know what it was like to be God…

He felt the excitement build in him like an electrical pulse as the helicopter buzzed into view: zigzagging across the canvas of sky that was changing minute by minute. He stepped back into the shadows. From here it was only ten floors up to the secret eyrie at the building's summit; to the room in which the power of the Triskellions would finally be unleashed.

A few steps away, no more. A few minutes…

He watched the chopper descend, the blades slow and the rush of air fall away. The helicopter door opened and he stepped out onto the landing pad to welcome Todd Crow, his eyes eagerly searching for the package he was expecting to see in the man's hands.

He saw nothing.

"Tell me they're still in the chopper, Crow," he said.

Crow said nothing; he just stood and stared. Over his shoulder the director saw others emerging from the helicopter. Laura Sullivan stepped down first, followed by Rachel and Adam. The pulse of excitement became a powerful surge of fury. He moved close to Crow and put a hand round his neck. "What the hell are *they* doing here? Since when did you stop following orders?"

Crow took hold of the director's fingers, bent them back and pushed the hand away from his neck. "Change of plan," he said.

The director's mind raced; his brain struggled to adjust to the new situation, to make new plans. He tried his best to summon the smile he knew the children would be expecting as they rushed towards him, their arms outstretched.

Their expressions were open and eager; their voices were unrestrained and full of joy: as happy as children on Christmas morning.

"Dad...!"

50

Laura hung back and watched, helpless and horrified, as Rachel and Adam ran past Crow towards the man on the landing pad. Their screams of excitement were shrill and felt painful above the sound of her own heart thumping.

The director of the Hope Project was Rachel and Adam's father.

Ralph Newman was the man who had recruited Laura ten years earlier. He had been the scientist who had befriended her, or had pretended to. The one who had encouraged her and had organized funding for her studies, drawing her deeper and deeper into a project that she had not fully understood until it was far too late; until there had been no way for her to get out.

Now Laura's mind was racing with dreadful questions. It couldn't have been a coincidence that the man in charge of the Hope Project's most secretive operation was also the father of the children it had hunted so mercilessly. Was it possible that the head of the Bureau of Extra-Terrestrial Activity just *happened* to be the father of the most special children in the world?

How could it have happened? How could anyone have planned it?

And the most horrifying question of all.

How could a father order the murder of his own children?

Ezekiel Crane's speech was coming to an end. As the crowd cheered and clapped, he bid his worshippers well and told them it was time to follow him. He ordered them to march from the park, to swarm down Broadway and gather together at the foot of the Flight Building.

He told them that they were doing something very special.

His followers began drifting towards the park's many exits, and Crane stepped into the basket of a hot-air balloon which had been slowly inflating throughout his speech and which now stood waiting for him at the side of the stage.

Brother Jedediah untied the mooring rope. "See you on the other side, Pastor," he said.

"I doubt it," Crane replied.

With a gust of flame from the burner, the balloon – vast and white and marked with the sign of the Triple Wheel – slowly began to rise. It was at this moment that Gabriel pushed through the front row of the crowd and climbed onto the stage.

He screamed at Crane, who was now receding into the distance as the balloon climbed into the sky, and the pastor peered down over the edge of the basket.

He froze when Gabriel pulled the Triskellion from his shirt and held it up for him to see: out of reach.

High above the park, the wind rushing in his ears, Ezekiel Crane could clearly hear the voice of the boy far below. The boy into whose eyes he had stared at the theatre in St Louis only days before.

"What is my name?" the boy had asked then.

Crane now knew perfectly well who he was, and he recognized the mockery, the *threat,* in the boy's voice as it rose up to taunt him: "It's a big day for both of us."

The relief, the happiness, that Rachel had felt on seeing her father had quickly given way to confusion and panic. Throwing her arms round him, she had felt only resistance. She and Adam had cried and babbled, telling their father how they had thought he was dead and that now they had found him, they could try and help their mother. Finally, they could be a family again.

He had looked at them as though they were ghosts.

"Dad?" Adam was pale and shaky and looked like he might collapse at any moment. "What's the matter?"

Rachel looked into her father's eyes, but they were fixed on the Triskellion round Adam's neck. She stepped back and turned to Laura, who just shook her head. Glancing over at

Major Crow, Rachel saw as much confusion on his face as she guessed was etched into her own.

"'Dad'?" Crow said. "I don't understand." He stared at Rachel, confusion mixed with sympathy and ... horror. "This is your..."

He didn't need to say it.

"You're the *director*?" Rachel was trying to stay calm, but she knew she was only moments away from breaking down completely; from weeping on her father's neck ... or clawing at it. Only seconds from throwing herself from the roof or at the face of the man who had turned her life upside down.

"I can explain, Rachel." There was a shadow of the smile she had been dreaming about; a hint of the concern in his voice that she had known and loved since she was a little girl.

"Daddy...?"

"Come with me and I'll tell you everything."

"Wait!" Laura shouted.

"You should come with us too, Doctor Sullivan."

The director walked across the tarmac to a metal door, which slid back to reveal the interior of a small lift. He beckoned to Rachel and Adam.

Adam took Rachel's hand.

What the hell's happening? she asked with her mind.

We need to go and find out, Adam said.

They walked to the lift and their father stepped aside to

let them in. A moment later Laura joined them. Ralph New-man gave her a sickly smile of welcome as she moved inside. The smile quickly died when Crow appeared in the doorway and Laura and the children moved to accommodate him.

"Where they go, I go," Crow said.

Ralph Newman nodded slowly, before reaching into the pocket of his jacket and producing a small black pistol. "Only room for four," he said.

Then, as the lift doors started to close, he raised his arm and shot Todd Crow dead.

51

Rachel, Adam and Laura were still screaming as the lift took them up the final few floors to the very top of the Flight Building. Ralph Newman stared at them impassively – simply interested in their *reaction* to the murder that had just taken place in front of their eyes and not in their *feelings*.

The observation tower was a conical structure, like the tip of a cigar. It was made entirely of glass and nestled between the outstretched metal wings on the roof. The lift doors hissed open, and Ralph Newman pushed his children and Laura Sullivan out, the gun still in his hand.

Rachel took in the three hundred and sixty-degree panoramic view of the city. She noticed the white hot-air balloon drifting towards the building between the skyscrapers.

"Sit," Newman said. He gestured at the leather chairs that were lined up by the windows.

Rachel and Adam did as they were told, but Laura, still

trembling with shock, managed a little resistance.

"What if I don't?" she asked. Her face was streaked with tears and spots of blood but she was defiant. "Are you going to shoot me, too?"

"Of course not," Newman said. "I've invested years of time and money in you, Laura. You know more about these things than anyone. Your research was, and still is, invaluable to me. Why would I kill my investment? Now sit down." Newman swiped the back of his hand across Laura's face, and she dropped quickly into her chair.

Rachel began to cry. She called out to Adam with her mind, but could hear nothing. As far as she could tell there was no blocking device in operation like the one at Alamogordo – perhaps she was simply too traumatized. She had just seen the man who had saved them from Alamogordo shot dead; she had just seen Laura Sullivan viciously slapped. Both of these acts of violence had been committed by the man she had grown up calling Daddy.

Newman stepped forward suddenly and grabbed the Triskellion from around Adam's neck.

"It's mine!" Adam shouted, attempting to wrestle his father off him.

"No, it's not." Newman slapped his son's hand away. "I've worked years for this. Now be a good boy." He pulled the amulet away, then reached out and grabbed roughly at the neck of Rachel's T-shirt. "Where's the other one?"

"I don't have it," Rachel cried.

He grabbed at Laura's shirt next, ripping it and tearing off buttons until he was satisfied that it was not round her neck. "Where is it?"

"We don't know," Rachel sobbed. "*We don't know!*"

"I don't believe you." He spoke close to her face. "If you don't tell me I'll…"

"What will you do? Kill me; kill us?" Rachel said. "How can you do this to your own children? You were there when we were born."

"You weren't born," Newman said quietly. "You were *bred*."

"What?" Adam said.

"You were bred," Ralph Newman repeated. "You were a government-funded genetic experiment. Your mother was identified as a carrier of a unique gene: one that had lain dormant for centuries in that ridiculous village she came from. I knew that any children she had would be … special, so I made sure that's what happened."

"But how did you know?"

"Because it was my *job* to know. I'd been researching this stuff for years and I knew all about the Wings and the Roots. I knew about the village of Triskellion and who your mother's real parents were. I knew because your grandfather couldn't be faithful to his wife," Newman spat. "And your grandmother was no better than a streetwalker."

Rachel flinched at the word.

Ralph Newman walked over to his desk and picked up

a card. He swiped it in the reader of a large steel safe-like structure built into the wall behind his desk. The door slid down electronically, revealing a black interior into which the shape of three Triskellions had been cut.

In one of the slots, a Triskellion glinted, gold and pulsating.

Newman placed the amulet he had ripped from Adam's throat next to it. They both began to glow and pulse in unison.

"You see?" he said. "They *need* to be together. Tell me where the other one is. Does the boy have it? Rafael ... or whatever he is calling himself ... Ariel ... *Gabriel*?"

Adam looked at Rachel before nodding.

"Very clever, keeping it separate from the others," Newman said. "But it must be here very soon." Glancing at the huge clock on the wall that detailed planetary movements and time zones across the globe, he ticked off the seconds. "I'm not too panicked. If he *does* have it, I know *he* needs the three of them together just as much as I do." He walked over to another door, behind his desk. "I suggest you 'reach out' with your minds and tell him to hurry up."

Adam looked at his father and attempted a defiant tone. "And if we don't?"

"Don't mess with me, Adam." Newman opened a door to the right of his desk and wheeled out a chair from inside. In the chair, her arms strapped and her mouth silenced by an ugly strip of duct tape, was Kate Newman.

The children's mother.

His own wife.

"I was true to my word, Laura," he said. "I got her out of jail... Out of the frying pan and into the fire, you could say."

Kate Newman struggled and wrestled against the tape, her eyes pleading with her children to do whatever was required.

"Now get those special brains working." Newman pressed the gun against Kate's head. "If you want your mother to stay alive."

There were several seconds of tense silence, broken suddenly by the chime of the lift arriving at the observation tower. All eyes turned to the opening doors, and it was clear from his expression that the man who emerged was used to welcoming committees.

His white teeth gleamed almost as brightly as his shiny silver suit. He spread his arms wide and strode confidently into the middle of the room, gradually taking in the tableau arranged around him.

"Well, I hadn't expected to see *quite* so many people," he said. "But it hardly matters. An event as momentous as this *needs* an audience."

Rachel and Adam both recognized the preacher whose face they had seen on billboards and television screens ever since they had arrived back in America.

"Ezekiel Crane," Adam whispered.

"I know that's the *name* he uses..." Rachel answered

slowly. Looking at him now – the taut over-pink skin, the peroxide hair, the smile that was as fake as everything else – Rachel had the uncomfortable feeling that he was someone she and Adam had met before.

Someone they knew very well...

From the look in Ezekiel Crane's piercing blue eyes, it was obvious he recognized them too.

"I should have expected you two to be here," he said. "Again, no matter. I can kill two very annoying little birds with one stone – when my business here today is complete, and everything has changed, the new world will take shape ... without either of you in it." His eyes held Rachel's for a few dreadful seconds, then flew to Laura's. "Nice to see you too, Doctor Sullivan. Dug up anything interesting lately?"

Laura stared, bewildered. "Who the hell *are* you?"

Crane grinned. "Oh, I've been all *sorts* of people..."

Rachel inched closer to Adam. She heard her brother gasp and in that instant she knew the preacher's real name. He was the man who had tried to kill them more times than she cared to remember; the man with whom they shared a dark history.

With whom they shared blood.

Then another voice spoke the name out loud.

"Hello, Hilary..."

Ezekiel Crane, who had once been Hilary Wing, span round to face Ralph Newman. The blood drained from the shiny plastic-looking face and his mouth was pale and thin suddenly. When he spoke, his lips trembled in fear and disbelief. "Rudi…?"

Ralph Newman nodded. "You can reinvent yourself all you like," he said; "but deep down you're still the same pathetic little runt you were when we were kids. Shame our mother isn't around any more or you could go running to her. You could bury your face in her apron and start blubbing, like you always used to."

The veins bulged, thick and blue, on Crane's forehead like angry worms beneath the skin, his fingers clawed, then folded into fists. He stepped towards Ralph Newman.

"I'm long past crying to anyone, brother," he said. "These days, *I'm* the reason people cry." He took a step closer. "And our mother is not around any more, because *you* killed her…"

52

Ezekiel Crane's words hung in the air. Rachel sat perfectly still, feeling spots of Todd Crow's blood drying on her face, as more images from the long-distant past came swimming through the murk into her consciousness.

Pictures from the past that lit up the present.

Rachel saw the anguished face of the young boy Rudi who would grow into the man Ralph – a man driven and scarred who would one day perversely father twins in the name of science.

She saw the thirteen-year-old Rudi snip a car's brake cables, a look of concentration on his face. She saw the expression morph into one of panic as the boy chased the shiny blue Packard. She listened to his screams, his pleadings for his mother to stop, knowing full well she was driving to her death.

The boy aged and grew in Rachel's mind. He … hardened. He was taken under the wing of those whose research he would eventually take over and extend. He became an esteemed and powerful scientist, and Rachel *felt* the terrible depths of his ambition as his plans took root...

Root. Wing.

Two families, whose long-forbidden union would one day produce Rachel and Adam, were the first step on a long and incredible journey from a small village to a dazzling glass tower.

"She was never meant to die!" Newman screamed, breaking into Rachel's visions. "*They* were. Your father and that woman." He pointed at Kate. "*Her* mother."

Crane shook his head and smiled. "But that's not what happened, is it ... *Rudi?*"

Crane and Newman continued to argue, and Rachel saw other pictures: the terrible snapshots of their lives. A child called Hilary – Rudi's half-brother – was taken back to England and raised in the village of Triskellion by his father. He grew into a sullen and damaged young man eager to lash out but unsure who his enemy was – unsure until twins had arrived in his village.

His own very *special* flesh and blood...

And in her mind Rachel saw the girl who would one day become her mother: Hilary Wing's half-sister, Kate. A girl who would grow into a woman eager to learn and desperate to spread her wings beyond the claustrophobic little village in which she had been raised. A woman who would travel to America, where she would meet a scientist and fall in love.

An older man called Ralph Newman.

But of course, that meeting would be far from accidental.

"Well, well, Kate." Finally turning from his brother, the anger was still clear on Ezekiel Crane's face when he looked at his half-sister – but it seemed to have left his voice at least. He turned and spread his arms wide. "This is turning into quite the family reunion."

Newman pointed the gun at Crane. "For the first and last time," he said.

"I don't know why I'm surprised," Crane said. "Just as it was my destiny to be here on this day, it was also yours. Although for very different reasons, of course. We have all been chosen to play one part or another. Mine is a little more important, that's all." He gazed at the steel case that contained the two Triskellions and counted off on his fingers theatrically. "One, two... Oh dear. We're still missing something very important, aren't we?" He leaned down towards Adam. "Your guardian angel has it, does he?"

Adam stood up. "Gabriel should have killed you when he had the chance."

"Sit down!" Newman shouted.

"Oh, I'm not very easy to kill," Crane said. "Not any more." He shook his head and pointed at Newman's gun. "You should put that away, brother; it will be of little use to you."

Ralph Newman barked out a laugh. "I don't know what it is you think you've turned into, Hilary – something rather sad, certainly – but I doubt if it's anything more than that."

"You cannot possibly grasp what has happened to me," Crane said. His voice grew louder and he addressed the room as if he were at one of his rallies. "You can't begin to understand what I have become, what I am *about* to become. I am special. I am *protected*."

Newman nodded, thoughtful. "Really?" he said, then he calmly put a bullet through Crane's kneecap.

The scream sounded unearthly, like something being dredged up from somewhere dark and hot, and Crane dropped to the floor, clutching his shattered leg. Blood running thick between his fingers, he dragged himself along, gasping for breath and struggling to gather up the tiny white fragments of bone that were now scattered across the observatory.

"It looks as though I've missed all the fun…"

Everyone looked up at the sound of the voice. Gabriel was standing in the corner of the room. Rachel shouted his name in relief; Laura reached over to take Adam's hand.

Gabriel calmly held up the third Triskellion, then tossed it from hand to hand like it was a cheap trinket. "I'm guessing you've all been waiting for this."

There was a sudden silence, a heaviness in the room, like all the air had been sucked out. All eyes were on Gabriel. Nobody saw him move, but as suddenly as he had appeared in the room, he was at the door of Newman's safe, reaching inside to slot the final Triskellion into place. "I hope this is not a disappointment."

The clock on the wall stopped.

The silence was broken by a low rumble that rose up and quickly became a deafening roar. The building began to shake and the sky suddenly went black.

Black ... and moving.

"Bees," Adam said. "Billions of them..."

The swarm spread across the sky, settling like a dark blanket, until bees covered every inch of every window in the observatory, and the room was plunged into darkness.

For a few seconds the only sounds were the low moan of agony coming from Ezekiel Crane and the ragged breathing of Kate Newman, who was struggling for breath beneath her gag. Then the observatory's emergency lighting system powered up and a narrow strip of light flickered on around a circle on the ceiling.

"Oh my God," Newman said. "I can't believe this is finally happening."

"Believe it," Gabriel said.

Rachel's eyes adjusted and she saw Ezekiel Crane clambering to his feet. Crying out in pain, he leaned against a chair to keep himself upright and waved a bloodstained hand at Gabriel. "You and I are the same."

"I don't think so," Gabriel said.

"We should be on the same side, at least."

Gabriel shook his head. "What is it that you think is happening here?"

"They're coming," Crane said. "That's what's happening.

You will tell them, won't you? When they get here." Desperation flashed in his eyes. "You will tell them that I am ready to
lead, here on earth? I have prepared the workers for them…
The *breeders*. They are ready to act on my command, ready
to be changed and moulded. You will tell them when they
arrive? Show them that I'm the one with the gifts; the one
who is willing to do what has to be done…"

Gabriel waited. "Have you finished?"

Crane nodded and lowered his head as though waiting to
be given an order, to receive his instructions.

"You are as deluded as your half-brother," Gabriel said,
pointing at Ralph Newman. "You have nothing. You offer
nothing. If things are going to change – and they will – it can
only happen when those who think as you do are gone for
ever. And how ever many people you think you have brain-
washed into following you, I guarantee not many of them
will shed a tear for you when you are gone." He dropped a
hand onto Adam's shoulder. "And Adam was right. I *should*
have killed you when I had the chance."

A growl rose up from Crane's throat and there was something murderous in his eyes – and even with Gabriel in such
an aggressive mood, Rachel was suddenly afraid for their
safety.

"I'm very sorry you feel that way." Crane's voice was fright-
eningly calm. "You have badly underestimated me. I will
show you what it means to be loved…"

Holding up one hand, he reached across with his other

and pressed a button on his brightly coloured wristwatch. A high-pitched alarm sounded. It was followed by the noise of other alarms – many thousands of them – which rose up from the streets seventy storeys below.

"No!" Gabriel said.

Rachel saw the look of horror on his face and realized that something terrible was happening.

Crane nodded. "I will show you just how much I am *loved*."

53

Barbra Anderson unfolded the tablecloth and sat Eden and Tammy down on the grass. The earth seemed to tremble beneath them.

They had not made it to the Flight Building. The crowds had been too dense and the children had been in danger of getting trampled, so they had stayed in Central Park.

Bob Anderson stood near by. He had been watching Pastor Crane's balloon journey on the big screens and had seen the gathering at the foot of the tower. There had been singing and banner-waving when the balloon had landed on the helipad high up on the glass building. He had felt a pang of regret that he wasn't with the rest of them, especially when the swarm of bees had appeared, darkening the sky and covering the building like it was a gigantic hive.

It had been a truly apocalyptic vision. A thing of biblical proportions, Bob had thought. The pastor had long promised such events, and now he was sending them the signal that meant they were to make the ultimate sacrifice. Bob had hoped things would turn out differently, but if the pastor told them to do it, then it must be the right thing to do.

The sky was rolling now and darkening with purple and black clouds ready to burst, until all at once a warm rain began spitting down on everyone. With their damp clothes sticking to their bodies, a strange silence fell across the whole park.

Bob looked again at the flashing red light on his Triple Wheeler's watch, listened to the piercing *beep-beep* of the alarm and knew that the time had come.

He sat down on the grass and hugged his children.

"What's happening, Daddy?" Eden asked.

"Nothing to be scared of, big fella."

"Are we going to die?" Tammy asked.

"Don't be crazy, honey." Bob squeezed her tight. "Pastor Crane wouldn't let us die. We're going to be reborn."

Barbra kissed and hugged her children. She then chastely kissed Bob on the lips and smiled at him. She opened the red lunch box on the cloth in front of her and took out the bottles. Then, along with thousands of other families gathered in the park around them, she began counting out the pills.

On the screens above, Brother Jedediah's huge, nervous and sweaty face appeared. He was speaking from a balcony a few floors up on the Flight Building, the Triple Wheel cameras trained on him. All around him the building was blackened by the swarm and the whole skyscraper vibrated with the collective buzzing of a billion bees.

This was Brother Jedediah's big moment.

"Tick-Tock." His voice trembled. "The time has come for you all to take the medicine, Brothers and Sisters. Pastor Crane has asked me to tell you that he is with you at this time. He will take you to the Promised Land…" He swatted something away with his hand.

"Pastor Crane loves us all and will deliver us—" Something else landed on Jedediah's face and this time it was not so easily dislodged.

A bee had woven its thorny legs into the hairs of his wispy moustache and was not about to move. Jedediah tried to continue. "As I speak, Pastor Crane is high up in this very building, negotiating with our new leaders…"

The rain began to fall more heavily, plastering the black strands of Jedediah's hair to his head, and more bees landed on his face and started to sting. The little man yelped and his squeals were broadcast across the whole city. Bees were peeling away from the Flight Building in vast numbers; swooping down, they clung to his hair and clothes until he was completely covered in a thick writhing black carpet. The buzzing was so loud that it drowned out his screams, and more and more insects flew around him, engulfing him in a vicious, spinning vortex – a tornado of bees.

The crowd gasped; the noise of the swarm grew louder and angrier, the spinning faster, until finally Jedediah was lifted bodily into the air and carried higher and higher above the crowd.

Then the bees dropped him.

Jedediah slammed hard onto the street below. Triple Wheelers screamed at the sight of their leader's second in command lying limp and broken on the pavement. A cloud of bees hovered around the body for a few seconds before darting into the crowds, stinging hands that were about to lift deadly medicine to lips. A column of bees, the size and volume of an express train, shot up Broadway, stinging and knocking vials of poison and bottles of pills from Triple Wheelers' hands, before descending on Central Park.

It was then that everybody began to wake up…

Bob looked at his wife, who was about to feed Eden and Tammy a handful of pills. In his own hand, he was holding a small vial of liquid barbiturate. He was getting ready to swallow it when a bee stung him on the neck. Then another stung his hand. The sharp pain pulled him up short. A coolness crept across his hand and up his arm as the venom spread through his bloodstream, quick and effective like a drug.

"Ow!' Barbra cried.

Bob saw that four or five bees had attached themselves to her hands and were stinging her, forcing her to drop the pills. Triple Wheelers yelled and squealed around them, and Bob suddenly saw the whole situation with a new clarity. The coolness in his veins spread to his brain and he dropped the vial on the ground and stamped it into the wet earth. Eden was crying; a bee had stung him on the arm. Bob picked his son up and kissed him while Tammy climbed to her feet and hugged her father tight, as if her life depended on it.

Which it did.

Bob ran around the neighbouring couples, slithering in the mud, shouting at them: "Drop the pills. Don't take the medicine. It's over…"

With the rain drumming down on the crowd, Bob quickly realized that the other families were doing the same thing he had done. Mothers who had dissolved pills into bottles of milk were looking quizzically at the poison they had been about to feed to their babies. It was as if the beestings had awakened them from the collective dream they had been moving through like zombies. People staggered around, slipping on the soaking grass, bleary eyed, as if recovering from a deep and troubled sleep.

The sky blackened further still. Bob grabbed his wife and held her tight. Her whole body was trembling and she was crying, her tears mingling with the pouring rain.

"What were we thinking, Bob?" she cried. "What were we thinking?"

"It's over, honey," Bob said. "Let's go home."

54

Four hundred and fifty metres above Broadway, in the Flight Building's secret observatory, Rachel and Adam, along with their mother, Laura, Gabriel, Crane and Newman had watched the events unfolding below them on the screen. They had seen the swarm descend on the crowd of Triple Wheelers. The venom had woken Ezekiel Crane's followers from their semi-trance and saved their lives.

Ralph Newman had moved to the window and stared out in wonder, seemingly oblivious to the others in the room with him once the heavens had opened. He still stood there, gazing at the darkening sky and the glittering web of orbs, which had begun to glow high in the distance above them, pulsing gently against the blackness.

"I didn't know it would be this … beautiful," he said.

Laura seized the chance to rush over and free Kate. She ripped away the tape from her mouth and helped her back to the other side of the room. Kate fell into the arms of Adam and Rachel.

"Mom. God… Mom…"

"I'm so sorry," Kate said. She stared, her eyes filled with hatred, at the man she had once loved; the man who had fathered her children as though they were no more than laboratory specimens and had then hunted them down.

"It's not your fault," Adam said.

Rachel pressed her face into her mother's neck. "How could anyone have known?"

Laura nodded, rubbing Kate's arm: doing her best to comfort her. "How could anyone have even *imagined*…?"

Gabriel stepped to the windows to stand at Newman's side. He looked out at the movement in the skies for a few seconds, then gestured down to the gun that was still in the director's hand. "You can get rid of that now," he said. "It won't work any more."

Newman glanced down at the gun as though he had forgotten it was there. He raised it casually, pointed it at Gabriel and pulled the trigger. There was an empty click. Newman tossed the gun down onto the floor, turned back to the window.

The orbs were getting bigger in the sky.

"What's happening up there?" he asked. For the first time there was a nervousness in his voice.

"Don't tell me you're scared?" Gabriel said. "Isn't this what you've been waiting for?"

Newman looked at Gabriel, saw the smile. "What is it? Why are you smiling?"

"I was just thinking about all those you've killed. You and the superstitious idiots who came before you. All those who were burned or beaten to death on flat black rocks; the ones you cut open while they were still alive."

Newman pressed his back against the window.

"They would have thought it was appropriate," Gabriel continued, "the way you're going to die…"

There was a sudden cry of pain from the other side of the room. Until now Ezekiel Crane had been watching transfixed as his plans had unravelled before his eyes. Moving closer to the huge screen, he cried out again, raising one hand and smearing blood down the glass while reaching out with the other to steady himself against the edge of Ralph Newman's desk.

Trembling, his knuckles white, his face rigid with fury and confusion, he roared, "I *am* Ezekiel One!"

"No," Gabriel said.

"I do not *need* the workers or the drones!" Spittle was flying from his lips. The skin looked like it was slipping on his face. "I will *still* rise up! I can *still* lead the new race when the time comes."

"Your destiny *was* to be here. In the City of Glass," Gabriel said, walking over to stand next to Rachel and Adam. "But you will not be *leading* anything."

Crane made a lunge for Gabriel, but his shattered leg gave way beneath him, and he crumpled to the floor, screaming. In his pain, he was unaware that someone had emerged from the lift behind him. Seeing the looks of amazement from Kate, Rachel and Adam and hearing the gasp from Ralph Newman, he turned to find out who they were all staring at.

Commodore Wing looked at his son. "It would have been better," he said, "if you *had* died…"

Crane climbed slowly back to his feet, never taking his eyes from the old man who limped past him to stand with Gabriel and the others: the daughter he had never been able to acknowledge properly and the grandchildren to whom he owed so much. He wanted more than anything to say sorry – to tell them he would do whatever he had to – but he was unable to find the words.

Rachel did not need to hear the words out loud. "It's OK, Granddad," she said.

Wing smiled and turned back to his son. "When I found out you were still alive, I was … happy. I have spent the last two years not knowing; living like someone who can't wake up from a nightmare. Now, though, seeing what you are…"

Crane's laugh was cold and empty. "What *I* am? I am not the useless old man who can barely walk. I am the one who is about to be reborn. Remade…"

Wing gazed past the son who had become a monster at Ralph Newman. A monster of a different kind and the stepson he had not seen for more than forty years. "If I had known all those years ago at Alamogordo what the two of you would become," he said, "I would have killed you myself.

I would have driven you away from the base and left you in the desert to die."

"Hindsight is wonderfully convenient, don't you think?" Newman said.

The blood rushed to the commodore's face and he raised his walking-stick.

"I may have cut those brake cables," Newman said, "but it's *your* fault my mother died."

"Watch your mouth, boy—"

Newman smiled. "If you had not been cheating on her with that woman, it would never have happened."

"*None* of this would be happening," Crane said. He pointed at Rachel and Adam. "Those two would not exist."

"Then I'm happy," Commodore Wing said. He beamed at Rachel and Adam. "More than anything in the world, I'm glad of that. Glad of *them*…"

Looking down at Rachel and Adam, he did not see Crane launch himself across the room at them; the perfectly manicured fingernails clawed at the air and a cry of naked fury rose up as he lunged in desperation at eyes, throats, *anything*.

Wing did not see, but Gabriel did.

Crane froze mid leap and the cry died in his throat when flames bloomed suddenly at his chest. He gasped in horror at Gabriel, seeing the reflection of fire in the boy's green eyes and the outstretched hand that had casually conjured it.

The fire spread quickly, catching easily in the synthetic

fabric of Crane's silver suit and licking down past his shattered knee and up towards his face.

He began to shriek and wheel around, only stopping when he was face to face with Ralph Newman. He held out his arms. His voice, taunting and mock-tender, was just audible above the crackle of the flames and the spit of burning flesh. "Come here, brother," he said.

"No, for God's sake…" Newman backed away, but there was nowhere for him to go and he was quickly gathered into the inferno, his own flesh blistering in the heat. They screamed in unison as Crane's artificial hair and face were consumed by the flames engulfing them both.

The temperature in the room was soon as unbearable as the smell. Rachel couldn't watch Crane and her father staggering around; she covered her ears to block out the noise of them bouncing off the glass walls. Adam and Laura looked away too.

"Please, someone stop this!" Kate shouted.

She was staring at Gabriel, but it was Commodore Wing who came forward. Moving as fast as he was able, he pushed and beat the human inferno with his outstretched walking-stick; pushing it back and hard against the window, which shattered into thousands of pieces. The sudden gust of wind that came through fanned the flames.

Their burning bodies entwined, the brothers rolled out onto the narrow walkway that supported the giant metal wings several storeys above the street. Ralph Newman thrashed and struggled to get to his feet, but the wind was high and strong and it blew him backwards until he was only centimetres from the edge. The soles of his shoes were melting and his legs gave way. Screaming, he slipped, grabbing on to Ezekiel Crane as he fell; he held on to Crane's burning leg and tried to claw his way back onto the platform.

Commodore Wing crawled gingerly out onto the walkway, and was just in time to see the weight of Ralph Newman pull the man who was once Hilary Wing slowly towards the edge. Crane pawed desperately at the metal, searching for a hand-hold, and for one brief moment Gerald Wing saw the pleading in his son's blue eyes. He saw something he recognized shining from the molten face. He saw the little boy who had cried by the lake.

"Hilary…" Wing yelled.

But the blackened fingers had lost their grip and the burning brothers fell together, their screams fading fast as the fireball span and tumbled towards the street below.

55

Wind howled around the skeletal steel framework that had held the glass of the observation tower in place and rain lashed through the void that was left. After what they had just witnessed, Kate was doing her best to comfort Rachel and Adam, who were in turn doing their best to comfort her.

A husband. A father. Gone...

Gerald Wing limped back across the room, horrified at his own actions, his hands held tightly to his head. Kate took his arm and pulled him towards her and the children. Suddenly, he looked very old.

"This is all my fault," he groaned. "Hilary and Rudi. God, I'm so sorry..."

"No. It was always going to happen," Gabriel said. "You know that."

They all knew. This moment had been predicted thousands of years ago by a Traveller in a cave in Morocco whose paintings has spelled out their destiny.

The orbs of light in the sky had been coming closer and closer and were now beginning to circle the tower. They weaved in and out of its frame, creating a lattice of light that protected those inside from the wind and the rain and bathed them in a warm golden glow.

Gabriel looked around. Triumphant. "We made it."

Adam straightened up. The tears he had shed for his father were drying on his face. "You always knew we would," he said. "Didn't you?"

"No. Even today, I thought I had failed, but you never failed *me*. And that's what made it happen."

They looked at the three Triskellions, pulsing with light and energy in Ralph Newman's safe.

"But what *has* happened?" Rachel asked.

Gabriel stepped forward and took her in his arms. "It's really what's about to happen," he said. And then he whispered something in her ear. Rachel pulled her head away so she was able to look into Gabriel's eyes. He nodded, and then he took Rachel's head between his hands and kissed her.

It was only a matter of seconds, but time – *everything* – seemed to stop, and Rachel could feel the new power surging through Gabriel's body.

"I need your help with one more thing before I go," he said, releasing her head. He took her and Adam by the hand and walked over to where the Triskellions glowed.

Kate Newman suddenly stepped in front of them, blocking Gabriel. She was crying. "Please don't take them with you," she pleaded. "They are all I have."

"It's OK," Gabriel said. "They're safe now. I'm not taking anyone."

"Take *me*," Laura said suddenly.

"You can't," Rachel said, shocked.

Kate and Adam looked equally horrified. They were both about to protest – but the expression on Laura's face stopped them. She was excited, buzzing.

"I've dreamed about something like this my whole life," she said. "I mean, digging up fossils is one thing, you know. But *this…*"

Kate Newman took her friend's hand. "We'll miss you."

The twins stretched out their hands towards Laura. She nodded. She did not need their powers to know exactly what they were thinking.

"I want to come with you," she said to Gabriel. "Wherever it is you're going. There's so much I want to know."

"That's your choice," he said. "It's not a decision I can make for you."

He took one of the amulets from the safe and asked Rachel and Adam to do the same. Standing in the centre of the tower, Gabriel held his hand out, a Triskellion resting in one palm. Rachel placed the second Triskellion on top of it and Adam placed the third on top of that. Gabriel briefly pressed his other hand down on top of all three and they began to spin.

They span in opposite directions until they hovered above

his palm, each of the nine blades shooting out beams of light that reached into the darkening sky, and then, like golden helicopters, the amulets swirled around the outside of the tower, creating triple wheels of light. The orbs that had been circling and weaving in the sky multiplied until they filled the tower, expanding and contracting.

Rachel could see the phosphorescent filaments inside begin to change. They transformed into faint images; transparent and ghostly, like X-rays.

Faces.

They circled Rachel and Adam, coming close to their heads, before spinning away again. Rachel was certain she saw the faces of Morag and Duncan; Jean-Luc and Jean-Bernard; Inez and Carmen inside them. Smiling.

Twins. Friends who had helped them, then sacrificed themselves so that the journey could be completed. Rachel could hear their voices chattering and laughing in her mind.

Other shadowy faces were materializing within the orbs. Faces she did not recognize, but which she guessed from the almond eyes were other Travellers like Gabriel: knights, saints and shamans whose energy had remained on earth after their deaths.

The Triskellions had generated three wheels of light that now began to intersect like a gyroscope; in the centre, one of the orbs stretched and grew. It floated in front of Gabriel. Limbs appeared to be pushing out from the inside, expanding and reshaping whatever membrane, or energy, it was that held the orb together. Arms developed first, and then legs. A torso, a head, until a translucent figure stood in front of them shimmering and not quite solid, skin building up over its body in layers of light…

And then Rachel knew who it was.

She looked around at the astonished faces in the tower, hovering over her grandfather's expression. He had dropped to his knees, and she realized that Gerald Wing also knew who it was; he had recognized the friend he had blown from the sky half a century before.

The memory of Gabriel weeping in front of the glass cylinder in the lab at Alamogordo popped into Rachel's head, and in a sudden, clear vision, she could see that that cylinder was now empty.

The figure in front of them had formed fully, jagged scars visible on its wet, naked body, its head fine and domed and its eyes almond-shaped. The same shape as Gabriel's.

She heard Gabriel's voice clear in her mind: *You weren't the only one looking for your father, Rachel.*

I'm so glad you found him.

I'm sorry that your search turned out the way it did.

It's not your fault.

Goodbye, Gabriel said. *I…*

Rachel did not need to hear *these* words to know what Gabriel meant. *Me too,* she answered with her mind.

Then the buzzing started. Bees in their billions were

flying over the building, forming a throbbing black cloud that threw the tower into darkness. The only illumination left was coming from the wheels of light created by the Triskellions.

Gabriel embraced the figure in front of him, and one of the Triskellions span a halo round their heads, joining them together, spiralling down their bodies until it reached their ankles. The second amulet did the same, weaving another ring round their chests.

Laura suddenly rushed at them, breaking through the bands of light and clinging on to Gabriel as the third Triskellion also bound them together. The three amulets spun faster and faster, the wheels rushing laterally and vertically until the figures were contained within a ball of tangled light moving so fast that it appeared to be in flames.

High above, the swarm began to regroup, creating a hole in the black cloud through which a shaft of bright white sunlight shone.

Like a door being left open.

Rachel could still just make out the three figures contained within the sphere. She saw the smiles, clear through the glare, just before a surge of power threw her to the floor. Just before the jagged stream of energy flew from the sphere and shot around the room's steel frame, dancing across the building's vast metal wings, arcing between them like a bolt of lightning.

Suddenly the sphere was taken. The orbs followed it; all

were sucked out of the tower by a huge vacuum. They popped and dispersed like bubbles of light in the slipstream.

Finally, the bees flew through the hole they had created and within seconds were all gone. It was as if they had evaporated or drifted away like dust into the beautiful blue sky that now stretched over the entire city. Bright as a summer's day, even though it was night.

56

Detective Angie Scoppetone had had better days. Earlier, she had received the news that Kate Newman had been mysteriously released from prison, which would mean one less collar on her record. On top of that, her working day had been pretty much screwed thanks to the tens of thousands of fruitcakes and other sad cases who were clogging up the city for some sort of festival or other. Now, like every other cop in the NYPD, she was being asked to do glorified traffic duty and help the self-same idiots who had flooded into Manhattan find their way out·again safely.

All this came on top of rogue swarms of freaking bees and the weirdest weather that anyone could remember. It was enough to give anyone an ulcer.

She stood in the centre of Broadway, shouting at stupid drivers, ushering pedestrians towards the subway stations and trying to keep the sea of people moving.

"Excuse me…"

Scoppetone turned round to see a family standing in front of her: a husband, wife and two children. They looked lost and bewildered, and like most of the people she had been dealing with for the last hour or so, their hands and faces were covered with beestings. She grunted, "What?"

"My name's Bob Anderson," the man said. "We're trying to get back home. I know it sounds stupid, but we can't remember where we left our car…"

Scoppetone sighed and started talking, unaware that another family was emerging on to the street from the building behind her: an old man, a woman and two sixteen-year-olds.

"It seems … calm somehow," Kate said.

They stood and watched for a minute or so. Sirens were wailing a few streets away on the other side of the building, and Rachel guessed that the emergency services must be in attendance where the bodies of Hilary and her father had landed. She shuddered.

"I'm starving," Adam said. "Can we eat?"

Just like her stupid, wonderful brother, Rachel thought. After everything they had seen and felt, after everything they had *lost,* he was still thinking of his stomach, or pretending to. He was still putting on a brave face.

Commodore Wing nodded. "Yes, let's find somewhere. We've got a great deal to talk about…"

Rachel watched her mother slip an arm through her grandfather's.

They began to walk.

A few hundred metres along the street Adam and Rachel had pulled ahead of the others. "What did Gabriel say?" Adam asked.

"When?"

"Up there." Adam gestured back up towards the huge metal wings that dominated the skyline above them. "He whispered something at the end. What did he say?"

"Same thing he said back in Australia." Rachel walked a few more steps, looked sideways at her brother. "Same thing Levi said that first day. 'They're coming.'"

epilogue

Zzzz … dnk. Zzzzz … dnk. Zzzzz…

The bee thumped lazily against the French windows and finding them open, buzzed out across the lawn and down towards the wild flowers by the lake.

"Looks like Jacob's hives are getting healthier," Adam said.

Rachel, who was stretched out on the sofa, lifted her head from the book she was reading and gazed out into the sunny garden. "Hmm," she said. She looked at the sunlight streaking in through the window, at the millions of tiny specks of dust caught in its beam, and breathed deeply. She caught the smell of dust, the freshly mown grass beyond and the comforting musty odour of the old house.

All were smells to which she had suddenly become ultra-sensitive.

They had been back in the village for two months and already their grandfather's house felt like home. The trauma of what had happened in New York, the memories of their father, were receding thankfully fast.

It was an ability they had used before.

Rachel heard the chink of teacups and their mother pushed the door open, then put a tray down on the floor by the sofa.

Kate sat down and stroked Rachel's hair. "You look pale, baby," she said. "Have some cake, or a sandwich. Get your sugar levels up." She began to pour the tea. "We're having roast beef for dinner when Granddad gets back from the cricket, so don't eat all the sandwiches, Adam."

Adam strolled over from his chair by the TV and took a stack of sandwiches. He kissed his mother on the head and she smiled at him indulgently.

"I'm going to start peeling the veg," she said, stroking her daughter's cheek before she went back to the kitchen.

Adam waited a moment. "When are you going to tell her?"

Rachel sipped her tea and frowned at her brother. "She'll know soon enough," she said. "She'll see it." She adjusted a couple of cushions behind her, then lay back and closed her eyes, stroking her stomach.

She heard another bee buzzing somewhere in the roses just outside the room – a monotonous buzz hypnotic and restful – and she realized that she had never felt happier in her life.

And as she drifted into a light sleep, she felt the two new lives stirring inside her.